The Black

Written By:

R.S. Rebecka

The Black Rook

Written By: R.S. Rebecka
Illustrated by Priyam Kuma deviantart.com/crimsonred4rtist
instagram.com/priyam.rawat/

ISBN: 9781967082735 (Paperback)
ISBN: 9781967082742 (eBook)

Library of Congress Control Number: 2025922393

Printed in the United States of America

BookButler Publishing Company
Upper Marlboro, MD 20774

TheBookButler.com

BookButler Publishing Company titles may be purchased in bulk for educational, business, fundraising, or sales promotional use. For information, please email:
info@thebookbutler.com

DEDICATION

For those whose inner world is
a universe of its own.

May you always find the space
and the courage to live out loud
what you see so clearly inside.

Table of Contents

Chapter 1

The brightly lit arena and the sound of the cheering crowd overwhelmed his senses. "Ox! Ox! Ox!" The pungent smell of unwashed bodies and spilled ale, a thick, cloying miasma, threw him into a dizzying, unfocused state of mind. He was biting the ragged edge of his thumbnail, a frantic, repetitive motion he couldn't stop, a ritual against the assault of the senses. He had been hit. Hard. A glancing blow to the side of the head that had felt less like a punch and more like being struck by a falling sack of bricks.

Then, out of nowhere, Marcus's ears were ringing like the sound of a violin string snapping. His world was fracturing.

The faces in the crowd, leering, jeering, and screaming, began to lose their detail. Their individual features, the missing teeth, the greasy hair, the ecstatic glint in their eyes, all blurred and smoothed away. They became identical, ovoid shapes, like eggs balanced on shoulders. Then, in a blink, they resolved into something he could understand. Something with rules. They became pawns. A gallery of identical, carved pieces, half of them stark white, half of them pitch black, their collective roar simplifying into a binary state, approval or disapproval. A white roar for the Ox, a black silence for him.

In the center of the pit, the sawdust-covered floor, stained with the grime and blood of a hundred other brutal contests, began to resolve. Lines, sharp and impossibly straight, shot across the ground, intersecting, forming a perfect grid. Eight squares by eight squares. Sixty-four squares of alternating light and dark, filtering in like building blocks, constructing a new, more logical reality over the chaotic filth of the old one.

He was no longer in the Rat Pit. He was on the board.

And he knew his own piece. He had always known it, felt it in his bones, in the rigid, straight line path of his desperation. He was a Rook. Unadorned, functional, powerful only in a direct line. His objective was not complex. It did not require the clever, L-shaped leaps of a Knight or the diagonal cunning of a Bishop. His objective was ten squares away. Ten silver crowns. A straight line from A to B. From this moment of agony to his mother's next breath.

His opponent was a different matter. The hulking brute across the grid was not a standard piece. In Marcus's fracturing mind, The Ox was a unique creation, a piece carved from blood-soaked granite and brute force. A Juggernaut. Its movement protocol was simple, advance, and crush. It possessed no subtlety, only overwhelming momentum. It stood on the board, a mountain of meat and muscle, clad in crude but effective armor, a thick leather cuirass studded with iron plates, and heavy greaves on its shins.

The Ox let out a triumphant roar, mistaking Marcus's dazed stillness for the onset of defeat. He stomped a foot, and the real-world floorboards groaned. On the board in Marcus's mind, the Juggernaut piece slid forward one square with a heavy, grinding sound.

The white pawns roared their approval.

Marcus's mind, now shielded within the cool, ordered logic of the game, began to work. The pain in his head became a data point, a status effect. The roar of the crowd was merely the sound of the game, no longer a personal assault. He analyzed the Juggernaut.

Strengths: Overwhelming power. The intimidation factor is high, causing fewer pieces to freeze or flee. Heavily armored on primary facings.

Weaknesses: The analysis came in a flash of cold clarity. Slow. Predictable trajectory. And the armor... the armor is a lie. It wasn't a lie of protection, but a lie of agility. It was heavy. Excessively so. The iron plates were crudely riveted to the thick leather, adding fifty pounds of dead weight. Weight meant inertia. Weight meant exhaustion. And armor, no matter how thick, had gaps.

The joints. The back of the knees. The neck. The armpits. The face.

The Ox charged, a human battering ram intent on ending the game in one final, brutal move. He lowered his shoulder, his fists like twin boulders, aiming to smash the Rook from the board entirely.

This was the core of the Juggernaut's strategy: to force the opponent to react to its power. But Marcus wasn't reacting anymore. He was playing. A Rook cannot outmuscle a stronger piece head-on. It must use the board. It must use its superior movement.

Instead of retreating, a move the Ox expected, Marcus moved sideways. A Rook's move. A quick, two-step slide along a straight line. The Ox, committed to his forward charge, thundered past, his momentum carrying him into the thick ropes that defined the pit. He struck them with such force that the entire platform shuddered.

The white pawns groaned. The black pawns remained silent.

Before the Ox could fully untangle himself, Marcus moved again. Another straight line, closing the distance. He didn't aim for the armored chest or the thick, bull-like neck. He targeted the foundation. With a sharp, snapping kick, he struck the back of the Ox's left knee. It was an unarmored, vulnerable space, a gap in the fortress wall.The Ox bellowed, a sound of surprise and pain, and his leg buckled slightly. He spun around, his face a mask of fury, no longer confident, now merely enraged. He swung a fist in a wide, sweeping arc. A Brawler's Hook. A desperate, undisciplined move.

Marcus was already gone, having retreated two squares back, out of range. He was using the entire board, forcing the slower, heavier piece to constantly turn, thereby expending energy and burning through its reserves. Each turn the Ox made, the heavy armor was a new burden. Marcus could hear the man's breathing now, coming in harsh, ragged gasps, the leather cuirass constricting his chest.

"Stand and fight, you little rat!" the Ox bellowed, his voice raw.

The white pawns echoed his sentiment, a wave of jeers and boos washing over the board. They wanted a bloody collision, not a tactical withdrawal. But Marcus was deaf to them. The game was all that mattered. The logic was pure.

He saw the pattern. The Ox would charge. Marcus would evade. The Ox would tire. It was a simple war of attrition. But attrition was slow, and time was a luxury he didn't have. His mother's face, pale and feverish, flashed behind his eyes. He had to force a mistake. He had to present a target the Juggernaut couldn't resist.

Marcus stopped moving. He stood in the center of the pit, his small frame looking fragile and exposed. He let his arms hang limp, a deliberate posture of exhaustion. It was a gambit—a baited trap.
The Ox grinned, a bloody, broken-toothed display of triumph. He saw victory within his grasp. He didn't charge this time. He advanced, slow and deliberate, a predator cornering its prey. He was savoring the moment, playing to the pawns, who roared their approval.

Marcus's world narrowed. The grid, the pawns, the roaring, it all faded into a peripheral haze. There was only his square and the adjacent square that the Juggernaut was about to occupy. He tracked the man's feet. The heavy, iron-shod boots. He tracked the swing of his arms, the shift of his massive shoulders. He tracked the rhythm of his labored breathing.

The Ox was two steps away when he lunged. Not a wild charge, but a powerful, deliberate lunge, his right hand grabbing, his left fist cocked for the final, finishing blow.

Now.

As the big man's hand reached for his throat, Marcus exploded into motion. He didn't retreat. He advanced. He dropped his weight low, ducking under the grabbing arm, and drove forward in a straight, hard line. He drove the heel of his right hand upward, not with the force of a punch, but with the sharp, precise impact of a targeted strike.

His target was the one part of the Ox's face that jutted out, unprotected and vulnerable, his nose.

There was a wet, crunching sound, sickeningly loud in the momentary lull of the crowd. The Ox screamed, a high, sharp sound of pure agony, stumbling backward. His hands flew to his face as blood gushed between his fingers, hot and thick. The Juggernaut piece on the board flickered, its granite form showing cracks. He was blinded by tears and pain, disoriented. He was, in the language of the game, in check.

The white pawns gasped. For the first time, the black pawns made a sound, a low, interested murmur that rippled through the gallery.

Marcus didn't give him a moment. He didn't press the attack on the man's head; that would invite a wild, retaliatory swing. He stayed low, a Rook sweeping across the lower ranks of the board. He kicked again, this time at the inside of the Ox's armored ankle. The heavy boot deflected most of the blow, but it wasn't about damage. It was about balance.

The Ox, blinded by blood and focused on the shattering pain in his face, stumbled. His weight shifted. And for a fraction of a second, all his mass was balanced on his uninjured right leg.

It was the opening. The fatal flaw in the Juggernaut's design, revealed.

Marcus launched himself forward. It wasn't a punch or a kick. It was a tackle, a shoulder-first drive with every ounce of his desperate, wiry strength. He didn't aim for the man's body. He aimed for the single, load-bearing pillar that was the Ox's right knee.

His shoulder connected with the side of the joint. There was a sickening, audible pop.

The Ox's scream was no longer one of pain and fury. It was a sound of pure, structural failure. His leg, his foundation, ceased to exist. He crashed to the sawdust-covered floor with the force of a felled oak tree, his huge body sending up a cloud of dust and filth. The Juggernaut piece on the board shattered into a thousand pieces of granite, leaving only a broken man in its place.

The game was over. The checkmate was complete.

But as the logical, ordered world of the chessboard dissolved, the hot, chaotic reality of the Rat Pit came rushing back in. The pain in his head returned with a vengeance. The roar of the crowd was no longer a binary force, but a deafening, terrifying wall of sound. And the man on the ground was not a broken game piece; he was a human being, screaming and clutching his ruined knee.

The sight of him, broken and defeated, should have been a victory. But it wasn't. The cold, analytical

Rook receded, and the desperate, terrified twelve-year-old boy took over. The image of his mother's gasping breaths filled his mind, and a firestorm of pure, desperate rage erupted in his chest. This wasn't enough. Winning wasn't enough. He had to finish it. He had to prove, to himself and to whatever cruel god was watching, that he could do what was necessary.

He fell upon the downed man. His small fists, hardened by a lifetime of street scuffles but untested in this kind of brutal final ty, became a blur of motion. He rained blows down cn the Ox's unprotected head and face. He wasn't thinking. He wasn't a player anymore. He was a machine of pure, frantic violence. Each punch was a coin he didn't have. Each impact was a breath his mother couldn't take. Each sickening, wet thud was a prayer to a heaven that had long since abandoned their corner of the world.

Chapter 2

The Scar did not have a dawn. It had a greying. The concept of light arriving was too generous, too active. Here, light did not so much arrive as it did admit defeat, seeping reluctantly into the narrow, grasping alleys that clawed their way between leaning tenements. It was a watery, pewter light that revealed no beauty, only the stark, unvarnished truth of decay. It was a thief. It stole the precious, concealing darkness and laid bare the grim reality of the world, assaulting the senses with a clarity that was a form of violence.

The light illuminated the damp rot in the wood, a smell like sour earth and spoiled mushrooms that was a constant, low hum in the back of Marcus's throat. It picked out the slick, rainbow sheen of refuse in the gutters, its odor sharp and ammoniac, a physical presence that made his eyes water. And it touched the pallor of the people who called this festering wound on the capital's edge their home, their skin the color of dirty parchment. For twelve-year-old Marcus, the greying was a signal that the protective shield of night was gone, leaving him exposed.

He'd slipped back in moments before, a phantom in the gloom, his heart a frantic, percussive drum against his ribs. The sound was too loud in his own ears, a frantic rhythm he was sure the whole tenement could hear. He pressed a hand to his chest, willing it to quiet. In his other fist, clenched so tightly his knuckles were white, was a small, corked vial nestled in a scrap of scavenged rag. It felt as heavy as a gravestone. Its weight was wrong, a dense, concentrated point of mass that felt alien in his palm.

Blood, warm and sticky, trickled from a fresh gash on his forearm, tracing a path down to his knuckles. The sensation was a thin, hot line against his cold skin. He ignored it. Pain was a currency in The Scar, a predictable transaction. He had just spent a little to purchase a sliver of hope. He crept to the corner that served as his bed, a pile of straw whose dry, dusty smell offered a small comfort, and a threadbare blanket that smelled of him and his mother, carefully unwrapped his prize. The rag was rough, its fibers scratching his skin. The vial was no bigger than his thumb, filled with a viscous, dark liquid that sloshed with a thick, syrupy sound when he tilted it. Medicine. Or so the back alley charlatan had claimed after Marcus had pressed a handful of pilfered coins into his grimy palm. The man's skin had felt like sandpaper, his breath a foul cloud of rotten teeth and cheap gin. The cut on his arm was from the baker's window he'd had to shatter to get at the coin box. The sound of the breaking glass had been a sharp, crystalline shriek that still echoed in his ears, a sound that felt like a tear in the fabric of the night. A small price.

From the room's only real piece of furniture, a sagging cot that groaned with every slight movement, came a cough.
The sound sliced through the quiet room, a jagged edge against the silence. It was not a strong, chest clearing sound. It was a weak, wet rattle, a sound like gravel being swirled in a bottle of thin oil. It seemed to catch in his mother's throat, leaving her gasping, a high, thin whistling sound that was the noise of a desperate, failing machine.

Abigail.

Her name was a memory of a softer time, of stories whispered about green fields and a life before The Scar had sunk its teeth into them. The name felt like a smooth, cool stone in his mind, something from another world. Now, it felt too beautiful for the gaunt, feverish woman lying on the cot. Her breath came in shallow, ragged little sips, as if she were afraid the air itself was too heavy, too thick to draw into her lungs.

Marcus moved to her side, his bare feet silent on the grimy floorboards. The floor was a landscape of its own, gritty under his soles, with slick patches he knew to avoid. The greying was strong enough now to show him the sheen of sweat on her brow, a glistening layer that caught the weak light. He could see the way her skin, once the color of warm cream, had taken on a translucent, waxy quality. Her once vibrant auburn hair, which used to smell of sunlight and wind, was lank and dark with sweat, plastered to her temples in stringy, damp curls.

"Ma?" he whispered. His voice was a raw crackle, the sound of a boy trying to sound like a man.

Her eyelids fluttered open. They seemed too heavy for her to lift, a monumental effort. Her gaze, clouded with the fog of fever, struggled to focus on him. The color of her irises, once a clear, bright blue, was now murky, like a summer sky seen through smoke. "Marcus...?" Her voice was a wisp, a thread of sound so thin that it barely disturbed the air, "You were gone."

"Just for water," he lied. The lie was automatic, a shield he used to protect her from the jagged edges of their life. He couldn't tell her he'd been out stealing, fighting, bleeding. His mother had raised him on tales of honor and goodness, tales that felt like cruel jokes in a place like this. Her goodness was a flickering candle flame, and he felt like a cupped, dirty hand, desperately trying to keep it from being snuffed out by the foul winds of The Scar.

He took the damp rag from her forehead. It was lukewarm and had a faintly sour smell. He dipped it into the bucket of murky water by the bed, the splash a loud intrusion. The water was yesterday's and already carried the scent of stagnation. A new bucket was his next task, another ritual in a day filled with them. As he gently wiped her face, the rough texture of the rag a counterpoint to the unnatural heat of her skin, she tried to smile. It was a pained twisting of her lips, a brief, failed gesture.

"My brave boy," she rasped, her bony fingers finding his wrist. Her touch was feather light, a ghost of its former strength, yet it held him fast. The skin of her fingers was dry and hot, like old paper left by a fire.

Guilt and a fierce, possessive love warred within him. The two emotions were a physical pressure in his chest. He was taking care of her by becoming the very thing she'd taught him not to be, a creature of the shadows, a thief with blood on his arm—a Rook, moving in straight, brutal lines toward a singular objective.

"You need to rest, Ma," he said, his voice thick, "I got... I got something. It'll help."

He uncorked the vial. The sound of the cork pulling free was a small, sticky pop. A bitter, herbal, and sharp smell instantly filled the air. It was the scent of crushed weeds and something acrid, like burnt tar. He held it to her lips, tilting it carefully. "Just a little. It's strong."

She coughed again, a spasm that shook her frail frame, but she managed to swallow a few drops of the dark liquid. She grimaced at the taste, her eyes watering. "Bitter," she whispered, the word a puff of air.

"It's supposed to be," he said, forcing a confidence into his voice that he didn't feel, "That's how you know it's working." It was a lie, but it was a rule. Strong medicine is bitter. That was a rule he could believe in.

He corked the vial and hid it carefully beneath a loose floorboard near his straw bed, his personal vault for anything precious. The medicine, a day's worth of stale bread, the smooth, grey stone she'd once given him from a riverbank long ago. His treasures. The act of placing them in their designated spot was a comfort, a small point of order in a world of chaos.

Abigail's breathing seemed to even out, or perhaps it was just his desperate hope painting illusions in the dim light. He sat by her side on the cold floor, the grit pressing into his legs, watching the almost imperceptible rise and fall of her chest, until the greying had fully given way to the miserable, overcast light of a Scar morning. Each breath she took was a victory. Each shallow gasp was a battle he felt in his own lungs. And he knew, with the cold, hard certainty of a boy forced to grow up too fast, that the few drops in the vial were not a cure. They were a reprieve—a stay of execution. And the clock was already ticking. To get more, he would need more coin. And to get more coin, he would have to wade deeper into the filth he was so desperate to shield her from.

The journey to the district well was a descent through the nine circles of urban hell. Marcus clutched the wooden bucket, its handle rough and splintered, biting into the flesh of his fingers. The weight and texture were familiar, providing a grounding sensation. He navigated the labyrinth of The Scar, a place that was less a district and more a living, monstrous organism of suffering.

The air was a thick soup of smells, a sensory assault that he had learned to parse and categorize. The sour stench of unwashed bodies. The acrid, nose-burning smoke from burning refuse. The cloying, sick sweetness of decay, a smell that clung to the back of the throat. And underlying it all, the ever-present, damp, earthy stink of the open sewer that sluggishly snaked its way through the heart of the district. He moved through it by rote, his mind focused on the task, filtering the overwhelming input into manageable streams.

Tenements, cobbled together from scavenged wood, mismatched stone, and sheer desperation, leaned against each other as if for support, blotting out the sky and creating canyons of perpetual twilight. Their sagging balconies were festooned with rags, a parody of festive banners. In the narrow, muddy lanes below, humanity teemed. Grim-faced men with hollow eyes huddled around small fires, their gazes blank. Women, old before their time, bartered scraps of food with voices worn thin by hardship. And the children... the children were everywhere. Some were feral, running in packs with the sly, cunning eyes of cornered rats. Others were unnervingly still, their bellies swollen from hunger, their gazes fixed on nothing.

Marcus kept his head down, his eyes scanning, assessing. He was part of this landscape, but he moved through it with a purpose that set him apart. He knew which alleys were controlled by the Sleeper gang, their territory marked by crude drawings of a closed eye. He knew which were the turf of the Luteras, marked by three overlapping circles. He knew which beggars were genuinely helpless and which were informants for the City Guards who occasionally patrolled the district's edge, their gleaming armor and dismissive sneers a mockery of the surrounding squalor.

He saw a flash of silver from the Citadel, the spire of the King's palace that pierced the sky far, far beyond the choking confines of The Scar. It was a needle of light, a constant, indifferent reminder of another world, a world of warmth and plenty, a world that had forgotten them. A surge of bitter resentment, hot and familiar, rose in his throat. It was a useless emotion. They had everything up there. He just needed enough to keep his mother breathing. That was a straight line. That was a problem with a potential solution. Resentment was a fog.

The well was the district's social hub, a place of conflict and fleeting community. It was controlled by a gnarled, one-eyed man named Riat, who had claimed ownership through brute force years ago and now charged a half-copper for every bucket drawn. Riat's voice was a low grunt, his single eye a milky, unsettling orb.

"Marcus," Riat grunted as the boy approached, "Your mother still kicking?"

The casual cruelty of the question was a physical blow. Marcus's fists clenched at his sides, his ragged nails digging into his palms. He forced the reaction down. An emotional response was a weakness. A transaction was not. "She's fine," he lied, his voice flat. He placed the bucket down. The sound of wood on stone was a solid, final thing. "I need a full one."

"Coin first," Riat rasped, extending a grimy hand.

Marcus's pockets were empty. He'd spent every last stolen piece on the vial. He had a plan—a straight line. "I'll work for it. Let me draw for the next five people. You keep the coin, I get my bucket."

Riat spat a brown stream of chew onto the ground near Marcus's feet. The glob landed with a wet smack. "Feeling generous today, are we? What's the catch?"

"No catch," Marcus said, meeting the man's single-eyed gaze without flinching. This was a negotiation. The terms were clear. He held the man's stare until Riat squinted, then shrugged.

"Fine. But you spill a drop, the deal's off."

For the next ten minutes, Marcus worked. The well bucket was heavy, the rope coarse and slick with grime. The repetitive motion was calming. Pull, coil, empty. Pull, coil, empty. He hauled it up time and again, his arms straining, the gash from the baker's window stinging with sweat and dirt. He focused only on the task, his movements efficient, his face a mask of grim determination. He ignored the burning in his muscles and the whispers of the others in line. He filled the buckets of a scabby-faced woman, a coughing old man, and a young mother with a listless child on her hip. Riat collected the coppers, his good eye glinting.

Finally, it was his turn. He drew his own bucket, taking care not to spill a single drop, and hefted it. It was a dead weight, sloshing with the precious, life-sustaining liquid.

"Pleasure doing business with you, boy," Riat sneered.

Marcus just nodded and turned away. The transaction was complete. He began the long walk back. The water was for his mother to drink, to clean her face, to dilute the bitter medicine. But the relief from the charlatan's potion had faded. By the time he returned to their room, the wet, rattling sound of Abigail's breath had returned, more pronounced than before. Her fever was climbing. The potion had failed. The transaction was void. He had paid, but the goods were faulty. A cold, sharp panic, like a shard of ice in his gut, began to spread.

He knew, with a certainty that felt like a block of ice in his stomach, that he was losing her.

Over the next two days, the panic solidified into a cold, hard dread. The vial was empty. His mother's brief moments of lucidity were becoming shorter, while the periods of feverish rambling were growing longer. She spoke of her childhood home, of a river that ran clear and cold, of a father with kind hands. She was retreating into a world he couldn't follow, and he was terrified she wouldn't come back.

There was only one place left to go—a place of rules and order. Master Elian's apothecary was situated on the very edge of The Scar, a cleaner, more solid-looking building that catered to the lower-tier merchants and artisans.

Marcus pushed through the door, a small bell tinkling brightly above him. The sound was clean and clear, a stark contrast to the muffled, chaotic noises of his world. The air inside was a revelation. It smelled of dried lavender, camphor, and something sharp and sterile. It was an organized smell, clean and purposeful. Jars of powders, liquids, and dried herbs lined the shelves, neatly labeled in a script he couldn't read. The order and cleanliness of the place were both a comfort and an accusation.

Master Elian, a thin, balding man with spectacles perched on his nose, looked up from a ledger. "Can I help you, boy?"

Marcus's heart hammered against his ribs. He felt grimy and out of place, a smudge on a clean page. "My mother," he said, his voice coming out hoarser than he intended, "She's sick. A lung fever. She can't breathe right, and... and she's burning up."

Elian listened, his gaze analytical. He asked questions, "How long? What have you given her? Is the cough dry or wet?"

Marcus described everything: the rattling sound, the night sweats, the charlatan's bitter medicine. Elian nodded slowly, his expression growing more grave.

"It sounds like the Wasting Lung," he said finally. The name was a pronouncement of doom. "The charlatan's brew likely did nothing but thin her blood and give you false hope."

"Can you help her?" Marcus's voice was a desperate plea, "Is there real medicine? Something that works?"

"There is," Elian said. For a fleeting moment, hope surged in Marcus's chest, a painful, unfamiliar sensation. "A tincture of silver leaf and crushed pearl dust, mixed with a distillation of mountain ginseng. It can fight the fever, clear the lungs."

"I need it," Marcus said, stepping closer.

Master Elian's gaze softened with something that might have been pity, but his voice was firm, clinical. A businessman stating terms. "The ingredients are exceedingly rare, boy. A full course of treatment... it would cost ten silver crowns."
Ten. Silver. Crowns.

The number hung in the air, vast and impossible. Ten silver crowns might as well have been ten thousand. He'd never even held a single silver crown. A silver crown was a lord's currency. The world, which for a moment had seemed to offer a path, a solution, suddenly erected a solid, insurmountable wall in front of him. The clean jars, the neat labels, the ordered shelves, they weren't a promise of healing; they were a display of things he could never have. The world was neatly divided into those who could afford to live and those who were left to die.
"I... I don't have it," he whispered, the admission tasting like failure, "I can work. I'm strong. I can clean, run errands, anything."

Elian sighed, a sound of genuine, weary regret. He removed his spectacles and polished them with a clean cloth. "Son, to earn that much, you would need to work for me for two years. Your mother doesn't have two years. She may not have two weeks. I am sorry. Truly. But I am a businessman, not a charity."

The transaction was over. The verdict was delivered.

Marcus backed away from the counter. The tinkling of the bell as he pushed the door open sounded like a death knell. He stumbled back out into the filth and stench of The Scar. Ten silver crowns. An impossible, mocking number.

He was standing at a precipice. Behind him was the certainty of his mother's death. Below him was a darkness he had not yet dared to explore. But as he stood there, the face of his mother, pale and gasping, filled his mind. And he knew he was going to jump.

There was one person in The Scar who dealt in impossible sums. A man who could turn desperation into opportunity and pain into coin. His name was Silas.

Marcus found him where he always was, holding court in the grimy back room of a tavern called The Leaky Mug. The air was thick with the smells of cheap ale, pipe smoke, and sweat. Silas was a man of contrasts. He wore a waistcoat that might have once been fine, though it was now stained and frayed. His smile was wide and welcoming, but his eyes were like chips of flint, constantly moving, assessing, calculating.

"Marcus, my boy!" Silas boomed as Marcus approached, "You look like you've seen a ghost. Pull up a crate."

Marcus didn't sit. He stood before the table, rigid. "It's my mother," he said, his voice low and urgent, "She's dying, Silas. The Wasting Lung. The medicine costs ten silver crowns."

Silas's smile didn't falter, but his eyes sharpened. He took a long drag from his clay pipe. "Ten silvers," he mused, "A king's ransom for a boy like you. Abigail is a good woman. Too good for this place."

"Can you help me?" Marcus asked, "I'll do anything. I'll work for you, steal for you. Anything."

Silas leaned back, studying Marcus. This was his art. He was a merchant of last resorts. "Stealing purses won't get you ten silvers in a lifetime, lad," he said, his voice soft and conspiratorial, "The kind of job that pays that much... it's not for boys. It's for men. Killers. You're not a killer, are you, Marcus?"

Marcus flinched. "No." The word was absolute. A rule. He did not kill.

"Didn't think so," Silas nodded, "But... there is another way. It just requires you to have a high threshold for pain." He leaned forward, his voice dropping, "There are men, wealthy men, who grow bored of watching horses race. They crave something more... visceral. They pay to watch men fight. Not soldiers. Brawlers. Bare knuckle. In a pit. No rules, no honor. The last man standing takes the purse. They call it The Rat Pit. A big score, for a boy with enough grit, could net you a silver crown. Maybe more."

The Rat Pit. A place of pure chaos. No rules. The opposite of the ordered world he craved. But it offered a path. A straight, brutal line. One victory =

one silver crown. Ten victories = ten silver crowns. The math was simple. It was clean.

"They let boys fight?" Marcus asked, his voice barely audible.
"They let anyone fight who's desperate enough to step into the pit," Silas corrected him. He smiled again, a predator's smile. "And you, my boy... you look desperate enough. I can get you in. Tonight. For a small finder's fee, of course. Say, twenty percent of your winnings?"

The offer was a lifeline thrown into a churning, black sea. It was monstrous, terrifying. It was a betrayal of every good thing his mother had ever tried to teach him. To spill his own blood, to break another man, for the amusement of rich gawkers. It was the ugliest part of their world, distilled into a single, blood-soaked ring.

But then he saw her face again. Abigail, her breath a fragile rattle. Ten silver crowns. An impossible number. And here, in this foul tavern, was a man offering him a chance, a bloody, brutal, soul-crushing chance to reach it.

He thought of the principles his mother had taught him. Honor. Kindness. Integrity. They were beautiful words. But they were luxuries. They couldn't buy medicine. They couldn't buy another breath.

Pain could.

Marcus looked Silas in the eye, the flinty, calculating eyes of the man who was offering to sell his pain. The boyish softness in his own face hardened, chipping away to reveal something colder, sharper, beneath. He was a Rook. He would move in a straight line, from one end of the board to the other. Ten squares. Ten victories. Ten silver crowns. It was the only move he had left to make.

"Get me in," Marcus said, his voice low but steady, a chilling echo of the man he was about to become, "Tonight."

Chapter 3

He didn't know how long he hit him. He was only dimly aware of other hands, strong and rough, pulling him off. He was hauled to his feet by the pit promoter's thugs, his chest heaving, his entire body trembling with a violent cocktail of adrenaline, exhaustion, and a dawning, sickening horror at what he had just done.

Below him, The Ox lay still, a broken mountain of a man, his face a swollen, bloody ruin.

A sudden, profound silence descended in Marcus's own head, more deafening than the crowd. He looked at his hands. His knuckles were split open, raw and bleeding, the skin torn away. He looked at the unconscious man at his feet, and a wave of nausea so profound it made his knees weak washed over him. He had done this. He had broken another human being for sport, for money. The line he had just crossed was a chasm, and he knew, with a certainty that felt like a block of ice in his stomach, that he could never go back.

A hulking man with a scarred face, the promoter, grabbed his arm and raised it high. "The winner... THE SHADOW!"

The roar of the crowd was for him now. They chant-
ed his new, hated name. However, the sounds were
muted and distant. He felt nothing. No triumph. No
pride. Just a cold, hollow ache that had nothing to
do with his bruises. The victory was as empty as his
pockets.

The promoter shoved a small, heavy leather pouch
into his hand. It clinked with the sound of his mother's life.

With trembling, blood-caked fingers, Marcus fumbled
it open. Inside, nestled amongst a few copper and
bronze coins that were his to keep for food, was the
prize. A single, gleaming silver crown.

It was beautiful. It was filthy. It was the price of his
soul.

He clutched it in his fist, the sharp edges of the milled
coin biting into his palm. It was real. He had done it.
He had won the first piece of her salvation.
His heart, which should have soared, sank like a stone.
A cold, stark piece of arithmetic, the only logic that
remained after the game was over, asserted itself
in his mind.

One down. Nine to go.

He had to do this nine more times. He looked down
at the broken man, then at the blood on his own

hands, and knew that the Rook had just begun its long, straight, terrible march across the boar.

The journey back from the pit was a descent into a different kind of hell. The roaring adrenaline that had sustained him through the fight drained away, leaving behind a sucking void filled with a symphony of pain. His head throbbed with a deep, percussive rhythm, a drumbeat of agony that matched the frantic hammering of his heart. His cheek was swelling, a tight, hot pressure that pulled at the corner of his eye. His knuckles, slick with his own blood and that of The Ox, screamed with a sharp, fiery protest.

He stumbled out of the repurposed brewery, pushing through a curtain of hot, stinking air and into the relative cool of the alley. The roar of the pit faded, replaced by the high, thin ringing in his own ears. Silas was there, materializing from the shadows, his face alight with a greedy, proprietary glee.

"I knew you had it in you, boy!" the man crowed, reaching for the pouch in Marcus's hand. "A magnificent performance! The crowd is already screaming for more. Now, about my finder's fee..."

Marcus pulled the pouch back, his movement sharp and jerky. He looked at Silas, but his eyes were a thousand miles away, still seeing the grid, still seeing the shattered Juggernaut on the floor. He said nothing. He simply held the man's gaze, and for the first time, Silas saw not a desperate boy, but something cold and empty and broken. The avarice in the older man's eyes faltered, replaced by a flicker of unease. Silas took a half step back.

Without a word, Marcus turned and limped away, leaving the man sputtering in the alley. The transaction was complete. Silas was irrelevant now.

The silver crown was a point of intense cold in his feverishly hot palm. He clutched it so tightly that its milled edges dug into his flesh, a sharp, grounding pain. It was a brand of his success and his sin. This was it. The first step. The first piece of the price. The thought gave him strength, a desperate, frantic energy that propelled him forward.

He moved through the labyrinth of The Scar, a ghost haunted by his own recent past. Every jarring step on the uneven cobblestones was a fresh negotiation with agony. The mud of the alleys sucked at his bare feet with a wet, greedy sound. The familiar sensory landscape of his home was warped, twisted by his new reality. The sour stench of bodies smelled like the pit. The acrid smoke from a barrel fire made him think of the greasy torches and the hungry, leering faces they illuminated. The distant sound of a drunken argument was a pale echo of the crowd's bloodthirsty roar.

He saw a mangy dog chewing on a bone in a doorway, and the wet, crunching sound it made sent a wave of nausea through him, bringing back the sound of

The Ox's nose breaking under his hand. He flinched, his stomach churning, and hurried past.

He was a creature of two worlds now, walking through the physical squalor of The Scar while his mind was trapped in the blood-soaked sawdust of the ring.

But hope was a powerful, driving force. It was a fever in his blood, hotter than any infection. I have it, Ma. I have the first one. It's real. The words were a silent mantra, a prayer he repeated with every agonizing step. He pictured her face, imagining the brief, lucid smile that might appear when he showed her the coin. He imagined her taking the real medicine, the powerful stuff from the clean apothecary. He pictured her breathing evening out, the rattling sound ceasing, the fever receding from her skin. These images were his fuel, burning away the pain, the guilt, the horror.

He finally reached his tenement, the leaning, patchwork building that was the center of his universe. He took the crumbling stairs two at a time, his battered body screaming in protest, his lungs burning. He ignored it all. He was a knight returning with the grail, a hero with a single, precious piece of salvation.

He reached their door and paused, his hand on the rough, splintered wood. He took a deep, shuddering breath, trying to calm the wild animal in his chest. He tried to wipe the blood from his knuckles onto his filthy trousers. He tried to compose his face, to erase the evidence of the pit, to become her brave boy once more.

"Ma," he whispered, his voice cracking, as he pushed the door open, "Ma, I got it. I got the first one..."

The silence hit him first.

It wasn't the quiet of a sleeping room. It was a different kind of silence. A solid thing, a pressure against his eardrums. For weeks, the soundtrack to his life had been the constant, painful, wet rattling of his mother's breathing. It was a sound he had grown to hate, a sound that haunted his sleep, but it was the sound of life. Of struggle.

Now, it was gone.

The room was filled with a heavy, profound stillness that seemed to absorb all sound, all life. The air was cold, stale. The single candle stub he had left burning was guttering in a pool of its own wax, its flame a weak, flickering pulse in the oppressive dark.

The weak light fell upon the cot.

Abigail lay there, on her side. But she was no longer struggling. The painful, rattling sound was gone. Her face, in the gentle, dying light of the candle, was peaceful. The lines of pain and fever that had been etched so deeply into her features were gone, smoothed away as if by an unseen, gentle hand. She looked younger, more like the mother he remembered from years ago, the one who told stories of green fields.

She was perfectly, utterly still.

Marcus stood frozen in the doorway, the silver crown suddenly feeling like a block of ice in his hand. The hope that had propelled him home, that had been a burning sun in his chest, was extinguished in an instant, plunging him into a darkness colder and more absolute than any night.

"Ma?" he whispered again, his voice trembling, a child's plea to a world that had suddenly gone deaf.

He took a step forward, then another, his bare feet making no sound on the floor. He felt disconnected from his own body, as if he were watching a stranger move. He reached the cot. He reached out a shaking hand, his fingers clumsy with dried blood, and touched her cheek.

The cold.

It wasn't the simple chill of the room. It was a deep, absolute cold that seemed to leach the warmth from his own fingertips, a cold that traveled up his arm and settled like a block of ice in his chest. A final cold.

The world shattered.

The silver crown, the symbol of his victory and his failure, slipped from his numb fingers. It fell to the floorboards, landing with a sharp, shockingly loud clatter. The sound echoed in the crushing stillness, a single, metallic laugh in the face of his grief. The sound broke the spell.

A noise tore itself from his throat. It wasn't a cry or a sob; it was a raw, animal sound of pure, unadulterated anguish. It was the sound of a soul being ripped in two. He collapsed to his knees beside the cot, the pain in his body completely forgotten, eclipsed by a cataclysm of grief so vast it threatened to swallow him whole.

He had been too late.

He had fought, and bled, and brutalized another man. He had sold a piece of his soul in that filthy pit. And for what? He had won the battle, but the war was already lost. The prize in his hand, the prize on the floor, was worthless.

He stayed there for hours, he didn't know how long, kneeling in the cold, dark room, his mother's cold hand clutched in his. The candle burned down and guttered out, the last spark of light winking out, plunging them both into a shared, final darkness. The numbness of shock eventually gave way to something else. The grief did not wash away. It froze. It hardened into something new. A white hot, consuming rage. It was a rage at the world, at the apothecary and his impossible price, at Griswold and the sneering faces in the crowd. A rage at Silas for showing him the way. And most of all, a cold, perfect, all-consuming rage at himself. For not being faster. For not being stronger. For not finding a way.

Sometime before the next greying stole the darkness, he stood up. His movements were stiff, robotic. His face, streaked with tears and grime, was a mask of cold, empty despair. He bent down and picked the silver crown up from the floor. He looked at it, this symbol of his failure, this monument to his lateness. Then, he walked out of the room, leaving the door open to the coming dawn, leaving his mother to the silence.

He found Silas at The Leaky Mug, even at this ungodly hour. The man was nursing a drink, a self-satisfied smirk on his face, no doubt calculating his future earnings.

"Ah, the conquering hero returns!" Silas greeted him, "I knew you had it in you, boy. Ready to celebrate?"

Marcus walked to the table and slammed the silver crown down. It spun, flashing in the tavern's dim light.

"She's gone," Marcus said. His voice was flat, dead, devoid of all emotion. The fury was still there, but it was now a cold, hard diamond of hate in his chest.

Silas's smirk faltered. The blood on Marcus's face, the deadness in his eyes, the finality in his voice. He understood. "Ah. Lad, I'm... sorry to hear that."

"I need another fight," Marcus said, his gaze unwavering, locking onto Silas.

Silas studied him. He saw the hollowed-out eyes, the absence of the desperate hope that had been there before. He saw the raw, brutalized knuckles. And he saw the cold fire that had replaced the fear. This was no longer a boy fighting for a cause. This was a weapon looking for a target. And a weapon was far more predictable, far more profitable.

A slow, calculating smile returned to Silas's face. This was better. A fighter fueled by grief and rage was a spectacle. Unpredictable. Vicious. The crowds would love it. The purses would grow.

"Of course, my boy," Silas said, his voice dropping to a conspiratorial purr, "Whenever you're ready."

From that night on, Marcus fought. He fought with a cold, terrifying ferocity that earned him the name 'The Shadow' in truth. He was a ghost in the pit, a relentless wraith of violence. He won again, and again, and again. The purses of coins grew heavier. Silas grew richer, skimming his twenty percent off the top.

But Marcus never spent a single coin on himself. The money was tainted, soaked in blood and failure. After each fight, battered and bruised, he would take the heavy pouch and walk to the other side of The Scar, to the district's only orphanage, a grim, crumbling building overflowing with the forgotten children of the dead and the destitute.

In the dead of night, he would leave the pouch on the doorstep, knock once, loud and sharp, a single, final sound. And then he would disappear back into the shadows before the door could open. He never saw their faces. He never wanted their thanks.

It wasn't charity. It wasn't kindness. It was penance. It was a desperate, futile attempt to wash the blood off his hands, to buy back the life he had failed to save by saving others he would never know. He would build a monument to his mother's memory out of the very currency of his own damnation. He had failed to save the one person he loved. So he fought, and he bled, and he gave away the spoils, fueling his own self-destruction to give a handful of faceless children a slightly better chance than he'd had. He was trapped in the pit, long after he stepped out of the ropes, his terrible, straight-line march continuing on a board with no king to save and no end in sight.

Chapter 4

Five years.

To a man like Gerald Felcher, five years was a unit of measurement, the value of which was entirely dependent on the context. Five years spent languishing in a forgotten border garrison was an eternity of dust and boredom. Five years spent orchestrating the silent, meticulous fall of a rival merchant house was a satisfying, well-paced campaign. For the boy he had come to observe, five years had been a crucible, a relentless hammer shaping a soul on an anvil of grief.

Gerald stood cloaked in the shadows of an archway, leaning on a cane he did not need, affecting a slight, age-induced tremor he did not feel. The wood of the cane was smooth and dark, a simple affectation of infirmity. The weighted core of solid iron within was a secret kept between him and the kneecaps of several unfortunate fools who had mistaken him for easy prey over the years. From his vantage point, he watched the river of human filth that was the main artery of The Scar.

He hated this place. His hatred was not the passionate revulsion of a moralist, nor the fearful disgust of the privileged. Gerald's hatred was the cold, pragmatic disdain of a master craftsman forced to work with shoddy, chaotic materials. The Scar was a tool, a hiding place, a recruitment pool, a sewer to flush unwanted things into, but it was an inefficient, unpredictable, and deeply unpleasant one. Its stench was an assault on the very concept of order. It was a physical miasma of failure, a chaotic symphony of desperation that offended him on a fundamental level. It smelled of sour gin, of unwashed wool, of rotting fish, of damp earth, and beneath it all, the sweet, cloying odor of human despair, a smell he knew better than any perfumer knew his oils.

His current task was a symptom of the same systemic disease that allowed places like The Scar to fester rot at the core of the kingdom. Whispers in the Royal Court had grown from the rustle of silk to the clang of steel on whetstones. A faction of powerful, reactionary nobles, men whose bloodlines were as ancient as their thinking, felt threatened by the young Prince Alexander's burgeoning idealism. They saw the boy's compassion for the common folk not as a virtue, but as a fatal weakness, an imbalance that would upend their centuries of entitlement. The whispers spoke of... removal. An accident. A tragic illness. A quiet knife in a quiet hallway.

Gerald, in his so-called retirement, had been discreetly tasked by the few loyalists who still remembered his true capabilities to locate assets. Not soldiers or knights who could be tracked through official channels, but ghosts. Weapons that could move through the shadows, untraceable, deniable. Weapons forged in the fire and filth of places like this.

His informant, a miserable wretch named Silas whose loyalty was tethered to a steady stream of coin and the mortal fear of his own sordid past being brought to light, had provided the name. "The Shadow." A pit fighter. For five years, the boy had been the bloody, beating heart of the infamous Rat Pit, a consistent earner for its promoter and a legend amongst the dregs who wagered coppers on human misery.

However, it was the other part of Silas's report that had truly snared Gerald's interest —the anomaly in the data that suggested a far more complex mechanism at work. The boy never kept his winnings. Every blood-soaked purse, without fail, was left anonymously on the doorstep of the city's most destitute orphanage.

That was not the behavior of a common thug. Greed, pride, addiction, those were simple, predictable motivators, easily manipulated and prone to failure. Penance, however, was a far more complex and potent fuel. It spoke of a wound, a deep, festering trauma that had shaped the boy into something more than just a brawler. It suggested a conscience, however twisted, and a conscience, Gerald knew, could be a powerful lever.

Following the low, guttural roar of the mob, a sound that vibrated in the damp air and rattled loose shutters, Gerald made his way to the abandoned brewery. The sound was a beast, a singular creature with a hundred mouths all baying for the same thing: blood. He paid the entrance fee with a casual toss of a coin, his hooded and stooped form drawing no more than a passing glance. He was just another old man seeking a vicarious thrill, another piece of flotsam in the tide. He found a position against a damp stone wall, the rough, cold texture a familiar anchor. He melted into the shadows, his eyes, sharp and analytical as a hawk's, scanning the scene.

The Rat Pit was exactly as he expected, a crude theater of brutality designed to extract coin from the base instincts of men. The air was a hot, suffocating wall, thick with the oily smoke of cheap torches, the stench of unwashed, sweating bodies, and the sharp, metallic tang of spilled blood that clung to the back of his throat. He saw the promoter, Griswold, a corpulent swine whose authority was built on brute force and a complete lack of scruples. He saw the crowd, a churning mix of the desperate from The Scar and the depraved from the upper city, their fine clothes looking obscene in the gloom. Their faces were slack with bloodlust, their eyes wide and hungry, reflecting the flickering torchlight. It was a microcosm of the world's worst impulses, contained and monetized. Gerald felt a familiar weariness. He had spent a lifetime navigating cesspools like this, both literal and metaphorical. The ones in the Royal Palace just wore finer clothes and smelled of lavender.

A rusty bell clanged, a harsh, discordant sound that seemed to split the air. A new fighter was shoved into the ring. Gerald's gaze narrowed, his focus sharpening to a fine point.

This was him—the Shadow.

He was seventeen now, no longer the scrawny, desperate boy Silas had first described. The years in the pit had hammered and honed him. He was lean, but corded with the dense, wiry muscle of a survivor. There was no bulk to him, no wasted mass. Every fiber of his being was calibrated for speed and endurance. His body was a roadmap of his profession, a tapestry of pale, silvery scars crisscrossing his arms and torso, testaments to hundreds of sloppy cuts and glancing blows. A more prominent, jagged scar cut through his left eyebrow, giving his face a permanent, brooding intensity. He moved with a liquid grace, a coiled tension that was utterly at odds with the lumbering brutes who usually fought here. He entered the pit not with a swagger, but with the quiet, deliberate purpose of a man clocking in for a day of hard, unpleasant labor.

But it was his eyes that confirmed Gerald's interest, that validated the entire journey into this sewer. They were the color of a storm-wracked sky, grey and deep and turbulent. And they held nothing. No fear. No excitement. No rage. Nothing at all. They were a chillingly, unnervingly empty void where a boy's spirit should have been. This was not a fighter; this was a ghost who had learned how to hit.

His opponent was a caricature of brutality, a hulking beast the crowd was calling "The Butcher." He was a head taller, easily fifty pounds heavier, with arms like tree limbs and a face that looked like it had been used to tenderize meat. He grinned, a broken-toothed display of malice, and cracked his thick knuckles, a sound like popping twigs. He clearly expected a quick and savage victory.

The bell rang.

The Butcher, like The Ox before him and countless others in between, charged. It was the only tactic men like him knew to overwhelm with brute force. Gerald watched, not as a spectator, but as an assessor. He was evaluating a potential tool for its strengths, weaknesses, and operational parameters.

Marcus, Gerald had made sure to learn his real name, did not retreat. Not this time. Five years had changed his strategy. He held his ground, his body sinking into a low, stable stance. At the last possible second, as the Butcher's massive fist swung for his head with a force that whistled in the hot air, Marcus pivoted. It was not a dodge; it was a fluid, economic movement, a redirection of energy learned through a thousand painful lessons. The Butcher's momentum carried him stumbling past. As he did, Marcus's leg snapped out in a low, vicious kick to the back of the bigger man's knee.

It was a strategist's move, not a brawler's. Gerald's eyebrow raised a fraction of an inch. Interesting. The boy wasn't just reacting; he was thinking, exploiting physics, attacking the foundation.

The Butcher roared in frustration and spun around, swinging wildly. Marcus flowed around him, a shadow indeed. He never stood still, never presented a solid target. He used the ropes, the corners, the very space of the pit as his allies. The fight became a strange, deadly dance. Marcus landed no devastating blows, but a series of short, sharp, irritating strikes, each one a calculated investment in future pain. A jab with his stiffened fingers to the throat, disrupting the big man's breathing. The heel of a hand to the bridge of the nose, a move designed not to break but to obscure vision with a sudden gush of tears and blood. A quick, chopping kick to the thick muscle of the thigh, again and again in the same spot, a relentless effort to deaden the nerve and slow the leg.

Gerald saw the pattern immediately. It was the combat philosophy of the outnumbered and outmatched, death by a thousand cuts. Don't try to shatter the fortress wall; dismantle it brick by brick. This required patience, discipline, and an intimate understanding of pain, both how to inflict it and, more importantly, how to endure it.

The crowd began to grow restless. This wasn't the straightforward carnage they had paid for. It was too much like work. They booed, they jeered. "Fight him, you coward!" a man in fine silks shrieked, his face red with wine and impatience, "Stop dancing!"

Marcus ignored them. His focus was absolute, his empty eyes fixed on his opponent. He was utterly deaf to the world outside the ropes, insulated by his own cold purpose. This, too, was a valuable trait. An asset who could not be swayed by popular opinion or intimidation was a reliable one.

The Butcher's face was now a mask of crimson, a mix of his own blood and incandescent fury. He was tiring; his lunging attacks were becoming slower and sloppier. His roars of anger were punctuated by great, heaving gasps for air. He was a beast of pure rage, and Marcus was the matador, calmly and methodically draining his strength, leading him around the ring by a thread of pain.

The end came with a sudden, brutal efficiency that was breathtaking in its precision. The Butcher, in a final, desperate gambit, lunged forward, his arms open wide, abandoning fists in an attempt to trap Marcus in a bear hug that would surely crush his ribs and end the fight.

Marcus didn't retreat. He moved forward, into the attack. He dropped low, a blur of motion, driving his

shoulder into the man's midsection while simultaneously hooking a leg behind the Butcher's ankle.

It was a perfect, beautifully executed trip, a textbook example of using an opponent's mass and momentum as a weapon against them. The Butcher's forward lunge became his own undoing. He crashed to the sawdust with the force of a felled tree, the air exploding from his lungs in a massive, agonized grunt.

Before the giant could even begin to process what had happened, Marcus was on him. And in that instant, the cold, disciplined fighter vanished, replaced by something else. Something feral.

Gerald watched, his expression unchanged, but his mind was cataloging. The boy had a switch. He possessed the discipline to fight smart, but he also had access to this wellspring of pure, unadulterated savagery. A potent, if dangerous, combination. The trick would be learning how to aim it.

Marcus's fists rose and fell in a relentless, percussive rhythm. There was no art to it now, no strategy. It was the same frantic, desperate violence he had unleashed on The Ox five years ago, but now it was honed, faster, more efficient. It was a storm of rage unleashed upon the downed man's face. Each blow landed with a sickening, wet thud that was audible even over the roar of the crowd, who had now switched from jeering to screaming in ecstatic approval. This was the carnage they had paid to see.

Griswold's men finally pulled Marcus off their unconscious cash cow. The boy stood, his chest heaving, his knuckles bloody. He looked down at the broken man at his feet, and Gerald saw it again, that flicker of utter hollowness in his eyes, like a man looking at a messy chore he had just completed. There was no triumph, no joy in his victory. The roar of the crowd, the chants of "Shadow! Shadow! Shadow!" meant nothing to him.

Griswold waddled into the ring, his jowls quivering with excitement. He grabbed Marcus's arm and held it aloft. Then he shoved a heavy pouch of coins into the boy's hand. Marcus took it without a word, his expression blank. He turned and slipped through the ropes, disappearing into the press of bodies, the cheers and adulation washing over him like water off stone.

Gerald Felcher allowed himself a small, internal smile, a cold, satisfying click of a lock falling into place. He had found it. Not just a tool, but a masterpiece of tormented potential. A boy forged in loss, hammered into shape by five years of brutality, and tempered by a grief so profound that it had burned away everything but a core of cold, hard rage and a desperate need for penance. He was an unclaimed weapon, lying in the filth, waiting for a hand to wield him.

"An investment," Gerald murmured to himself, the word tasting of future possibilities. A pawn, yes, but a pawn with the potential to become a rook. A Black

Rook, capable of moving in the shadows and striking with decisive, linear force.

He pushed himself off the wall, the feigned tremor gone, his movements now precise and purposeful. He knew where the boy was going. He had followed him twice before. The ritual was always the same. First, the fight. Then, the purse. Then, the long, lonely walk to the orphanage on the eastern fringe of The Scar. After that, he would return to Silas, the parasite, to arrange the next descent into hell.

The time for observation was over. The time for acquisition had begun.

He made his way through the throng, his path weaving with an unnatural ease, people seeming to part for him without realizing why. He intercepted Silas near the ale-stained bar, the man's face flush with vicarious victory and the promise of his cut.

"Silas," Gerald said, his voice a low rasp that cut through the noise like a blade.

The informant turned, his greedy smile freezing on his face when he saw who it was. The blood drained from his cheeks, leaving them a pasty, mottled gray. Fear, cold and immediate, replaced the avarice in his eyes.

"L Lord Felcher," he stammered, bowing slightly in a gesture that was both servile and terrified. "I... I didn't know you were in attendance."

"The boy," Gerald said, cutting him off, his voice flat and non-negotiable. "The Shadow. He's mine now. His contract with Griswold is terminated. You will inform the promoter of this. You will receive a final, generous payment for your services, and then you will forget his name, my name, and this conversation. Am I understood?"

Silas swallowed hard, his Adam's apple bobbing in his scrawny neck. He knew Gerald's reputation. He knew that the man's "retirement" was a fiction whispered in the darkest corners of the underworld. To refuse was not an option. "Y yes, my lord. Understood. But Griswold... he won't like it. The boy is his biggest draw."

A flicker of amusement, as cold and brief as winter sunlight, crossed Gerald's face. "I am not concerned with what Griswold likes," he said softly, "Tell him... a prior investor is calling in his stake."

With that, Gerald turned and walked away, leaving Silas trembling in his wake, a man who had just been handed a death sentence to deliver to a much larger, more violent man. It was, Gerald reflected, a fitting end to their business relationship.

He stepped out of the foul, hot air of the brewery and back into the cool, damp night. He knew Marcus would be back soon, his soul a little lighter from his act of penance, his body aching, his mind empty and ready for new instructions.

Gerald didn't leave. He made his way back into the now-emptying pit. The crowd was dispersing, their bloodlust sated, leaving behind a mess of discarded cups, spilled ale, and the lingering stink of their excitement. He found a vantage point on the rough wooden benches overlooking the now-empty ring. He sat down, the posture of a man settling in to wait. From a deep inner pocket of his coat, he pulled a small, hard apple.

He began to eat it with slow, deliberate bites. The apple was crisp and clean, its sharp, sweet scent a stark, defiant contrast to the cloying atmosphere of the pit. The crisp snap of each bite was a small, orderly sound in the decaying silence.

He would wait. He was a patient man. He was about to make a significant investment, after all. And he wanted to inspect the merchandise up close, after it had been stripped of its purpose, at its most vulnerable. He was looking forward to seeing the boy's empty eyes fill with something new when he finally revealed the scale of the game he was about to be forced to play. Confusion, then fear, then, hopefully, a spark of the cold, strategic intelligence he'd seen

in the ring. Yes, this would be a most interesting acquisition.

Chapter 5

The knock was a solitary, percussive sound in the sleeping city. A single, hard rap of bruised knuckles against solid, weathered oak. It was a declaration. Here is the price. The transaction is complete. He didn't wait for the sound of the bolt being drawn, for the creak of the door, for the gasp of the night matron who would find the heavy leather pouch on the step. He was already gone, melting back into the shadows from which he was born.

The air outside the orphanage walls was different. It was cleaner, carrying the faint, soapy scent of lye and washed linen from the laundry room, a smell so alien it was almost painful. It was the smell of order, of a life he was paying for but could never touch. As he moved back toward the festering heart of The Scar, the clean air was stripped away layer by layer, replaced by the familiar, complex perfume of his world. First, the smell of coal smoke from the respectable artisans' quarter, then the sharp tang of the tanneries, and finally, the thick, cloying miasma of The Scar itself, a fusion of decay, stale spirits, and unwashed humanity.

He was a ghost moving through his own haunted house. The purse was gone. The ritual was complete. And the hollow space it left behind was a cavern, vast and echoing. The pain in his body, a dull, throbbing map of the fight, was a distant country. His mind was a smooth, grey, empty plain. This was the state he sought: a blank slate, a perfect void where the screaming memories of a boy and his dying mother could not find purchase. He was not Marcus. He was The Shadow, a function, a mechanism for converting violence into anonymous charity.

His bare feet, calloused and tough as old leather, knew the path back to the squalid room he slept in. It was a pilgrimage in reverse, away from the act of penance and back toward the tomb. The ground was a sensory landscape he read without thinking: the slick, treacherous feel of a patch of spilled gin, the sharp, surprising bite of a loose piece of gravel, the soft, yielding suck of the mud in the main gutters.

He rounded a corner into a narrow passage between a derelict tannery and a leaning tenement, a place where the darkness was so absolute it felt like a physical substance. And he stopped.

A new scent had been added to the air. It cut through the familiar stink of The Scar with the clean, sharp edge of a razor. It was the smell of cheap, cloying pipe tobacco, sweet and foul at the same time. The smell of a parasite.

"Twice in one night. You're making Griswold a rich man, lad."

Marcus didn't flinch. His senses had registered the man's shuffling footsteps, the soft scrape of worn leather on stone, seconds before the voice. He didn't bother to turn. The voice was as familiar as the ache in his own bones. Oily. Self-satisfied. Leech-like.

"He takes his cut," Marcus said, his voice a low, flat rasp that held no inflection. He continued his slow, deliberate walk. The blank slate of his mind remained, for the moment, undisturbed. Silas was part of the ritual, the unpleasant but necessary component that arranged the next transaction.

Silas scurried to keep pace, a frantic, shuffling energy emanating from him. He was a small, stooped man, his face a web of fine lines etched by drink and worry. But his eyes were the same as they had been five years ago — small, calculating, and gleaming with an avarice that never dimmed. The smoke from his clay pipe curled around his head like a foul, spectral halo.

"He does," Silas agreed, puffing, "But the purses could be heavier. The real money isn't in the winning, my boy. It's in the performance."

The word, performance, was a stone thrown into the still, grey pool of Marcus's mind. It created ripples.

It was a violation of the rules. The fight was not a performance. The fight was a transaction. It was an equation. Pain inflicted, pain endured, equals one purse. One purse equals one small act of atonement. To introduce the concept of a "performance" was to contaminate the math with a lie.

Marcus stopped. He picked up a rough scrap of burlap from a refuse pile, a familiar motion, and began to wipe the grime from his hands, the coarse fibers scraping against his raw, split knuckles. The friction was a grounding sensation. "The crowd gets their blood. That's the performance."

"Ah, but they crave a story," Silas insisted, stepping closer. The stench of him, a mix of stale smoke and unwashed wool, was a physical intrusion, making Marcus's nose twitch in disgust. "Imagine this. The Shadow, undefeated for five years, faces a new challenger from the docks. A brute. A killer. The odds are stacked. The wagers fly. But in the third round... you take a fall. Just for a moment. Long enough for the smart money to shift. Then, a heroic comeback. The crowd goes mad. The purses double. Triple, even."

Marcus stopped wiping his hands. He turned his head slowly, and for the first time that night, he fixed Silas with his gaze. His eyes, the color of a storm-wracked sky, were not empty now. The grey, placid plain was gone, replaced by a gathering thundercloud.

"No," he said. The word was flat. Absolute. Unbreachable.

Silas blinked, his smug expression faltering. He had misread the room. "No? Don't be a fool, Marcus. This is how the world works. It's a bigger score. We both stand to profit handsomely."

"I don't care about the score," Marcus said, his voice dropping even lower. A familiar, cold fury, the same fury that he unleashed in the pit, began to uncoil in his gut. This was the first rule of his wretched existence: the fight was sacred. It had to be real. The pain had to be real. The victory, hollow as it was, had to be earned. To fake it, to turn his penance into a cheap pantomime for a few extra coins, was to defile the only meaningful thing he had left. It was a violation of the system. "You find the fights. I take them. That's the arrangement. It doesn't change."

"The arrangement can be improved!" Silas hissed, his greed warring with his caution. The avarice won. "You're a tool, lad, a bloody magnificent one, but you're not seeing the bigger picture! I have an investor, a man of considerable means, interested in maximizing the return on,"

"Find another tool," Marcus cut him off. The fury was a cold, sharp thing now, honed to a fine point. He turned his back on Silas, a gesture of pure, final dismissal.

"You arrogant little whelp!" Silas's voice cracked with frustration and wounded pride. "After all I've done for you! I picked you out of the gutter! I gave you a way to…"

"You gave me a cage and charged admission to watch the animal," Marcus snarled, whirling around. His lean frame, corded with the dense, wiry muscle of a survivor, was coiled like a spring, radiating a palpable aura of menace. For a moment, the empty fighter was gone, replaced by the cornered rat, all teeth and feral intensity. "Don't forget your place, Silas. You're the man who feeds the animal. Nothing more."

He spat on the cobblestones near Silas's feet. A raw, contemptuous sound that sizzled in the quiet alley. He saw fear flash in the older man's eyes, a genuine, primal fear, quickly masked by bluster. That was their dynamic. Marcus was the weapon Silas was the trembling hand that pointed it.

"Is that how you see all your benefactors, boy? As zookeepers?"

The voice was new.

It came from the deeper shadows that Silas had just vacated, but it was nothing like Silas's reedy, gin-soaked rasp. This voice was calm, cultured, and carried an undercurrent of solid iron. It was a sound that did not belong here. It was a sound of clean lines and hard edges in a world of rot and decay. The sound slid down Marcus's spine like a shard of ice, and a primal instinct, honed over five years of violence, screamed at him. Danger. Anomaly. A piece on the board that doesn't belong.

Out of the archway stepped a man who, at first glance, seemed utterly out of place. He was old, leaning on a simple, dark wood cane. He wore a heavy, hooded cloak of good quality, but it was well-worn, showing none of the ostentatious wealth that Marcus associated with the upper city slum tourists. His face, half hidden in the shadow of his hood, was a mask of placid wrinkles. He seemed frail, a dry leaf that a strong wind could carry away.

But his eyes... his eyes were like chips of obsidian. Sharp, analytical, and utterly devoid of the feigned warmth or overt greed Marcus was used to. They swept over Marcus, not as a man, not even as a fighter, but as an object. They assessed his weight, his muscle tension, his stance, the raw state of his knuckles, and the weariness in his posture. It was the dispassionate, calculating gaze of a craftsman examining a tool. For the first time since he had become The Shadow, Marcus felt a sensation he hadn't experienced in years. He felt like prey.

Silas audibly squeaked, a small, pathetic sound like a mouse in a trap. He took a shuffling step back, his face draining of color, the clay pipe slipping from his trembling fingers to clatter on the stones. The sound was sharp, brittle, final. "L Lord Felcher," he stammered, bowing in a clumsy, servile gesture, "I... I did not know you were... here."

The old man, Felcher, ignored Silas completely, as one would ignore a piece of furniture. His gaze remained locked on Marcus. "A fine specimen," he murmured, more to himself than to anyone else, "A potent combination of disciplined rage and... something else. A profound, self-renewing wound." He took a slow, deliberate step forward, his cane making a soft, solid thump on the cobblestones. The sound was quiet, yet it seemed to dominate the sonic landscape of the alley. "Your association with Griswold is concluded. Your services are no longer for hire. You work for me now."

The audacity of the statement was so absolute, so breathtaking, it momentarily stunned Marcus. The cold fury he'd felt toward Silas was instantly magnified a hundredfold, redirected at this intruder. All his life, he had been a creature of The Scar, kicked, used, and forgotten by the powerful. Five years in the pit had at least given him a semblance of autonomy. A grim, terrible autonomy, but his own. He chose to fight. He chose to give the money away. He followed his own brutal rules. No one told him what to do. No one owned him.

A harsh, grating laugh tore itself from Marcus's throat. It was a rusty, ugly sound. "'You work for me now,'" he mimicked in a derisive, snarling tone. He took a step forward, deliberately entering the old man's space, radiating the aura of barely contained violence that had sent larger men than this stumbling backward. This was his territory. This was his board. "Did you not hear me, old man? I don't have keepers." He leaned in, close enough to smell the faint, clean scent of wool and cold iron, his voice a venomous whisper, "Go find some other dog to put on a leash. Before I decide to break that fancy walking stick over your head."

Felcher's expression did not change. The placid mask remained. There was no anger, no fear, not even surprise. There was only a flicker of something in his obsidian eyes. Disappointment. Or perhaps, the clinical observation of a failed test.

"Insolence," Felcher said, his voice still unnervingly calm, as if he were remarking on the weather, "A flaw to be corrected."

It happened faster than Marcus could process. It defied the laws of physics as he understood them. The world seemed to slow, then lurch sideways. The man didn't move like an old man. There was no creak of bone, no hesitation. There was only a fluid, economic shift of weight, a blink and you miss it rotation of the hips. The dark wood cane, which had been resting placidly on the ground, became a blur. It wasn't a wild swing. It was a precise, targeted strike, a piston of dark wood that moved with a speed that defied his age, his posture, his very appearance.

Marcus's instincts, honed by a thousand near misses in the pit, screamed a moment too late. He tried to recoil, to twist away. But the cane was already there. It didn't strike his head or his arms, the places a brawler would aim. It connected with the soft, vulnerable space of his solar plexus.

The sensation was not just pain. It was an implosion.

A white hot supernova of agony erupted in his chest, incinerating the air in his lungs. His entire nervous system shrieked a single, incoherent message of pure, catastrophic shock. His muscles, a moment ago coiled and ready for violence, became useless spaghetti. The world dissolved into a swirling tunnel of gray. His gasp for breath became a choked, strangled off grunt as his diaphragm seized in violent, crippling protest. He tasted hot, coppery blood and the acrid burn of bile rising in his throat.

He folded, not by choice, but by a complete and total systems failure. His knees buckled, and he crashed to the hard, grimy cobblestones. He landed on his hands and knees, his body convulsing, his stomach heaving, trying to expel something that wasn't there. He couldn't breathe. He couldn't think. The universe had been reduced to this single, all-consuming point of agony, and the desperate, futile struggle of his lungs to remember their function.

Through the haze of pain, he was dimly aware of two things. The first was the sound of Silas scrambling away into the darkness like the rat he was. The second was the soft, solid thump of the cane planting itself on the stones mere inches from his head.

He forced his watering eyes open, looking up through a curtain of sweat and tears. Lord Felcher stood over him, his expression utterly unchanged. He looked down at the wheezing, broken boy at his feet with the detached interest of a biologist observing a specimen under a microscope.

"The first lesson," Felcher said, his voice as level and cold as a winter tombstone. "Power is not about the strength in your fist. It is about the will to use it, and the knowledge of precisely where to strike." He nudged Marcus's shoulder with the tip of the cane. It wasn't a violent gesture, but it was heavy, proprietary, an act of ownership. "You are strong. You are fast. You are predictable. And you are, at your core, ruled by sentiment. This makes you a flawed, but potentially valuable, asset."

Marcus finally managed to drag in a ragged, shallow breath. It felt like swallowing broken glass. The rage was still there, a smothered ember under a mountain of pain and humiliation.

"Go... to... hell," he managed to gasp, the words broken and weak, a pathetic defiance.

Felcher allowed a thin, bloodless smile to touch his lips. It held no humor, only a chilling certainty. "I have been there, boy. I am one of its chief architects. It is from there I have come to recruit." He paused, letting his words hang in the foul air. "I know who you are, Marcus. I know about the fight with The Ox. I know about the single silver crown that fell from your numb fingers."

Ice. Pure, soul-deep ice flooded Marcus's veins, colder and more terrifying than any physical pain. That moment, that silent, holy, horrific moment in the dark with his mother's body, was his. It was a sacred, private horror, the genesis of his entire existence. The thought of this... this thing... knowing about it, speaking of it so casually, was a violation far more profound than the blow from his cane. He had been seen. Not just his actions, but his deepest, most secret wound had been cataloged.

"And I know about the orphanage on the eastern fringe," Felcher continued, his voice relentless, each word a precisely aimed dart. "I know of the anonymous donations. A touching, if futile, gesture of penance for a failure that was never yours to begin with. You tried to buy a breath for your mother, Abigail. And now you spend your nights trying to buy back a piece of your own soul with the blood of other men."

The smothered ember of rage flared into a conflagration. With a guttural snarl that was pure animal, Marcus tried to lunge, to launch himself at the man from his hands and knees, driven by a fury that eclipsed all pain, all reason.

Thump.

The cane jabbed down again, this time pressing firmly into the pressure point where his neck met his shoulder. A new, electric shock of pain lanced through him, a white hot spike that bypassed his muscles and went straight to his nervous system. His body went limp, his cheek smacking against the cold, wet stones. He was utterly, completely helpless, a puppet with its strings cut.

"Second lesson," Felcher's voice was now directly above him, a low, conspiratorial murmur. "Information is the truest currency of power. And I am a very, very wealthy man." He removed the cane. "You have a choice. You can stay here, in this cage of your own making. You can continue your little ritual, fighting brutes for the amusement of degenerates, earning scraps to salve a wound that will never heal. You can rot in this sewer, and in ten years, you'll be a broken-down husk with a drunkard's liver and a punch-addled mind, and no one will even remember your name, let alone your mother's."

He let that sink in, the casual cruelty of his words more debilitating than any physical blow.

"Or," he said, his voice dropping further, becoming a thread of dark promise, "you can come with me. You can take this rage, this skill, this pain, and forge it into a real weapon. I will give you a new target for your anger. A bigger cage, with much more dangerous animals. I will teach you how to fight in a war of shadows, where a single whisper can kill more men than a sword. I will give your pain a purpose beyond this... sad, little spectacle."

Felcher stepped back, giving Marcus room. He was no longer pressing, no longer dominating. He was offering. An escape. A different hell.

Marcus lay there for a long moment, the world slowly coming back into focus. The pain in his chest was a dull, persistent fire. The cobblestones were cold and unforgiving beneath his cheek. He could taste blood and grime and the bitter ash of his own shattered pride. He thought of the five years of ceaseless, repetitive violence. The faces in the crowd, all blurring into one leering mask. The meaningless clink of coins. The empty room. The cold ritual. He had thought he was his own master. He was a fool. He was just a ghost, haunting the memory of his own failure, walking in a straight, endless line on a board of his own design.

This man, Felcher, offered him something new. Not hope. Hope was a lie he no longer believed in. He offered him a direction. A target. A chance to aim his bottomless well of rage at a world that deserved it, a world of men like this, powerful, cruel, and untouchable. A chance to stop being a ghost and become a blade.

Slowly, his muscles protesting with every movement, Marcus pushed himself up. He rose to his knees, then, shakily, to his feet. He was unsteady, his body screaming, his pride shattered. He stood before Lord Felcher, not as a defiant pit fighter, but as something new. Something broken and remade.

He looked at the small leather pouch of coins he had dropped during the scuffle with Silas. The price of another broken body. Another pointless offering. He left it there, lying in the filth.

He met Lord Felcher's obsidian gaze. His own eyes, for the first time in five years, held something other than emptiness. It was a cold, nascent flicker of resolve. He didn't speak. He didn't need to. The transaction had already been made.

Felcher gave a curt, satisfied nod. "A wise investment," he murmured.

He turned and began to walk away, his cane thumping
a slow, steady rhythm on the cobblestones. Thump.
Thump. Thump. The sound was no longer just a sound.
It was a beat. It was a command. It was the tolling of
a funeral bell for the boy he had been.

Without a word, Marcus fell into step behind him, a
shadow tethered to a new master, leaving the roar
of the pit and the ghost of The Shadow behind him
in the filthy, unforgiving darkness of The Scar.

Chapter 6

The first step was a declaration of war against his own body. Every nerve ending shrieked in protest, a chorus of fire and shattered glass. The world dissolved into a gray haze of pain, so profound and absolute that it threatened to drown him. He put a hand against the grimy alley wall to steady himself, the slick, cold brick a temporary anchor in a sea of agony. His breath came in ragged, shallow gasps. Sweat, cold and slick, beaded on his forehead, mingling with the dirty water from the trough.

He was a fighter. He knew pain. He had endured broken ribs, dislocated fingers, cuts that went to the bone. He had learned to wall it off, to put it in a box and continue functioning. But this was different. The strike to his solar plexus wasn't the dull, blooming ache of a blunt impact; it was the sharp, specific, and intimate violation of his body's core command center. It felt precise. It felt surgical. It felt like an insult delivered in the language of anatomy, a lesson taught by a master who knew exactly which nerve clusters to address.

Gerald Felcher stood ten feet away, his back partially turned, waiting. The old man's patience was in itself a form of torment. It wasn't the restless impatience of a master with a slow servant; it was the placid, unconcerned certainty of a predator that knows its prey is crippled and has nowhere to run. The silence stretched, amplifying the sound of Marcus's own wheezing breaths and the frantic, unsteady beat of his heart.

"Hurry up, boy," Felcher said without looking back, his voice cutting through the damp air. "The dregs of this place are drawn to the scent of wounded animals. You are currently perfumed with it."

The casual dismissal, the reduction of him to a bleeding piece of meat, stoked the embers of Marcus's rage. It was a fury born of humiliation and powerlessness, the only warmth he had left in the chilling landscape of his new reality. He forced his legs to move, taking another agonizing, shuffling step. His teeth ground together so hard he felt a sharp pain in his jaw, a deep ache in the roots.

"Go to hell," Marcus rasped, the words torn from his throat. It was a pathetic show of defiance, a pebble thrown at a fortress wall, but it was all he had. It was a reflex, a desperate attempt to redraw the lines of their engagement.

Felcher stopped. The steady thump... thump... of his cane ceased. He turned, not with anger, but with the measured calm of a teacher addressing a particularly slow student. He closed the distance between them in three silent steps, his form eclipsing the weak light at the alley's end. He loomed over Marcus, who was leaning heavily against the wall, panting like a winded dog.

"Impulse," Felcher said, his voice a low, instructional murmur that was more chilling than any shout. "The bane of the untrained mind. You mistake a raw emotional response for a show of strength. It is the purest form of weakness. A signal flare announcing your vulnerabilities to the world."

Before Marcus could process the words, the tip of Felcher's cane moved. It was a flicker of motion, a barely perceptible twitch. It didn't swing. It didn't strike with force. It simply moved forward, a precise, targeted jab, connecting with the outside of Marcus's left knee.

A lightning bolt of pure, unadulterated agony shot through Marcus. It was a white hot spike driven directly into the joint, a blinding flash of pain that was completely different from the implosion in his chest. This was a structural failure. He felt a sickening, grinding pop, a sound that seemed to echo inside his own skull, as the kneecap was brutally dislocated. His vision went white, then black, then exploded in a shower of desperate, swimming stars. A sound, a high, strangled cry, escaped his lips before he could clamp his jaw shut. His body went rigid, every muscle locked in a cataclysm of pain, and he slid down the grimy wall, his good leg no longer able to support him. He ended up in a heap on the ground, a whimpering, shuddering mess.

"Third lesson," Felcher continued, his voice as calm as a frozen lake, unmoved by the cry he had just elicited. He was a physician diagnosing a symptom he had just induced. "Your tongue is a weapon. As is your temper. Wield either without discipline or thought, and you will cut only yourself. That was an impulse. It earned you pain. The next time, it might earn you a knife in the guts because you insulted the wrong man and didn't have the sense to see he had friends hiding in the shadows. Do you understand the principle?"

Marcus couldn't speak. He lay on the filthy ground, curled around the throbbing, incandescent sun of his knee, tasting blood and the sour burn of bile. He understood. He understood that every word, every action, had a consequence in this man's world. He had just paid the tuition for his first, brutal lesson in this new, terrifying school. He had been a king in a cage of sawdust. Here, he was less than a novice.

"Get up," Felcher commanded. The tip of his cane nudged Marcus's shoulder, a firm, insistent pressure.

This time, the climb was an exercise in pure, abject misery. The initial shock of the knee injury had worn off, replaced by a deep, throbbing, nauseating ache that radiated up his thigh and down his shin. He used the wall as a crutch, his fingers scraping against the slick, moss-covered brick, and dragged himself upright once more. He didn't look at Felcher. He couldn't. The humiliation was a physical weight, heavier than any fatigue, pressing down on him, stealing the air from his lungs. His own body was now a foreign country, a landscape of betrayal and pain.

The journey began. A slow, agonizing procession of two through the labyrinthine heart of The Scar. Marcus hopped, limped, and stumbled, his world narrowed to the few feet of muddy, refuse-strewn ground in front of him and the steady, relentless tap... tap... tap of Felcher's cane. That sound became his new reality. It was the tick of the clock in his new prison.

The familiar sights and smells of his home were now instruments of his shame. Gaunt-faced men with hollow eyes, huddled around flickering barrel fires, watched them pass. Their gazes, usually blank and inward-looking, now held a flicker of interest, of contemptuous pity. They saw him, The Shadow, the undefeated king of their miserable little pit, now a broken cripple being led on an invisible leash by a strange old man. He felt their stares like hot brands on his skin. His ears burned with a heat that had nothing to do with his exertion.

He saw a lookout for the Sleeper gang, a wiry youth with a shaved head and dead eyes, perched in a tenement window. He saw a known cutthroat named Zev leaning in a doorway, his hand resting on the hilt of the long, curved knife he was famous for. This was Marcus's world. He knew the predators, knew their territories, knew how to navigate the complex, unwritten laws of this urban jungle. This old man, with his clean coat and arrogant bearing, should have been a walking invitation to be robbed and murdered. The fact that he wasn't, the fact that these predators simply watched him pass, was more terrifying than any threat.

"You're lost, old man," Marcus snarled, the words a low, bitter hiss. He needed to reassert some semblance of control, to prove he still knew this world better. "You're a lamb trotting through a wolf pack. That little trick with the cane won't work when there are three of them, and one is slitting your throat from behind."

Felcher didn't even break stride. "Your senses, while sharp for your environment, are miscalibrated for the broader world," he replied, his voice a dispassionate lecture. "You are looking for the obvious threats. Zev, the Sleeper lookout. They are loud dangers, advertised and known. They are, therefore, irrelevant."

He made an abrupt, unexpected turn into a narrower, darker alley that reeked of stale gin and rotting fish. Marcus stumbled after him, his leg screaming in protest at the sharp change of direction.

"You failed to notice," Felcher continued, pointing with his cane toward the mouth of the alley they had just left, "the trio of sewer scrapers who began shadowing us the moment you cried out in the first alley. Not hard men. Just opportunists. One with a weighted sock, one with a sharpened bit of scrap iron. You were so focused on my presence in front of you that you missed them entirely."

Marcus risked a glance back. The mouth of the alley was empty. "You're lying."

"No. I am observant," Felcher corrected him, his tone holding the finality of a mathematical proof, "They peeled off the moment we entered this particular passage. Because they, unlike you, recognize the markings of this territory." He gestured with his cane toward a faded, barely visible symbol chalked on the wall, three overlapping circles. "The sign of the Luteran Tong. This alley is their property. No freelance thief would dare operate here. They would lose a hand for it."

Marcus stared at the symbol. He had seen it a hundred times and never given it a thought. It was just another piece of graffiti in a landscape that was already covered with them. His vaunted street smarts, the keen awareness he had cultivated over years—the very skill that had kept him alive—were suddenly revealed to be shallow. Pathetic. He had been looking at the board, but Felcher knew the rules of every single piece, even the ones that weren't moving. The humiliation deepened, curdling into a cold, sick dread in the pit of his stomach.

"Another lesson, boy," Felcher said, his voice echoing in the narrow passage, "Your awareness is tailored to a twenty-foot ring of sawdust. It is designed to track one opponent. In the world we are entering, threats are layered. They come from all sides, from above and below, and the most dangerous ones are those you never see at all. Your perception must be widened from a spotlight to a sphere. If it is not, you will be a corpse before your education is complete."

They continued in silence for what felt like an eternity. The sounds of The Scar began to recede. The chaotic symphony of screams, drunken shouts, and desperate arguments was replaced by the more structured, rhythmic noises of the city proper. The distant, metallic clang of a far-off smithy. The rumble of wagon wheels on stone. The sharp cries of merchants hawking their wares. The air changed. The thick soup of human misery and decay thinned, giving way to a new set of smells, each one sharp and distinct to Marcus's overstimulated senses. The warm, yeasty smell of baking bread from a shop, so potent it made his stomach clench. The sharp, mineral tang of coal smoke. The rich, earthy scent of horse manure. They were leaving The Scar. With every agonizing step, Marcus felt as though he were being dragged out of a familiar darkness into a blinding, hostile light.

They emerged onto a wider, better-kept street. The tenements here didn't lean on each other for support; they stood, grudgingly, upright. Gas lamps, not greasy torches, were perched on iron poles, their steady, yellow light casting long, clear shadows. People bustled past them, merchants and apprentices, couriers and city watchmen. They paid the strange duo no mind, a hobbling youth and a stern old man, just another fleeting sight in the endless motion of the city. To be ignored here felt different than in The Scar. There, it was a form of survival. Here, it was a mark of his own insignificance.

Felcher led him to a drab, unremarkable three-story building, sandwiched between a cooper's shop, from which came the rhythmic thump thump of a mallet on wood, and a boarding house that smelled of boiled cabbage. A simple sign, its letters faded and peeling, read "J. FENNIMORE, PROVISIONER." Felcher produced a key, a complex, dark iron thing, and opened a side door that led into a narrow, dark staircase.

The air inside was cool and still, smelling of dust, dry rot, and old paper. Felcher ascended the stairs without a word, the tap of his cane the only sound in the confined space. Marcus followed, hauling his wrecked body up each step, his hand sliding along the gritty wall for support. His rage had burned itself out, leaving behind only a cold, hollow exhaustion. He was a million miles from the pit, from the only life he had known. He felt like he was climbing the steps to his own scaffold.

They reached the third floor. Felcher unlocked another door, pushed it open, and stood aside.

Marcus limped into the room, and for a moment, he could only stand and stare, his breath catching in his throat.

It was a simple, modest attic room. A narrow cot with a neatly folded grey blanket. A small table with a single chair. A washbasin with a pitcher of water. A single, unlit candle in a pewter holder. And it was clean. Impossibly, aggressively clean. The floorboards were scrubbed to a pale, worn blond. The air was free of any scent but that of old wood and beeswax. There was a small, grimy window that looked out over the slate roofs of the city.

After the constant, suffocating filth of The Scar, the room felt as sterile and alien as the surface of the moon. It was the antithesis of everything he was. He felt his own grime, his own stench of blood, sweat, and despair, as a physical desecration of the space. It was not a sanctuary. It was a holding cell. It was the cleanest, quietest, most terrifying cage he had ever seen.

The fight finally drained out of him, replaced by a deep, shuddering wave of confusion and a bone-deep weariness that had nothing to do with his injuries. He turned to Felcher, who was standing in the doorway, observing him with that same analytical gaze. A scientist watching a rat navigate a new maze.

"Why?" Marcus whispered, the word barely audible. It was not a challenge. It was not a question of logistics. It was a plea for meaning in a world that had just been rendered meaningless. "Why me? What's the point of all this?"

Felcher stepped into the room, closing the door behind him. The click of the lock was a sound of absolute finality. He walked to the table and set his cane against it. "I told you. You are a weapon. And weapons, like all tools, require maintenance, calibration, and proper application."

He looked at Marcus, his obsidian eyes seeming to pierce the gloom. "You ask 'why you' as if it is a matter of destiny or fate. It is not. It is a matter of pragmatism. I require an instrument of singular, untraceable violence. One motivated not by greed or loyalty, which are fleeting and corruptible, but by something deeper. Something permanent."

He made a gesture that encompassed Marcus's entire broken state, "Your grief is a powerful, self-renewing fuel. I watched you for weeks. You fight with a discipline born of endless repetition, and you finish your opponents with a rage born of a wound that will not heal. Your desire for penance, this need to atone for a failure that was never yours to begin with, can be repurposed. It can be aimed. Instead of atoning for one life you couldn't save, you can be used to preserve a future that is currently in peril."

His voice was a cold, unassailable logic, a butcher appraising a side of beef. "I have no interest in your soul, boy. I am interested in your skills. Your pain has made you sharp. Your loss has made you expendable in your own mind. You are the perfect raw material—a perfectly forged blade left to rust on a dunghill. I am not your savior. I am simply a craftsman who recognizes a fine tool when he sees one and intends to put it to its proper use."

The utter lack of malice in his voice was more terrifying than any threat. Marcus felt a profound chill seep into his marrow. He wasn't a person to this man. He was an object—a thing to be aimed and fired.

"Sit," Felcher commanded, gesturing to the cot.

Marcus obeyed, his body screaming as he lowered himself onto the coarse, clean blanket. The texture was rough against his skin.

Felcher lit the candle. The small flame pushed back the shadows, revealing a small, leather-bound satchel he had placed on the table. He opened it, and Marcus saw not weapons, but medical supplies. Clean linen bandages, a vial of dark, antiseptic-smelling liquid, a wicked-looking needle threaded with dark gut, and two small, polished pieces of wood.

"Give me the leg," Felcher ordered.

Marcus hesitated, then slowly, gingerly, extended his savaged leg.

Felcher knelt, a strange and unsettling sight. He worked with a swift, impersonal efficiency that was more terrifying than any overt cruelty. He cut away the filthy fabric of Marcus's trousers around the knee. The joint was swollen to the size of a small melon, a grotesque, discolored mess of purple, blue, and an angry red.

"A simple dislocation of the patella, combined with torn ligaments," Felcher diagnosed, his fingers probing the swollen flesh with a firm, knowing touch that sent fresh waves of agony through Marcus. "Painful, but not permanently debilitating, if set properly. You were lucky. Had I used the weighted core of the cane, your leg would be useless forever." He looked up at Marcus, his eyes cold and clinical. "Another lesson. Always know the capabilities of your weapon, and never use more force than is required for the task. Restraint is the hallmark of the professional."

He uncorked the antiseptic and poured the stinging liquid over the joint. Marcus hissed, his muscles clenching, but he didn't cry out. He would not give this man the satisfaction.

"Bite on this," Felcher said, handing him a rolled-up piece of leather. It was old and tasted of oil and salt. Marcus took it and clamped it between his teeth.

"This will be unpleasant," Felcher stated, a masterpiece of understatement.

He placed the two small wooden blocks on either side of the knee. Then, with one hand pressing down on Marcus's thigh to hold the leg immobile, he grasped the joint with the other.

"Breathe," he commanded.

And then he pushed.

The world exploded—a universe of pure, white hot, screaming pain. The piece of leather in his mouth was the only thing that stopped him from howling like a tortured animal. He felt a sickening, grinding pop as the kneecap was forced back into its groove. His vision went black. He distantly felt himself thrashing on the cot, but Felcher's grip was like iron, holding him fast.

When he came back to himself, seconds or minutes later, he was slick with sweat, trembling violently, and the world was a blurry, tear-streaked watercolor. Felcher was already wrapping the knee tightly with clean linen bandages, his movements quick and economical. The sharp, catastrophic pain had subsided, replaced by a deep, oceanic throb that was almost a relief by comparison.

Felcher finished his work and stood up, wiping his hands on a clean cloth. He placed a small tin cup of water and a piece of hard, dry bread on the table beside the cot. Beside them, he left a small, corked vial filled with a clear, syrupy liquid.

"The water and bread are for now," he said, "The vial is laudanum. It will dull the pain and allow you to sleep. Rest. Your body must heal. I have paid for this room for one night."

With that, Felcher turned, walked to the door, and stepped out. The lock clicked shut, the sound echoing in the profound silence of the room, a final, metallic punctuation mark.

Marcus lay on the cot, alone. The clean, quiet room felt like a tomb. His leg throbbed in time with the frantic, terrified beat of his own heart. He was a prisoner. A tool. A weapon being serviced by its new owner. The rage was still there, a cold, hard ember deep inside him, but it was banked by a terrifying clarity. He couldn't fight this man. Not yet. He had to learn. He had to listen. He had to understand the rules of this new, monstrous game. He had to let the craftsman sharpen his blade.

He looked at the vial of laudanum, then at the grimy window. He had left The Scar, but he had just entered a much deeper, much more dangerous pit. And this time, he wasn't sure he would ever be able to climb out.

He resisted the laudanum at first, the vial sitting on the table like a silent dare. He knew about it. It was the milk of the poppy, the slum's favorite poison, a sweet, numbing solace for those who wished to forget. He equated it with surrender.

But the pain in his leg had its own insistent rhythm, a throbbing drumbeat of misery that made thought impossible. After hours spent staring at the cracks in the ceiling, each one a branching tributary on a map of desolation, he succumbed. He uncorked the vial and swallowed the cloying, bitter liquid, chasing it with the stale water.

Sleep did not come for him. It ambushed him.

One moment, he was lying on the cot, aware of the coarse blanket and the distant, muffled sounds of the city. The next, he was unmoored, adrift in a sea of thick, viscous darkness. The air tasted of damp soil and forgotten memories. It pressed in on him, a palpable weight. He was suspended in the very mud of The Scar's gutters, his limbs leaden.

There was a faint, watery light ahead, and in it, a silhouette. A woman's form, slender and achingly familiar. Ma?

The silhouette turned. It was Abigail, but not the gaunt, fever bright woman of his nightmares. This was the mother from a softer time, her auburn hair vibrant, her eyes clear. A wave of love so fierce and painful it felt like a physical blow washed over him. He tried to move toward her, but it was like running through waist deep mud.

Then, another figure stepped into the weak light, emerging from the darkness at his side. It was Gerald Felcher. The world tilted. His mother was talking to Felcher, her voice a low hum he couldn't decipher. Her expression was one of earnest, heartbreaking appeal. She placed a hand on Felcher's arm, a plea in the gesture. An impossible, paradoxical image.

The scene shifted, and they were at the public pump, the one where he had washed his bloodied hands a thousand times. The water gushing from the spout was not murky brown but thick and red. His mother dipped her hands into the blood and held it out to Felcher, her gaze beseeching.

What is this? he tried to shout, but his mouth was full of mud. What are you saying to him?

His mother finally turned her gaze to him. Her eyes were filled with an infinite, weary sadness. "He has to be kept safe," she mouthed, the words a blade in his chest. The "he" was a dizzying vortex. Was she talking about him? Or someone else?

The murky ground beneath him gave way completely. He was falling. Flashes of his life flickered past the pain of the cane, the crunch of The Ox's nose, his mother's hand on his brow, the gleam of a silver crown. He fell through it all until he landed with a sudden, jarring finality.

The impact was on something smooth, cool, and unyielding. He was standing on a vast, polished surface of alternating light and dark squares that stretched to a hazy, infinite horizon. A colossal, world-sized chessboard.

He looked down at himself. He was clad in armor of a dark, smoky gray, almost black. It was sleek, unadorned, the articulated plate of a knight, but it held no heraldry, no allegiance. In his hands, he held a tower shield. He was a chess piece. The Black Rook.

A voice, like mountains grinding together, rumbled from above. "Interesting. The grief remains potent. The will to obey, however, is nascent. Still too much... resistance."

He looked up. Towering over the board, his head lost in the twilight of the sky, was Gerald Felcher. A god, a primordial force clad in shadows, his eyes twin dying suns. A great, shadowed hand, the size of a city block, descended, and its fingers closed around him.

He was lifted. The world swooped away. He dangled thousands of feet above the board. He saw the other pieces arrayed across the vast expanse, ghosts carved from gray smoke, their forms vague and unimportant. Only two others held any substance. On his side, cloistered behind phantom pawns, stood a single King carved from white, luminous alabaster, shining with a soft, internal light. Across the chasm of empty squares stood another King, this one of grim, pitted obsidian.

Felcher's colossal face leaned closer, his breath a cold wind. "The game is simple," his voice rumbled. "Their King is rigid, predictable. Our King... our King wishes to change the rules. A noble, but dangerously naive, philosophy." The giant hand moved, placing Marcus down with a solid, echoing click onto a new square, far forward, exposed. "Your role is also simple. You are a rook. Power in straight lines. A blunt instrument. You will move where I tell you. You will clear the board of threats. You will be my Black Rook, and you will cast a long, long shadow."

A gray, smoky pawn on the opposing side began to slide forward.

"Protect the King," the voice of Felcher thundered from the heavens, a command that was also a prophecy, a judgment, and a curse, "That is all that matters. Do not fail."

The final words were a hammer blow. He woke with a choked, violent gasp.

His heart was a frantic drum against his ribs. The cramped attic room. The dirty light of dawn. The dull, throbbing ache in his leg. He was back. A sound cut through the silence. The click of a leather strap.

Across the room, his back to Marcus, stood Felcher, methodically packing his satchel. He was preparing to move. The dream clung to Marcus like a shroud. He looked at the old man and saw a colossal, cosmic player moving pieces on a board he couldn't comprehend.

"The dream..." Marcus croaked.

Felcher didn't turn. "The laudanum has its side effects," he said, his voice clipped, "Fantastical dreams are common. A pointless waste of energy." He finally turned, the god of the dream replaced by the infuriatingly calm man, "It doesn't matter. Get dressed. We leave in five minutes."

Marcus stared at him, the memory of being lifted, of that thunderous, damning command, more real than the solid floor beneath him. Do not fail.

The words echoed in the deepest, most wounded chamber of his heart. Felcher hadn't just taken him from the pit; he had looked into the raw, festering wound of his soul and named the disease. He hadn't just broken his leg, he had dismantled his very identity and was now reassembling it into something of his own design.

He was a rook. He was a weapon. And the game had already begun.

With a grunt of pain and a surge of cold, terrifying resolve, Marcus swung his legs over the side of the

cot and began the agonizing process of getting ready
for the first move.

Chapter 7

The world was a throbbing symphony of pain, conducted by the relentless, jarring rhythm of his own limping gait. Every step on the cobblestones was a fresh insult to his knee, a jolt of fire that traveled up his spine and exploded like a firework behind his eyes. The clean, bandaged joint felt alien, a foreign object grafted onto his body, and with each movement, the torn ligaments within sent out their own sharp, insistent protests. He had been given no crutch, no assistance, only a terse command to "walk it off, the muscles will thank you for it later." It was less a piece of advice and more a continuation of his torment, a lesson in enduring misery without complaint.

He was dressed in a set of clothes Felcher had produced from a bundle: simple, gray wool trousers, a rough-spun linen tunic, and worn leather boots that were a size too large and chafed his ankles with every agonizing step. The fabric was coarse and unfamiliar against his skin, a constant, abrasive reminder of his new station. It was a uniform for his new role as... what? Prisoner? Apprentice? Weapon in training? He felt like a stray dog that had been deloused and collared, but was a stray dog all the same. The loss of his old, filthy clothes, which had carried his own scent, the scent of his mother, the scent of his life, felt like being stripped of his own skin.

"You'd think for all your grand pronouncements, you could afford a carriage," Marcus muttered, his voice a low, bitter rasp. The bravado was a flimsy shield, but it was the only one he possessed. He pitched his voice to be just loud enough for Felcher to hear, a small act of rebellion in a world where he had no power, a pebble flicked at a mountain. "Or is making the cripple walk part of the grand lesson plan, you sadistic old goat?"

Felcher, walking a few paces ahead, didn't stop or turn. His cane tapped its relentless, steady rhythm on the stones, a sound that was beginning to permanently etch itself into Marcus's brain. "Insolence," he stated, his voice carrying back to Marcus, as devoid of emotion as a ledger entry, "Another debit against your account. As for a carriage, they are slow, conspicuous, and reek of bourgeois complacency. They are for merchants showing off their new wealth or nobles too fat to walk. We are neither."

"So we're just... poor, then?" Marcus shot back, a sneer in his tone. He shifted his weight, and a fresh jolt from his knee made him wince, a physical punctuation that undercut his defiance.

"We are invisible," Felcher corrected without inflection, "A state that requires speed, subtlety, and an avoidance of unnecessary attention. Principles you have yet to grasp." He came to a halt at the intersection of two narrow, unfamiliar streets, where the buildings huddled close, casting the morning in a perpetual gloom. The air here was thick with the smell of damp brick and chimney soot. "Wait here."

Before Marcus could formulate another sarcastic retort, Felcher put two fingers to his lips and emitted a sound that was less a whistle and more a piercing, complex birdsong. It was a short, thrilling melody that seemed to cut through the ambient noise of the city — the distant rumble of wagons, the shouting of vendors — sharp and clear as a shard of glass. It hung in the air for a moment, an anomaly of sound in the urban cacophony.

For a moment, nothing happened. The street remained empty save for a few stray cats and a woman shaking a rug from an upper-story window. Marcus watched, a cynical curl on his lip. Was this another one of the old man's tricks? A magic whistle to summon a flock of pigeons to peck his eyes out?

The shadows detached from the wall of the alleyway across from them.

It was the only way to describe the phenomenon. They didn't emerge; they simply materialized. One moment, there was a solid brick wall, stained with damp and age. The next, three figures stood there, silent and still as statues in a graveyard. They were wrapped in dark, ragged cloaks that seemed to drink the light, their faces entirely obscured by deep hoods that left nothing but a black void where features should be. They were street wraiths, creatures of the city's underbelly, but they moved with a disciplined cohesion that spoke of something far more organized than mere thuggery. They were not a gang, they were a pack, their stillness a shared, predatory language.

Marcus's hand instinctively twitched, a useless, in-grained reflex from the pit. He took a half step back, his heart thudding against his ribs with a heavy, pan-icked beat. These men radiated a silent, predatory stillness that made the loud, posturing thugs of The Scar seem like boisterous, clumsy children.

One of the figures led a horse.

And that was when Marcus forgot the pain, forgot the silent, menacing men, forgot his own bitterness and humiliation. He forgot everything but the horse.

He had seen horses before, of course, but always from a distance, objects in a world that did not belong to him. They were the property of the City Guard, stomping nervously in formation, their tack jingling, their breath misting in the cold. Or they were tired, sway-backed dray horses, their ribs showing, their heads hanging low as they pulled heavy wagons of goods into the markets. They were part of the landscape, like buildings or birds, things that existed in a world apart from his own.

But this horse... this horse was a living myth. It was a creature pulled from a forgotten, more epic age.

It was immense, a creature of midnight and muscle, its coat a deep, lustrous black that seemed to absorb the watery morning light and hold it captive. It wasn't the glossy, pampered black of a nobleman's parade mount; it was the matte, formidable black of a thundercloud —a darkness that promised power. It stood a good hand taller than any guard horse Marcus had ever seen, its chest broad and powerful enough to break a shield wall, its legs thick with cabled sinew that spoke of incredible strength. A faint web of old, silvery scars patterned its flank and neck, not the random nicks and scrapes of a working animal, but the precise, grim lacework of old battles, lines that told stories of blades and arrows. One of its ears was notched, and a thin, white line traced its way down from just below its eye, a duelist's scar.

The horse radiated an aura of immense, coiled power, but also a profound, world-weary calm. Its eyes, large and dark and unnervingly intelligent, surveyed the street with a serene disinterest. They flickered over Marcus for a second, the gaze assessing him as no threat, and then dismissed him with the casual certainty of a king ignoring a peasant. This was not just an animal; it was a veteran.

Felcher approached the horse, and for the first time, Marcus saw something akin to warmth touch the old man's severe features. The hard lines around his mouth softened almost imperceptibly. He reached out and ran a hand down the horse's powerful neck, his fingers tracing the line of a thick, ropy muscle.

"Euphrates," Felcher murmured, his voice softer than Marcus had yet heard it, the syllables imbued with a rough affection. The horse turned its great head and nudged Felcher's shoulder with a soft nicker, a sound like old leather and rumbling earth, a private communication between old comrades.

Awe, pure and childlike, pierced through the layers of Marcus's cynicism. It was a foreign, almost painful sensation, a muscle he hadn't used in years. He had spent his entire life in a world of decay and brutal utility. He had never seen something that was, in its own way, so perfectly and terribly beautiful. The horse was like a piece of a forgotten, more epic age, a living embodiment of the strength and certainty he had never known.

One of the hooded figures stepped forward and handed the reins to Felcher. The reins were not fancy, just thick, well-oiled leather. "The package is secured at the Rookery, my lord. No complications."

The man's voice was a low, toneless rasp, devoid of any identifying character. It was a voice designed to be forgotten.

"And Silas?" Felcher asked, his eyes still on the horse, his hand still stroking its neck.

"He delivered his final report. And then he... retired. Also, no complications."

A cold sliver of understanding slid through Marcus, sharp and chilling. Silas was gone. Not run off, not paid off. Retired. In the parlance of the shadows, a word he was beginning to learn, that meant only one thing. The man who had put him in the pit, the parasite who had fed off his pain for five years, had been erased from the board. It should have felt like justice. It should have felt like a victory. Instead, it just felt... cold. An administrative detail. Another debit cleared from Felcher's ledger. A loose end tied up with ruthless efficiency.

"Very good," Felcher said, "Return to your watch. Await my signal."

The three figures nodded in unison. They did not walk away. They simply receded, melting back into the alleyway from which they had come, the shadows swallowing them whole until the street was empty once more. One moment, they were there; the next, they were not.

Felcher turned his attention to Marcus, his brief moment of warmth gone, the stern tutor back in place. "The horse's name is Euphrates. He served with me in the Fourth Border Legion for twelve years. He has seen more battles, possesses more courage, and is demonstrably more intelligent than any man you have ever fought. You will treat him with respect." He swung himself into the saddle with a fluid ease that belied his age and supposed frailty, a motion as practiced as breathing. From his new perch, he looked down at Marcus, his authority magnified by his height. "Up."

Marcus stared up at him, then at the vast expanse of the horse's back. It looked as high as a rooftop. "Up where?" he scoffed, the instinct to resist, to push back against this total domination, kicking back in. "I'm not a sack of potatoes for you to sling over your shoulder."

"That is precisely what you are at the moment," Felcher said flatly, his voice a low rumble. "A troublesome, but necessary, piece of luggage. Do you intend to walk to the capital? At your current pace, we might arrive by winter. Your leg will have healed, but my patience will have expired. I assure you, you do not want to see my patience expire. Now, up."

He reached down a hand. It was a lean, wiry hand, the skin dotted with age spots, but the grip looked as strong as forged iron.

Grumbling, feeling his ears burn with a fresh wave of humiliation, Marcus acquiesced. This was impossible. There was no way he could haul his own dead weight, let alone with his wrecked leg, up the side of this mountain of a horse. But defying the order, he was quickly learning, was a far worse alternative.

He reached up and took Felcher's offered hand. The old man's skin was dry and cool, his grip firm. And the world tilted.

Felcher pulled. There was no visible strain in his arm, no grunt of effort, no shifting in the saddle. It was a single, fluid, upward motion, as easy as lifting a jug of water. Marcus, all one hundred and thirty pounds of wiry muscle and bone, was lifted off the ground as if he were a child's doll. He let out an involuntary yelp of surprise as he was hauled upward, his feet dangling in the air. For a dizzying moment, he was airborne, held aloft by the impossible, steel-like strength of this deceptively frail old man.

He was deposited onto the horse, seated in front of Felcher, his back pressed against the old man's firm chest. He landed with a clumsy jolt that sent a spike of white hot pain through his knee. The horse, Euphrates, didn't so much as twitch at the sudden addition of his weight, his powerful body as solid and unmoving as a stone monument.

Marcus sat there, stunned and breathless. The sheer, casual display of power was more intimidating than any blow from the cane. This wasn't the deceptive speed of a well-placed strike; this was raw, undeniable strength, hidden beneath a mask of old age. Felcher was a fortress, and Marcus realized he had only been chipping away at the outermost wall.

The world looked different from up here. Higher. The perspective shifted. He was above the heads of the other pedestrians. The city spread out around him, a maze of stone and slate and motion. He could feel the immense warmth of the great animal beneath him, a living furnace, the subtle yet powerful shift of its muscles as it breathed. He was acutely aware of Felcher's presence behind him, a wall of stern disapproval at his back, the man's arms on either side of him as he held the reins. It was the most secure he had ever felt in his life, and also the most trapped.

"Hold on to the pommel," Felcher ordered, his voice a low rumble just behind Marcus's ear. The proximity of the sound, the vibration of it against his own back, was unsettling.

Euphrates began to move. It wasn't the jarring trot of the city guard's mounts. It was a smooth, ground-devouring walk, each hoofbeat a steady, powerful rhythm that was felt more than heard. They moved through the city streets with an unnatural ease. The crowds of people, the carts, the chaos, it all seemed to part before them, not out of fear, but as if acknowledging a superior presence, a force of nature that was not to be impeded.

As they rode, Marcus's initial awe began to morph into a boyish curiosity that he couldn't entirely suppress. He ran a hesitant hand along the horse's neck. The hair of its mane was coarse, like rough rope, but its skin beneath was like warm satin stretched over stone. He could feel the power vibrating through its body, a low hum of contained energy. He thought of the roaring, sweaty, stinking pit. The claustrophobic cage of blood and sawdust. And now this, this feeling of moving, of gliding through the world on the back of this magnificent beast. It felt like a kind of freedom, even though he was a prisoner.

"He likes apples," Felcher said suddenly, his voice startlingly close.

Marcus snatched his hand back as if he'd been burned, his face flushing with heat. "I wasn't, I was just."

"He is also fond of carrots, but has a curious disdain for pears. When he was younger, in the border garrisons, he developed a taste for cheap ale. He once consumed an entire bucket left unattended by a careless stable hand and spent the afternoon attempting to sit in the captain's chair." For the briefest of moments, a flicker of something that sounded almost like wry amusement touched Felcher's voice, before it was immediately smoothed away into his usual flat tone. "An appalling lack of discipline."

Marcus couldn't help it. A small, involuntary smile touched his lips. He imagined the great, stoic warhorse, drunk and trying to squeeze into a captain's chair. The image was so absurd, so profoundly at odds with the terrifying, epic beast he was riding, that it was hilarious. He quickly smothered the smile, remembering who he was with, but the moment had happened. A tiny, almost microscopic crack had appeared in the wall of his resentment.

They rode on in silence for a long time. The city's dense heart began to thin, the stone buildings giving way to more modest timber and plaster homes, then to walled estates with glimpses of green gardens within. They were heading toward the Spire, the glittering needle of the Royal

Palace that was a constant, indifferent presence on the horizon, a symbol of a world that had forgotten The Scar existed.

Marcus felt the exhaustion settling deep into his bones. The jarring ride, the constant, throbbing pain in his knee, the whirlwind of the last twelve hours... it was all catching up to him. His head began to nod, his body slumping forward against the horse's powerful neck. The smell of the horse was clean and animal, a scent of hay, sweat, and warm leather.

He felt Felcher shift behind him. A firm hand settled on his shoulder, not pushing, not punishing, but simply steadying him, keeping him from toppling over. The hand was a point of immense, solid reality against the sea of his fatigue.

"Sleep, boy," Felcher's voice was a low, non-negotiable command. It was not a suggestion; it was an order to be obeyed. "The journey is long. Your body is broken, and your education has barely begun. There will be more pain. More lessons. More fury. Conserve your strength. You are going to need all of it."

Marcus didn't want to obey. He didn't want to show this weakness, to give in to the exhaustion. It felt like another surrender, another piece of himself he was ceding to this man. But the steady, rhythmic gait of the horse was a lullaby of power, a slow, deep rhythm that resonated in his bones. The firm hand on his shoulder was a tether to this new, terrifying reality. And the vast, aching weariness was an enemy he could no longer fight.

His world narrowed to the feel of the horse's warm neck beneath his cheek, the steady thud thud thud of its hooves on the road, and the undeniable, solid presence of the monster at his back. For the first time since he had charged headlong into his new life, Marcus surrendered completely. He closed his eyes and let the darkness take him, a passenger, a prisoner, a boy on the back of a legend, riding toward a future he could not begin to imagine, a future that smelled of apples and old battles and the cold, clean scent of iron.

Chapter 8

Sleep was not a gentle tide this time, not the slow, creeping mercy of laudanum. It was an ambush. One moment, Marcus was a passenger in the waking world, his consciousness a flickering candle flame against the wind of his own fatigue. He was aware of the rhythmic, swaying gait of Euphrates, a living metronome that rocked him deeper into stupor. He could feel the unyielding presence of Felcher at his back, a solid wall of iron will that was both a prison and a strange, unwelcome form of security. He could smell the world passing by, the clean scent of cut grass from a nobleman's estate, the sharp tang of woodsmoke, the rich, animal musk of the horse. The next moment, the sensory input of the physical world was violently severed, like a rope cut with a sharp knife. He plunged.

He was back.

The sensation of arrival was a physical shock, a silent thud as his consciousness was slammed back into the cold, unyielding form of the rook. He stood on his starting square, a tower of smoky black iron on a vast, polished chessboard that stretched into a misty, indeterminate horizon. The weight of the armor was immense, a physical manifestation of his new, inescapable purpose. It didn't just rest on his shoulders; it was fused to his very being, a cage of duty. His shield felt as heavy as a gravestone. The air was thin and cold, carrying a scent he was beginning to recognize as the signature of this place — the smell of ozone after a lightning strike, and sterile, ancient dust, the scent of a lifeless world waiting for a game to begin.

He was in the back rank, positioned in the corner of the board, the traditional starting square for the Queen's Rook. To his left, stretching out in a formidable line, stood the other pieces of his army, the forces of shadow. The pawns were a solid, unbroken wall, their forms identical, their faces indistinct and featureless, like figures carved from hardened smoke. They were pure potential, a shield of lesser lives waiting to be spent. Next to them stood the major pieces, each with its own distinct, menacing character. There was a knight, its form not that of a noble destrier, but of a lean, vicious wolf, its head low, its muscles coiled as if ready to spring. There was a bishop, whose sharp, angular cowl was pulled low, its form suggesting a severe and unforgiving faith, a creature of rigid, diagonal dogma. And beside the King stood the queen, a figure of terrible, cold majesty, her form tall and slender, radiating an aura of silent, lethal power. They were his army. They were all silent, all motionless, emanations of a single, unified, shadowy will.

And at the center of their line, cloistered behind the wall of pawns, stood his King.

Again, the King was carved from what looked like alabaster, but today its light seemed dimmer, more vulnerable. A shimmering haze, like heat rising from a road on a sweltering day, blurred its edges, making its features impossible to discern. Marcus knew, with a certainty that required no thought, that this hazy, indistinct figure was the nucleus of his entire existence. The command from his previous dream echoed in the hollows of his mind, not as words, but as a fundamental law of this universe: Protect the King. He felt the purpose of it as a physical pull, a chain forged of duty and iron will that connected his square to the King's. His role was absolute: be a fortress, a spear, a shield of last resort.

Then, his gaze was drawn across the board.

Across the sixty-four squares of checkered desolation, the opposing army was arrayed in a perfect, mirror-image formation. But where his side was forged of shadow and night, theirs was carved from bone. They were not a gleaming, pristine white, the color of heroism or purity. It was the color of old, bleached skeletons, a dry, porous ivory that seemed to suck the very light out of the air. Each piece, from the smallest pawn to the towering King and Queen, radiated a palpable aura of corruption. It was a cold, sickly energy, a miasma of decay and righteous, self-assured malevolence that washed across the board in invisible waves. It was a presence that felt fundamentally wrong, like a discordant note in the music of the universe. It smelled of dust and dry graves, of rot that had long since been scoured of moisture, leaving only a brittle, hollow shell.

It was the Ivory Blight.

The name blossomed in his mind, unbidden but utterly correct. These were not mere opponents. They were a disease. Their goal was not just to win the game, but to infect every square, to drain the life from every piece, to turn the entire world into their own sterile, bone-white necropolis. A shudder, not of fear but of pure, instinctual revulsion, ran through him. His purpose was not just to protect his King, but to halt the spread of this plague.

For a long moment that stretched into an eternity, nothing moved. The two armies faced each other in absolute, thrumming silence. The tension was a physical thing, a high-frequency vibration that hummed just at the edge of hearing, making the nerves in his teeth ache. The game was poised on the knife's edge of its beginning, a breath held before the first, irrevocable move.

Then, a movement.

A pawn in the center of the white army slid forward. Not one space, but two, a bold, aggressive opening gambit. It moved with a smooth, silent hiss, its ivory base gliding over the polished board as if lubricated by its own corruption. It came to a rest in the very heart of the battlefield, a stark white sentinel planted deep in neutral territory, a declaration of intent, a flag planted in conquered land.

As it settled onto its new square, the featureless, generic form of the pawn began to waver, to shimmer like the King's form, but this was a different kind of distortion. This was not a haze of mystery; it was a transmutation of malice. The smooth, carved bone seemed to melt and run like hot wax, its contours shifting, reshaping themselves with a sickening, plastic slowness. The

sound it made was not a sound at all, but a psychic squelch, the noise of reality being forcibly reshaped.

Marcus watched, his hand tightening on the grip of his heavy shield until his knuckles were white. The pawn was transforming. The featureless head grew thin, wisps of carved hair appearing on a balding pate. The body elongated, taking on the stoop of a man perpetually bent over a counter, a posture of false humility. The smooth surface of its face puckered and folded, forming a long, thin nose upon which perched a pair of delicate, spectral spectacles. The form re-solved itself with a final, soft click into a perfect, bone white effigy of Master Elian, the apothecary.

His face wore an expression of calm, clinical pity — the same look he had given Marcus in his shop, what felt like a lifetime ago. His voice echoed across the vast board, not a shout, but an intimate, insidious whisper that bypassed the air and wormed its way directly into Marcus's mind, coiling in his memory like a venomous snake.

"The ingredients are exceedingly rare, boy," the ivory apothecary whispered, its words a symphony of con-descending regret, each syllable a perfectly polished stone of dismissal. "Pearl dust doesn't come cheap. A full course of treatment... it would cost ten silver crowns."

Rage.

It was a white hot, volcanic surge of it, so powerful it almost buckled his knees. The memory was not a memory; it was a fresh, bleeding wound, ripped open and filled with salt. This man, this piece, was the face of the system that had condemned his mother. The face of cold, polite, well-reasoned cruelty. The face of a world where life had a price tag, and his love hadn't been enough to pay it. This was the voice of the locked door, the insurmountable wall, the casual, business-like sentence of death. This was the calculated, devastating reason he had been sent into the pit in the first place.

This was the first move of the Ivory Blight. Not a faceless soldier, but a memory. A tailored, personalized strike aimed directly at the deepest crack in his soul. They weren't just playing a game; they were dissecting him.

An impulsive, animal snarl built in Marcus's throat, a low, guttural sound of pure hate. His mission was to protect the King, but this... this was an affront that could not be borne. The board, the King, the game, it all receded into a red-tinged periphery. All he saw was that face, that calm, reasonable monster, and all he felt was an overwhelming, primal need to smash it into a thousand pieces of ivory dust.

He moved.

He braced his feet against the cool, smooth surface of his square, intending to charge forward in a straight, furious line. A rook's move. The only move he truly understood. He would cross the board, a black thunderbolt of retribution, and obliterate that ivory pawn before the game could even truly begin. He would show them what happened when they stirred the ghosts of his past.

He took a single, lurching step. His armored foot came down on the next square with a resounding, echoing clang. And stopped. Not by his own volition.

A force, immense and irresistible, clamped down on him. It wasn't the giant, physical hand from the previous dream. It was a psychic restraint, an unyielding imposition of will that froze him in place, locking every joint in his armor, paralyzing every muscle in his body. It was the presence of his player. It was the cold, dispassionate will of Gerald Felcher.

"Impulse," the thought boomed in his mind, not a word, but a pure concept, a wave of cold, disapproving logic that crashed against the incandescent shores of his rage. "The bane of the untrained mind. You mistake a raw emotional response for a show of strength. It is the purest form of weakness. A flare fired in the dark, showing the enemy exactly where you are and how to wound you."

The memory of the lesson, and the phantom agony of the cane in his solar plexus and his knee, lanced through him. He fought against the restraint, straining with every fiber of his being. It felt like being encased in a block of ice. He could see the Apothecary Pawn standing there, exposed, mocking him with its passive existence. The urge to destroy it was a physical hunger, a gnawing emptiness that only the crunch of its ivory form could fill.

"Analyze," the mental command from Felcher was sharp, cutting through his rage like a scalpel. It forced his eyes open, forced his mind to work. "Observe the board. Your move is a reaction, not a strategy. It satisfies your anger, but what does it achieve? You would trade your Rook, a major piece of power and control, a pillar of our defense, for a single pawn. An uneven exchange. They would welcome it. They would celebrate your foolishness as they remove you from the game."

Forced to be still, his gaze widened, compelled to see past the red haze of his anger. He saw the board as a whole again. He saw the Ivory Blight's pieces, poised and waiting, their silence no longer passive but predatory. He saw a bone white Knight, just a few squares from the Apothecary Pawn, its wolfish form tense and ready to leap. He saw a Bishop, its diagonal line of attack aimed like a drawn bowstring at the very path he would have to take. If he charged, he might destroy the pawn, but he would be immediately captured, a black rook falling to a white knight. Removed from the board in the second move of the game. His King, his primary objective, would be left without one of its most powerful defenders. The Blight had not just presented him with a target; they had laid a trap, using his own history as the bait. And he, in his blind, wounded fury, had been about to walk right into it.

The realization was a dousing of ice water on the fire in his soul. The rage did not vanish, but it cooled, condensing from a wild, roaring inferno into a hard, cold, heavy stone of hate in his gut. The fury was still his, but the impulse was no longer in control. He had been played. He had almost been defeated by a memory. It was the most profound humiliation he had ever felt.

"Better," Felcher's thought was devoid of praise. It was a simple statement of fact, a confirmation that the desired result had been achieved. "Emotion is a fuel. It can power the engine. It can provide the force for the hammer's blow. But it must never, ever be allowed to touch the steering wheel. Logic. Calculation. Purpose. These are what guide a successful campaign."

The invisible restraint on him did not vanish. Instead, it shifted, turning from a rigid hold into a guiding push. He felt his base begin to slide across the board, not of his own volition, but steered by the will of his player. He was being moved, a piece in the hand of a master.

He didn't charge forward into the trap. Instead, he slid sideways, a long, swift movement parallel to his own back rank. He glided past the indistinct form of his own Bishop, past the terrible, cold majesty of his Queen, until he came to rest on the square right beside his hazy, indistinct King. The King's Square.

The King moved.

It slid two squares toward him, a quiet, almost shy maneuver, moving away from the center and toward the corner fortress he was now positioned to create.

And then Felcher castled.

With a final, decisive movement, Marcus was lifted, a strange, weightless sensation, and seemed to pass through the ethereal, shimmering form of his King. He was set down with a solid, echoing clang on the square on the other side. The maneuver was complete. In a single, fluid sequence, his King was now tucked safely into the corner of the board, sheltered behind a wall of three pawns, and he, the Black Rook, stood sentinel beside it. The most powerful fortifications on the board had been erected. His rage and impulsiveness had been subverted and redirected into a maneuver of ultimate defense. He was no longer a lone agent of vengeance; he was a fortress wall, a guardian, a promise of brutal retaliation for any piece that dared to approach.

The Apothecary Pawn still stood in the center of the board, its clinical, pitying gaze a constant, silent provocation. The stone of hatred in Marcus's gut was a cold, dense weight. But now, he understood. The destruction of that piece was not the goal. It was a potential milestone, a target of opportunity, in a much longer, more complex war. His anger was not a tool for immediate gratification. It was a weapon to be sharpened, aimed, and deployed with cold, dispassionate, and utterly devastating precision when the time was right.

He looked at the King he was now guarding, nestled behind him in its newly formed fortress. The shimmering haze that surrounded it seemed to lessen for a moment, a brief parting of the psychic clouds, and he almost caught a glimpse of the face within. It was a young face, a boy's face, not much older than his own, etched with a startling, almost painful nobility. It was a face that held a profound, unwavering belief in the good of others, a face full of an idealism that seemed dangerously out of place on a battlefield as brutal as this. It was the face of someone who believed the game could be played with honor.

Then the haze swirled and thickened again, obscuring it completely. Marcus wasn't sure what he had seen, if it was real or just a projection of his own desperate need for a cause worth this much pain. The identity of the King remained a frustrating, vital mystery. But his mission was clearer than ever. He was the shadow that would allow the light to survive. He was the wall of night that would hold back the bone white dawn. He was The Black Rook, and he was anchored to his post, a silent, waiting tower of rage and iron. The Ivory Blight had made its move. Now, it was Felcher's turn to answer. And Marcus would be his instrument. The game had begun in earnest.

Chapter 9

They had truly left The Scar now. The city had unfolded around them not as a single entity, but as a series of distinct, jarringly different territories. They rode through quarters where the air smelled of money, the dry, papery scent of ledgers, and the metallic tang of coin counting houses. They passed through districts where the air was thick with the rhythmic clang of a hundred hammers and the acrid smoke of forges, a landscape of raw, industrial power. Each new zone was a fresh sensory assault, a new set of rules to be learned, and Marcus's mind, accustomed to the monolithic squalor of his home, struggled to categorize the overwhelming flood of new data.

His body was a separate country of misery. The thrumming ache in his knee had become a constant companion, a dull, hateful beat that accompanied the steady rhythm of Euphrates's hooves. The exhaustion was a physical weight, a leaden cloak he couldn't shrug off. He had dozed fitfully, slumping against Felcher's back, only to be jolted awake by a sharp turn or a loud noise, his dreams a chaotic fugue of ivory chess pieces and the scent of his mother's sickroom.

Now, a new wall loomed ahead, grander and more formidable than any he had ever seen. This was not the crumbling, patched-together boundary of The Scar. This was a statement of power, a curtain of massive, granite blocks that rose high into the sky, patrolled by men in gleaming, standardized armor. Banners, heavy with embroidered sigils he didn't recognize, snapped in the wind, the sound a sharp, percussive crack. This was the Western Summer Gate, the main artery into the true heart of the kingdom. The air here smelled of stone dust, horse sweat, and the oiled leather of a thousand harnesses. It smelled of authority.

The shouts from the gate watch, the sudden tension in the air as bows were drawn on the parapet, Marcus tensed, every instinct screaming danger. The shift in atmosphere was instantaneous and absolute, a physical drop in temperature. His gaze flicked upward, his mind, a machine honed by the pit, automatically assessing the threat. He counted the archers. He noted their firing angles. He assessed the thickness of the gate, the positioning of the pikemen. He was already calculating escape routes, however futile they might be from horseback and surrounded by professionals. The board had changed again, and he was in a check he could not see a way out of.

"HALT! IDENTIFY YOURSELF! BORDER PASSES READY!" The voice from the gate captain was a bellow, a raw, impersonal sound of institutional power, a voice that expected and received immediate obedience.

Felcher did not slow Euphrates. He simply raised a hand, a calm, almost lazy gesture.

Then the gate captain's tone shifted. It was as if a string inside the man had been violently tightened, pitching his voice a full octave higher. The aggression vanished, replaced by a sudden, almost fearful deference that was more shocking than the initial challenge. "My apologies, Commander! I wasn't aware you were returning through this post..." The man's voice trailed off, thick with a nervous dread.

Commander?

Marcus froze, his earlier discomfort on the horse, his annoyance, all of it vanishing, replaced by a cold, sharp shock that ran deeper than Felcher's earlier pronouncements. His internal system of categorization, the only thing that gave him a sense of control, shattered. He had mentally upgraded the "old man" from a simple retired soldier to someone with connections, someone who could command the shadowy figures in the alley. But "Commander?" That was a different echelon entirely. That was a title that belonged at the apex of the military pyramid. It was a word that meant serious power, absolute authority. The kind of authority that could crush a boy from The Scar like an insect without a second thought, and no one would ever ask why.

The casual way Felcher, he had to remember the name now, Gerald Felcher, waved his hand, his calm,

"Calm down, Captain. It's just Gerald Felcher now. I'm retired," did nothing to lessen the impact. It amplified it. The soldiers' reaction was raw, genuine. The fear was a scent of an animal in the air. They didn't see "just Gerald Felcher." They saw their Commander. Marcus watched, his eyes wide, as men scrambled on the wall, bows being un-drawn with clumsy haste, and the massive iron-bound gates began to grind open with a speed born of terror.

The pieces clicked into place with an alarming, terrifying clarity the instant obedience of the hooded figures, the quality of the warhorse, the sheer, breathtaking audacity of plucking a pit fighter from The Scar for some unknown, high-stakes purpose. It all made a horrifying kind of sense now.

He felt a new wave of apprehension wash over him, colder and more profound than before. He wasn't just in the hands of a tough old soldier offering a hard path out of hell. He was in the hands of a Commander, someone who likely navigated the dangerous currents of power at the highest levels of the kingdom. The "deal" he'd made felt suddenly more binding, the stakes infinitely higher. He realized with a sickening certainty that if a Commander wanted him, then "no" had probably never been a true option on the board. He had been captured long before the cane had struck him.

He swallowed hard, his throat dry as dust. The promises of a warm bed and three meals a day now seemed like very small crumbs offered by a very large, potentially dangerous wolf.

As Euphrates began to move forward through the now opening gate, into the relative brightness and what he assumed was the capital proper, Marcus finally found his voice. It was quiet, carefully neutral, all traces of his earlier sarcasm or defiance stripped away by the raw display of power he had just witnessed.

"Commander, huh?" he said, the word feeling heavy and foreign in his mouth. He wasn't challenging, wasn't questioning Felcher's attempt to downplay it. It was a simple, flat statement of fact, an acknowledgment of a newly revealed and very significant truth. He looked at the strong, straight back of the man in front of him with a new, much deeper, and far more unsettling level of respect. This changed everything. Or perhaps, it just clarified what everything had been from the start.

The ride through the capital was a sensory onslaught that made The Scar seem almost peaceful in its monolithic misery. Here, the world was a chaotic tapestry of a thousand competing sensations. The sounds were sharper: the crisp jingle of coins, the murmur of educated conversations, the high, clear laughter of well-fed children, the clip-clop of dozens of horses on clean-swept stone. The smells were a dizzying array: roasting meats from cook shops, the sweet, heady perfume worn by passing ladies, the clean scent of soap, and the acrid tang of ink from a printer's shop. It was too much. His mind, used to a limited palette of decay and desperation, felt bruised by the sheer variety of the input. He felt small, out of place, a creature of mud and shadow suddenly thrust into the full, blinding glare of the sun.

Felcher navigated the bustling main thoroughfares with the same unhurried purpose he had shown in the alleys of The Scar. He seemed to be an expert in every landscape. Eventually, he turned Euphrates down a quieter side street, and the sensory volume of the city lowered. Here, the buildings were smaller and more intimate, with brightly painted shutters and window boxes spilling over with flowers.

And then, the most alien scent of all hit him.

It was the overwhelming, complex perfume of a flower shop. Not the faint, wild scent of a field, but a concentrated, intoxicating cloud of a thousand different blossoms. He could pick out the sweet, almost cloying scent of lilies, the spicy, peppery fragrance of carnations, the delicate perfume of roses, and beneath it all, the green, wet smell of cut stems and damp earth. It was a smell so profoundly alive, so bursting with color and vitality, that it felt like a physical blow against the grey, desolate landscape of his soul.

Felcher dismounted in front of a small, almost quaint apartment built above the shop. "We're here," he said, his voice retaining its flat, neutral tone. He gestured to a small, well-kept barn at the back of the property, tucked into a narrow alley. "Tie the horse securely. Use a double slip knot. Ensure there's fresh water in the trough."

Marcus slid clumsily from Euphrates's back, his injured leg screaming in protest as it took his weight. He gritted his teeth and nodded once, a silent acknowledgment of the order. He moved to do as he was told, leading the great warhorse into the cool, hay-scented dimness of the barn. He focused on the task, his hands moving with practiced efficiency on the rope, ensuring the knot was secure, just as Felcher had implicitly demanded. This was a valuable animal; carelessness would not be tolerated. The simple, repetitive motions were a comfort, a small ritual of order in a world that had become utterly chaotic.

As he finished, a new sound cut through the quiet. A woman's voice, warm and full of delighted surprise. "Gerald! You're back!"

Marcus paused, mid-straightening from checking the water trough. He froze for a split second, an observer hidden in the shadows of the barn entrance, his mind struggling to process the scene unfolding outside. An older woman, her hair streaked with grey but her face full of a vibrant energy, had come out of the apartment's side door. She rushed to Felcher and wrapped him in an affectionate embrace, standing on her toes to plant a firm kiss on his cheek.

Marcus's mind struggled to reconcile this warm, domestic scene with the stern, powerful "Commander Felcher." This was... different. Intimate. Another piece that didn't fit any model he had built.

He watched Alyvia, her name registered as Felcher spoke it, her tone a mix of concern and gentle scolding. When her gaze flicked to him, a brief, curious glance, he remained perfectly still, his expression carefully neutral, his eyes meeting hers for a fraction of a second before dropping respectfully to the ground. He was an unknown quantity, a "guest," as Felcher had put it. Her immediate, motherly concern, "You should have told me! I would have gotten the room ready and had food on the table when you got back," was another alien concept. People didn't prepare for him. People didn't worry about his comfort. People in his world either used him, feared him, or ignored him.

He stayed where he was, near the horse, giving them space, adhering to the unspoken but clear understanding that he was an appendage to Felcher, not an active participant in this reunion. He was watching, listening, as commanded. And what he was seeing was a side of Felcher that hinted at a life beyond commands and military strategy, a life with... affection. It was another piece of the puzzle, another layer to the complex man who now controlled his fate. He wondered briefly what "off-center accommodations" meant in the context of this cozy-looking flower shop.

The tender gesture, Felcher tucking a stray strand of hair behind Alyvia's ear, and the soft, affectionate words, "My wife, looking as beautiful as ever..." sent another jolt through Marcus, stronger than the last.

Wife.

The word resonated, adding yet another, even more baffling, layer to the enigma of Gerald Felcher. Commander, retired soldier, influential figure, spymaster, and now... a husband, capable of gentle affection. Marcus stood silently by the barn, the familiar, solid presence of Euphrates beside him, and felt like an intruder on a scene he had no right to witness.

The contrast was staggering. This was the same man whose chilling smile had frozen his blood, whose casual pronouncements dictated his entire future, who spoke of "failure not being an option" with absolute, terrifying finality. And here he was, speaking with a softness, a tenderness, that Marcus could never have imagined existed in his emotional vocabulary.

He watched them, his face carefully blank, but his mind was reeling. It didn't make Felcher less dangerous. In fact, it might make him more so. A man with something to protect, something he loved, could be far more ruthless than a man who had nothing. The world he'd been thrust into wasn't just black and white, authority and obedience. There were shades here, personal connections, emotions that seemed out of place with the stern military façade.

Alyvia's easy affection, Felcher's gentle response, it was a glimpse into a life utterly removed from Marcus's own, where such tenderness was a forgotten luxury, if it had ever existed at all. He thought of his own mother, her love a fierce, protective thing born of hardship and fear. This soft, settled affection was different, a language he didn't speak.

He kept his gaze low, not wanting to stare, not wanting to intrude further. He was the "guest," the "spindly thing from The Scar," an outsider to this domestic warmth. He waited, silent and still, for his next instruction, his mind trying to reconcile the disparate images of Gerald Felcher, the ruthless Commander, the perceptive strategist, and now, the affectionate husband. It made predicting the man and understanding him even more difficult. And in his precarious position, understanding was crucial for survival.

Felcher's sharp command, "Boy, come over here and introduce yourself!" cut through the quiet domesticity like a knife.

Marcus reacted instantly. He gave the knot one final, firm tug, then moved from the shadows of the barn entrance towards Felcher and Alyvia. He walked with a measured, deliberate pace, not too fast to seem eager, not too slow to seem reluctant. He stopped a respectful distance away, not wanting to crowd them, particularly Alyvia, whose warmth felt like a heat he was unused to.

He stood straight, his hands loosely at his sides, his gaze briefly meeting Alyvia's before flicking to a point just past her shoulder, a habit of deferential address he was quickly adopting. He was acutely aware of his rough appearance, the dust of the road, and the ingrained grime of The Scar still clinging to him, a stark contrast to the clean flower shop and Alyvia's neat, homespun dress.

"Ma'am," he began, his voice low and even, addressed to Alyvia but loud enough for Felcher to hear clearly. He made sure to keep any trace of his Scar accent subdued, aiming for a neutral, respectful tone that revealed nothing. "My name is Marcus."

He offered nothing more. No surname, no explanation of who he was or why he was there. Felcher had called him a "guest." His introduction was simply to put a name to that label. He waited, silent and observant, for whatever came next, acutely aware of both Felcher's and Alyvia's scrutiny. He was a puzzle piece being presented, and he knew his every word and gesture was being noted and filed away.

Marcus stood frozen, his carefully constructed composure momentarily shattered. "Gerald Philip Felcher!" Crack. The sound was sharp, definitive, and utterly shocking. He watched, wide-eyed, as Alyvia, this soft-spoken woman who smelled of flowers, not only berated Commander Felcher but also smacked him smartly on the back of the head. And Felcher...

took it. He didn't flinch, didn't react, just stood there as his wife continued her tirade. "Look at the poor thing! He's a child, not one of your toy soldiers! I bet you dragged him all over kingdom come without a moment's rest!"

The world tilted again, more violently this time.

Alyvia's words about his sleepless nights, her genuine, fiery concern, were a shock. People didn't notice him like that; they didn't see the exhaustion behind his empty eyes, let alone express care for it. It was disorienting. He felt his ears grow warm, a hot flush of embarrassment and confusion spreading across his face.

He kept his gaze carefully neutral, not daring to look directly at Felcher's reaction to being disciplined by his wife, yet he was hyperaware of the Commander. This was a power dynamic he had never conceived of. The fear Felcher inspired was still very real, a cold knot in his stomach, but seeing him on the receiving end of such familiar, almost maternal, authority was... utterly bewildering. It was a new piece on the board, a piece with rules he couldn't begin to fathom.

"A hot meal and a bath are what you two need," the words echoed Alyvia's earlier concern and Felcher's own conditional promises. Now they were being presented as an immediate order, not from the Commander, but from his wife.

Marcus didn't move. He didn't speak. He was the "boy," the "guest." He looked towards Alyvia respectfully when she spoke of him, then his eyes flickered to the floor. He waited. His orders came from Felcher. Even if Alyvia was giving the commands now, he wouldn't presume to act without a cue from the man who had brought him here, the man who had stated, unequivocally, that failure was not an option.

His mind was a whirlwind. This apartment, above a flower shop, this woman who could command a Commander, this unexpected display of domesticity and concern — it was a world away from the cold, hard logic of the pit and the chilling pronouncements of his new master. He was still watching, still listening, and the lessons were becoming more complex and contradictory by the minute.

As Alyvia herded them towards the stairs, herding being the only appropriate word for her determined fussing, Marcus followed a step behind Felcher. He kept his eyes down, but his senses were on high alert, taking in the interior of the apartment. The contrast between the quaint exterior and the modernized interior was striking. The stone bathtub he glimpsed in a side room, a built-in cast-iron stove in the main living area; these were not the rustic fittings he might have expected. They spoke of comfort, of thoughtful design, of a home built for living, not just for show. The air inside was warm and smelled of stewing meat, of drying herbs, and of the lingering scent of Alyvia's flowers.

And then, as they moved further into the living space, another realization, more profound than the modern amenities, more shocking than the head smack, struck Marcus with the force of an epiphany.

Felcher. Commander Gerald Felcher, the man who could command secret police with a snap of his fingers, who could have guards at a major city gate backpedaling in fear, who had plucked him from the deepest pit of the city for a purpose so important that it demanded absolute obedience... chose to live here. Above a flower shop. With his wife.

He could have had a mansion in the capital's most opulent district. He could have been surrounded by a retinue of servants, living in a fortress that was a reflection of his undeniable power. But he hadn't. He had chosen this, a quiet, relatively modest life, a haven of domesticity filled with the scent of flowers and simmering stew.

The thought was staggering. It recontextualized everything Marcus had seen. The affectionate banter, Alyvia's easy command, Felcher's uncharacteristic submission to her fussing — it wasn't just an oddity; it was a deliberate choice. This quiet life wasn't a sign of diminished status; it was a preference. This was the fortress he had built for himself, a fortress not of stone and steel, but of warmth and normalcy.

Marcus looked around the comfortable, well-appointed room, his mind struggling to reconcile this with the image of the ruthless strategist who was reshaping his life. The chilling smile, the absolute authority, those were real. But so was this. This chosen simplicity.

It didn't make Felcher less dangerous. If anything, it made him more unpredictable, more complex. A man who wielded immense power but chose not to flaunt it, who sought refuge in a quiet life... what were his true motivations? What did he truly want from Marcus?

He kept his face impassive, his gaze sweeping the room before returning to a neutral point on the floor. He was still the silent observer, the "guest." But his understanding of his benefactor, his captor, his Commander, had just shifted dramatically. This wasn't just about military service or protecting a prince. There was something deeper at play in Gerald Felcher's life, and Marcus had just stumbled upon a significant piece of it. The quiet life didn't mean weakness; it might, in fact, be a sign of a different kind of strength, a different set of priorities. And Marcus was now, inextricably, a part of it. The board was infinitely more complex than he had ever imagined.

Chapter 10

The command, "A hot meal and a bath are what you two need," was delivered with the unassailable authority of a queen addressing her court. It was not a suggestion. It was a decree. Alyvia herded them towards the stairs that led up to the apartment, and Marcus found himself following a step behind Felcher, a silent, grim shadow in the wake of this bewildering domestic whirlwind.

His mind was a maelstrom of conflicting sensory data. The scent of the flowers from the shop below was a constant, almost dizzying presence —a perfume of life so potent that it felt like a judgment on the stench of death and decay that clung to him. As they entered the apartment proper, new scents joined the chorus: the rich, savory smell of a meat and root vegetable stew simmering on the stove, the sharp, clean fragrance of dried herbs hanging from the rafters, and the warm, comforting scent of beeswax from polished wood. It was the smell of a home, a concept so alien to Marcus that it was like trying to imagine a new color.

He was acutely aware of the space around him. The floorboards were smooth and solid under his worn boots, not creaking or groaning like the treacherous, half-rotten wood of The Scar. The light that streamed through the clean glass of the windows was soft and golden, illuminating dust motes dancing in the air like tiny, benevolent sprites. Everything was ordered, clean, and purposeful. It was a physical manifestation of a life lived by rules he could not comprehend.

Alyvia turned, her hands on her hips, her expression a mask of affectionate exasperation aimed squarely at her husband. "Gerald, you look like you've been sleeping in a ditch. And you," she said, her gaze softening as it fell upon Marcus, "you look like you've been living in one. The bath is through there. It's already drawn. Go on."

Felcher, the Commander who made gate captains tremble, merely gave a slight, almost imperceptible nod. He looked at Marcus, "You heard her." The command was simple, but layered with meaning. It meant, Obey her as you would obey me.

Marcus's heart gave a hard, painful thud against his ribs. He looked from Felcher's impassive face to Alyvia's expectant one. The path to the bathroom door seemed a mile long. Every instinct he had, every lesson learned in a world where vulnerability was a death sentence, screamed at him to resist. To be stripped of his clothes, to be submerged, to be helpless, it was a nightmare scenario. But the fear of Felcher, a cold, rational, and overwhelming force, was greater than the instinctual terror. Failure, as the Commander had so clearly stated, was not an option.

He gave a jerky, single nod and turned toward the indicated door. He walked with his stiff, limping gait, each step a small agony, feeling their eyes on his back. The bathroom was small, but like the rest of the apartment, it was a marvel of clean, efficient design. A stone tub, large enough for a grown man to soak in, was built into the corner. Steam rose from its surface in gentle, fragrant clouds, carrying the clean, sharp scent of lye soap and something herbal, perhaps rosemary. The floor was tiled in small, hexagonal pieces of grey and white stone. The air was warm and humid, a stark contrast to the cool dampness of his entire existence.

He stood there for a long moment, just inside the closed door, his hand still on the latch. He was alone, but he felt as though he were on a brightly lit stage. He could hear their muffled voices from the other room, Alyvia's warm tones and Felcher's low, rumbling responses. He was supposed to undress. The thought sent a jolt of panic through him.

He was seventeen. In The Scar, at seventeen, you were a man, or you were dead. He had fought men twice his size, had felt the crunch of bone under his fist, had walked through alleys where a wrong glance could get you a knife in the ribs. He was The Shadow, a creature of violence and cold purpose. And he was being told to take a bath like a recalcitrant child. The indignity of it warred with the primal fear of disobedience.

It's just a bath, he told himself, his internal voice a harsh rasp. It's a command. Follow the command. He peeled off the rough-spun tunic, the unfamiliar fabric scraping against his skin. He unlaced the ill-fitting boots. As he stripped away the layers, he felt as if he were peeling away the hardened shell he had built around himself for five years. His body, when he finally stood naked in the warm, steamy air, was a pale, wiry thing, a tapestry of old scars and new bruises. He felt horribly exposed, vulnerable, a thing of filth and violence in this pristine, sweet-smelling room.

He stepped into the tub. The water was hot, shockingly so. For a second, his muscles seized, the heat a searing pain against his cold skin. Then, as he sank deeper, the heat began to work its magic, seeping into his bruised muscles, into his aching joints, into the very marrow of his bones. It was an intense, overwhelming sensation —a pleasure so profound that it was almost indistinguishable from pain. He let out a long, shuddering breath and sank down until the water was up to his chin, the steam wreathing his face. He closed his eyes. For the first time in five years, he felt something other than cold.

The door opened without a knock. Marcus's eyes snapped open, his body instantly tensing, ready to fight, to flee. Alyvia stood there, a thick towel over one arm, a stiff bristle-brush in one hand, and a coarse block of lye soap in the other.

"You can't possibly get clean just by sitting in it," she said, her tone practical, leaving no room for argument. "Turn around."

Panic, cold and sharp, lanced through him. "I can do it," he said, his voice a low, strangled croak.

"Nonsense," she said, and her voice was firm, but not unkind. It was the voice of a woman who had raised sons and knew every excuse they could offer. "I've bathed scraped-kneed boys and battle-wounded men, and they all say the same thing. You're no different. Now, turn around before the water gets cold."

He was trapped. His mind raced. To argue further would be to defy her, and by extension, to defy Felcher. The potential consequences of that were unthinkable. To obey was to submit to an intimacy, a level of maternal care, that his mind recoiled from in terror and a deep, buried longing. He was warring inside, the hardened pit fighter feeling the humiliation of being treated like a grubby child, while a much younger, more wounded part of him, a part he thought had died with his mother, felt a tremor of something else entirely.

Fear won. He turned slowly, presenting his back to her, his shoulders hunched, his muscles knotted with tension. He stared at the tiled wall in front of him, his jaw clenched so tightly it ached.

He heard her set the soap and towel down. He felt the water shift as she knelt on a small stool beside the tub. Then, the brush was on his back. It was stiff, merciless, scraping away years of ingrained filth. The sensation was shocking, a rough, abrasive scouring that felt like it was taking off the top layer of his skin. He flinched.

"Hold still," she chided gently. Her other hand, warm and firm, rested on his shoulder to steady him. Her touch was not clinical like Felcher's. It was... a human touch.

She worked with practical, no-nonsense efficiency, scrubbing his back, his shoulders, and his arms. The lye soap had a clean, sharp smell that cut through the herbal scent of the steam. It was the smell of erasure, of washing away the past. As she worked, some of the tension began to leak out of him. The roughness of the brush was aggressive, but the hand on his shoulder was steady and sure. It wasn't a gesture of control, but of support.

"Goodness, child," she murmured, more to herself than to him. "It's like trying to scrub a statue that's been left in a sewer."

Her hand moved to his head, her fingers gently probing his scalp as she began to lather the soap into his matted hair. And then she stopped. He felt her fingers go still. He could feel the change in her posture, a subtle shift in the atmosphere.

"Oh, you poor thing," she whispered. Her voice was filled with a soft, genuine pity that was a thousand times worse than any revulsion. He knew instantly what she had found. The telltale signs of the things that thrived in the filth of The Scar. Lice. A fresh wave of hot, burning shame washed over him, so powerful it made him feel dizzy. He wanted to sink under the water and never come up.

She said nothing more about it. There was no gasp of disgust, no sharp intake of breath. She simply finished washing his hair, her touch now even gentler than before. She rinsed the soap away with pitchers of clean, warm water.

"Alright," she said, her voice back to its practical tone. "Stay put. I'll be right back."

She left the room, closing the door behind her. Marcus sat in the tub, motionless, the water beginning to cool around him. He felt stripped bare, not just of his clothes, but of his pride, his defenses. He was just a boy from The Scar, full of filth and vermin.

The shame was a suffocating blanket. He needed to escape. His eyes were fixed on the wall in front of him. The hexagonal tiles. Grey and white. A repeating, predictable pattern. Order in a world of chaos. He began to count them. One, two, three... he traced their shapes with his eyes, focusing on the crisp, dark lines of the grout that separated them. Seven, eight, nine... it was a ritual, a way to build a wall in his mind, to retreat into a place where things made sense. Ten, eleven...

The tiles began to shift. The grout lines sharpened, brightened, forming a perfect, luminous grid. The hexagonal shapes flattened, squared off, turning into the familiar alternating pattern of light and dark. The sound of the water dripping from his hair faded away, replaced by the profound, humming silence of the dream space. He was back on the board.

He stood as the Black Rook anchored to his post beside his King in the castled corner. The air was cold and sterile. Across the board, the Apothecary Pawn stood unmoving in the center, a constant, mocking presence. The stone of hatred in his gut pulsed with a dull, cold ache.

The Ivory Blight made its next move.

From its back rank, a Bishop piece slid forward. It moved with a smooth, diagonal hiss, its ivory form shimmering as it advanced. Like the pawn before it, it began to transmute. The pointed, cowl-like head of the piece softened, flattened, becoming the balding, greasy pate of a man. The rigid body stooped, taking on a subservient, wheedling posture. A frayed, spectral waistcoat appeared on its form, and a phantom clay pipe materialized in its hand. It resolved into a perfect, bone white effigy of Silas.

The Silas Bishop came to rest on a square from which it commanded a long, open diagonal, aimed like a poisoned dart toward Marcus's side of the board. Its whisper slithered across the checkered expanse, a sound of oily conspiracy and self-interest.

"Twenty percent, my boy," the piece hissed, its voice an echo in Marcus's mind. "A small finder's fee. It's how the world works. You're a tool, lad, a bloody magnificent one, but you're not seeing the bigger picture..."

Another memory. Another ghost summoned to the battlefield. The insidious voice of the man who had sold him to the pit, the parasite who had profited from his every moment of agony. This was a different kind of attack. The Apothecary was a wall he had run into. The Silas Bishop was a poison, a slow corruption, a voice of cynical pragmatism that sought to undermine the very concept of a just cause.

Again, the hot rage flared. But this time, it was tempered by the memory of the last lesson. He felt the invisible restraint of his Player, but it was looser now, a guiding pressure rather than an iron clamp. He did not move. He forced himself to analyze.

The Bishop was a powerful piece. Its diagonal reach was immense. But it was also limited.

"Observe the threat," the thought from Felcher was calm, instructional. "Understand its nature. A Bishop, no matter how powerful, is forever bound to the squares of a single color. It can never touch the other half of the world. Its influence is powerful, but it is inherently flawed, inherently incomplete. It sees the world only in black or only in white. It cannot comprehend the whole board."

Marcus looked at the Silas Bishop, a creature of the dark squares, its influence a diagonal scar across the battlefield. It could threaten, it could harass, but it could never directly attack his King, now safely ensconced on a white square. It was a nuisance, a poison, but not a direct threat to the core objective. Its power lay in its ability to distract, drawing his focus away from the true dangers.

"Do not react to the noise," Felcher's thought continued, "Control the space."

The guiding pressure returned, and his Rook began to move. He slid forward, out from his defensive position beside the King, moving down the open file. One, two, three, four squares. He came to a halt in the center of the board, a black tower of power now controlling the entire vertical line. From this new position, he exerted a huge zone of control. He pinned down enemy pawns. He restricted the movement of the enemy Queen. He wasn't attacking anything directly, but his very presence had reshaped the strategic landscape. He had seized the open file. He was no longer just a wall; he was a weapon in waiting, a promise of future devastation.

The Ivory Blight responded. A Knight, its form a hulking, brutish shape reminiscent of The Ox and The Butcher, made a jarring, L-shaped leap. It landed with a heavy, echoing thud on a square that threatened one of his forward pawns. It was a move of pure, uncomplicated aggression. A direct physical threat.

So this was their strategy. A multi-pronged assault. A psychological attack with the Apothecary.

An insidious, corrupting attack with the Bishop. And a brute force attack with the Knight. They were testing all of his weaknesses at once.

He felt the presence of his Player considering the move, the silent, humming tension of a master contemplating his response. And then...

The door opened again. The chessboard dissolved. The tiles snapped back into sharp focus. The silence was broken by the sound of Alyvia's soft footsteps. The real world, warm and smelling of rosemary, rushed back in.

Alyvia returned, carrying a small wooden bowl and a fine-toothed metal comb. She set them on the stool beside the tub. In the bowl was a pungent, vinegary-smelling liquid.

"This will sting a bit," she said, her voice soft. "But it will do the trick. Lean your head back."

He obeyed without a word. He was no longer the Black Rook, a tower of strategic power. He was a boy in a tub, about to have his hair combed for lice. The jarring transition left him feeling dizzy and disconnected.

Alyvia dipped the comb in the liquid and began to work through his tangled, wet hair. Her touch was methodical and incredibly gentle. She worked in small sections, her fingers carefully untangling knots, the fine teeth of the comb scraping softly against his scalp. It was a slow, patient, painstaking process. The vinegar solution did sting, a sharp, clean burn, but it was nothing compared to the pain he was used to.

He closed his eyes, overwhelmed by the sheer, unexpected sensation of it. The gentle tug of the comb.

The warmth of her hands against his scalp. The quiet, rhythmic sound of her breathing. He couldn't remember the last time anyone had touched him with such care, not since his mother. The memory rose up, unbidden and painful, his mother, her hands still strong and healthy, combing his hair as a small boy, her voice humming a soft, tuneless song. A lump formed in his throat, thick and hot. He swallowed it down, forcing the memory away.

"Does that hurt?" Alyvia asked softly, her voice breaking the long silence.

"No," Marcus managed to say, the word a rough whisper.

She continued her work for a few more minutes in silence, the only sounds the soft scrape of the comb and the dripping of water.

"You're a quiet one," she observed. It wasn't an accusation, just a statement of fact. "Gerald said you were from The Scar. That can't have been an easy life."

Marcus said nothing. He didn't know how to respond. The Scar wasn't a life; it was a state of being, a war of attrition against hunger and filth and despair. It wasn't something you could explain to a woman who smelled of flowers.

Alyvia seemed to understand his silence. She didn't press. Instead, she changed the subject. "Gerald, you know, for all his stern looks and his Commander voice, he's a big soft fool for my stew. Burns his tongue every time because he's too impatient to let it cool. Complains about the vegetables being too soft, then eats three bowls." She chuckled, a warm, fond sound. "Don't tell him I told you that."

A strange, unfamiliar sensation fluttered in Marcus's chest. He pictured the Commander, the man who had crippled him with a cane, complaining about soft vegetables. It was another piece that didn't fit, another contradiction in the impossible puzzle of this man. It almost made him want to smile.

"What's your full name, Marcus?" she asked, her tone still light and gentle.

"Just Marcus," he said automatically. He had no other name. Surnames were a luxury, a sign of lineage and belonging. In The Scar, you were who you were, nothing more.

"Just Marcus," she repeated softly, "Well, Just Marcus, it's a good, strong name."

She finished the combing, rinsing his hair one last time with clean water. "There," she said, her voice full of satisfaction. "All done. I think we got them all. Now, out you get. There's a clean towel there, and I've left some clothes for you on the bed in the guest room. They were my youngest son's. He's long since outgrown them, but they should be a better fit for you."

She stood up and left, closing the door behind her. Marcus sat in the now tepid water, his mind a quiet, echoing space. He felt... clean. Not just on the surface. It was a deeper feeling, a lightness he hadn't known was possible. The scent of the rosemary soap clung to his skin. He touched his hair; it was soft and untangled.

He slowly stood up, his body feeling strangely light and new. He wrapped himself in the thick, soft towel. It smelled of sunlight and wind. He walked into the small guest room Alyvia had indicated. On the bed was a set of clean, soft clothes: a linen shirt and well-mended wool trousers. They were simple, but they were a world away from the rough, ill-fitting uniform Felcher had given him.

He dressed slowly, the soft fabric a balm against his skin. He was still a prisoner. He was still a weapon being honed. But for a brief, bewildering hour, in a warm, steam-filled room, he had been something else. He had been a boy being cared for. And the memory of it, the geometry of that simple, unexpected kindness, was the most complex and disorienting puzzle he had yet to face.

Chapter 11

Dressed in the borrowed clothes of a ghost, Marcus stepped out of the small guest room and back into the main living space of the apartment. The soft, worn linen of the shirt felt alien against his skin, a caress where he was accustomed to the abrasive scrape of rough-spun wool. The trousers, though mended, were of a fine, tight weave, and they fit him with a startling accuracy that was in itself a form of intimacy. He was wearing the past of Alyvia's long-gone son, a life he couldn't imagine, and the sensation was deeply unsettling. He felt like an imposter, a crow dressed in a robin's feathers.

He stood in the doorway, a silent, uncertain figure, his habitual instinct to retreat into the shadows warring with the fact that there were no true shadows here to retreat into. The room was filled with the warm, inviting light of late afternoon, a light that seemed to search out every corner, leaving no space for a creature like him to hide.

His eyes, seeking a pattern, a system, a set of rules to grasp onto, began to roam. The apartment, which had initially seemed merely cozy and domestic, proved upon closer inspection to be a far more complex environment. It was a repository of a life, of two lives, lived with depth and purpose.

One entire wall was dominated by bookshelves, crammed not with the neat, uniform bindings of a rich man's decorative library, but with a chaotic, well-used collection of tomes, scrolls, and leather-bound codices. Their spines were cracked, their covers worn, some held together with what looked like twine. He saw piles of books stacked on the floor, on side tables, even on a windowsill, their pages filled with a dense, elegant script he couldn't begin to decipher. He had never learned to read. Letters were just abstract shapes, complex and meaningless, like the squiggles of a madman. To him, these books were locked boxes, filled with treasures he could never access, a stark and sudden reminder of a world of knowledge from which he was utterly barred.

Beside the bookshelves, a large table was buried under a landscape of old maps. They were hand-drawn on vellum, their edges curled and stained with age and what might have been spilled wine. He saw the familiar, jagged coastline of the kingdom, but also charts of lands he had never heard of, places with strange, musical names. Pins with small, colored heads were stuck into the maps at various points, suggesting strategic planning, campaigns fought and won or lost long ago. Scattered amongst the maps were old notebooks, dozens of them, filled with the same elegant, impenetrable script as the books, their pages dense with notes, diagrams, and calculations. This was not a living room; it was a command center, a war room disguised with floral curtains and the smell of stew.

In one corner, leaning against the wall, was a simple, unadorned wooden rack. It held not decorative swords or ceremonial polearms, but a collection of practical, deadly looking training weapons. There were weighted wooden wasters, blunted sparring daggers, a quarterstaff of dark, heavy ironwood, and a light, recurved bow with a quiver of feather-fletched but un-tipped arrows. It was the armory of a man who practiced his deadly craft with the same diligence as a scholar studied his texts.

His gaze dropped to the floor. He noted the closet, its door slightly ajar, revealing a glimpse of more cloaks and boots. And then he saw it. Under the bed in the guest room from which he had just emerged, peeking out from beneath the simple dust ruffle, was a pair of boy's shoes. They were small, well-made, but heavily worn, with the toes scuffed and the leather cracked from countless hours of running, playing, and living. They were the shoes of the boy whose clothes he now wore. A boy who must have been here a long time ago. A ghost. Another piece that didn't fit. Where had that son gone?

He felt a profound sense of dislocation, of being out of place on a molecular level. He was a creature of straight lines and brutal simplicity, of survival and instinct. This place was a world of layers, of history, knowledge, love, and hidden violence, all tangled together in a way he couldn't parse. The sheer complexity of it was overwhelming.

He came to stand in the archway of the kitchen, his designated waiting position, a silent sentinel awaiting his next command. His eyes, desperate for order, found a pattern in the floorboards, counting the long, straight lines of dark wood, tracing their parallel paths across the room. One, two, three, four... The familiar, mindless ritual was a small, steady anchor in the churning sea of new information. His hand, of its own accord, came up to his mouth, and he began to bite at the ragged edge of a thumbnail, the small, repetitive act a pressure valve for the anxiety building inside him.

"Stop that," Felcher's voice was sharp, cutting through his concentration.

Marcus's hand dropped to his side as if burned. He stood rigidly, his eyes fixed on the floor.

"You're not in the pit, boy. You're in a home. Try to act like it. Sit down," Felcher gestured with his chin to the small wooden table in the center of the kitchen.

Marcus moved, his steps stiff, his body still a map of aches. He pulled out a chair and sat, his back ramrod straight, his hands placed flat on his thighs under the table. He did not feel like he was in a home. He felt like he was undergoing an inspection.

Alyvia came from the stove, carrying two steaming, earthenware bowls. The rich, savory aroma of the stew filled the air, so potent that it made Marcus's stomach clench with a hunger so fierce that it was almost painful. She placed one bowl in front of Felcher, and then one in front of him. Then she went to a breadbox and took out a loaf of dark, crusty bread. The loaf was still warm, and the yeasty, wholesome scent of it was a new and wonderful torture. She sliced off two thick, ragged heels and placed one on the rim of each of their bowls.

"There," she said, her voice full of simple, unadorned satisfaction. "Eat. Before he," she nodded at Felcher, "tries to inhale it."

Felcher, who had already picked up his spoon, shot her a look of mock indignation. "I do not inhale my food, woman. I appreciate it with... efficiency." He dipped his spoon into the bowl, blew on it once, a perfunctory gesture at cooling it, and took a large, hasty mouthful.

He immediately winced, a sharp intake of breath hissing through his teeth. "By the gods, Alyvia! It's hotter than a forge!" he rasped, fanning his mouth with his hand.

Alyvia just smiled, a knowing, triumphant little smile. "As I said," she murmured, pouring them both a cup of water from a pitcher, "Impatient old fool."

Marcus watched the exchange, his face impassive. But inside, a small, strange bubble of amusement formed. It was exactly as she had predicted. The Commander, the man who commanded armies and orchestrated silent retirements, had been defeated by a bowl of hot stew. He found the thought deeply and secretly amusing. His hand, hidden beneath the table, began to tap a silent, rhythmic beat against his thigh, a subconscious release of the tension and the tightly controlled amusement.

He looked down at his own bowl. The stew was thick, with chunks of tender meat, soft carrots, and potatoes, and a dark, savory gravy. The bread on the rim was already beginning to soften, soaking up the juices. He hadn't seen food like this in his entire life. Food in The Scar was about survival: a hunk of stale bread, a questionable meat pie, and a thin, watery gruel. This was... a meal.

He picked up his spoon. The spoon was heavy, made of real pewter, not the bent, tinny things he was used to. He hesitated. He looked at Felcher, who was now eating more cautiously, then at Alyvia, who was watching him with a soft, expectant look.

"Go on, Just Marcus," she encouraged gently, "It won't bite."

He dipped his spoon into the stew and brought it to his lips. The flavor exploded on his tongue. It was rich, complex, and deeply savory. The meat was so tender it melted in his mouth. The carrots were sweet, the potatoes soft and earthy. It was the most delicious thing he had ever tasted. He took another spoonful, then another, a lifetime of hunger asserting itself. He tore off a piece of the bread and sopped up the gravy, the taste a revelation.

He ate in silence, focusing on the simple, overwhelming sensory experience of the food. He was aware of Felcher and Alyvia talking, their voices a low, comfortable murmur in the background. He didn't try to follow their conversation. He was focused on his own task, eating the stew.

"...the appointment is secured, then?" Alyvia was saying.

"It is," Felcher confirmed, "The Prince's new adjutant was... receptive to my recommendation. Young Lord Vaelen will be promoted to the Northern Garrison by week's end, leaving a vacancy on the Prince's personal staff. A training position."

"And the boy?" Alyvia's voice was lower now, "You're sure about this, Gerald? Taking him from that life and throwing him into... that one? It's trading one pit for another, and the new one has sharper teeth."

"The new one also has a purpose," Felcher said, his voice hard, "He has the raw material. The rage. The resilience. He just needs to be shaped. Tempered."

"He needs a childhood," Alyvia retorted softly but firmly, "Which he's clearly never had."

Marcus kept eating, his spoon moving with a steady, mechanical rhythm. They were talking about him as if he weren't there, dissecting his life, his trauma, his future. He was the "raw material." A thing to be shaped. It should have made him angry, but he was too overwhelmed by the stew, by the warmth, by the sheer alien nature of the situation, to feel anything but a distant, detached sense of surreality.

"He will have a warm bed, three meals a day, and an education that will make him more than a brute," Felcher stated, his tone brooking no argument. "It is a better chance than he would have had. That is all any of us can offer."

There was a moment of silence, broken only by the scrape of their spoons against the bowls.

Marcus finished his stew. He had cleaned the bowl completely, using the last of his bread to wipe up every drop of gravy. He placed his spoon neatly beside the empty bowl and put his hands back in his lap. He waited.

Alyvia looked at his empty bowl, then at him. A soft smile touched her lips. "Would you like some more?"

He wanted to say yes. His stomach, after a lifetime of being half empty, was screaming for more. But he didn't know the rules. Was it polite to ask for more? Was it a sign of greed? He looked at Felcher. The Commander was still eating, his gaze fixed on his bowl. No help there.

"It's alright if you do," Alyvia said, seeming to read his hesitation. "I made plenty. My youngest, Thomas, always had a second bowl. Said it was the only way to be sure he'd have good dreams."

The mention of her son again, the ghost whose clothes he wore. Marcus felt a pang of something he couldn't name.

"Yes, ma'am," he said, his voice quiet, "If it's not a trouble."

"It's no trouble at all," she said, her smile widening. She took his bowl and went to the stove to refill it.

As she did, Felcher finished his own meal. He pushed his bowl away and fixed his gaze on Marcus. The shift from domestic husband to Commander was instantaneous and chilling.

"Tomorrow, your education begins in earnest," he said, his voice flat and all business, "You cannot read or write." It wasn't a question. It was a statement of a deficiency he had already noted. "That is unacceptable. An effective weapon must be able to receive written orders, read intelligence reports, and study maps. From tomorrow, Alyvia will instruct you in your letters and numbers for three hours every morning."

Marcus's head snapped up. He looked at Alyvia, who was returning with his refilled bowl, then back at Felcher. Him? Learn to read? The thought was absurd, impossible. The letters were a secret code he could never crack.

"But," he started to protest.

"There are no 'buts'," Felcher cut him off. "You will learn. You will apply yourself with the same focus you use in a fight. Is that understood?"

"Yes, Commander," Marcus said, his voice barely a whisper.

"Good," Felcher stood up, "For the rest of the day, you will rest. Your body needs to heal. Tomorrow, after your lesson with Alyvia, you and I will begin your physical conditioning in the barn. We need to correct the flaws in your fighting style. You are fast and you are vicious, but you are sloppy. You rely too much on instinct and not enough on technique. We will break you of your bad habits."

He looked at Marcus, his obsidian eyes seeming to see right through him, to see the fear, the confusion, and the buried rage. "This is your new life, boy. It will be harder than anything you have ever known. But if you survive it, you will be more than just a ghost from The Scar. You will be a weapon in the hand of a Prince. Do not disappoint me."

With that, he turned and left the kitchen, leaving Marcus alone with Alyvia and his second bowl of stew.

Alyvia placed the steaming bowl in front of him. She didn't say anything about Felcher's speech. She just sat down across from him. "Don't mind him," she said softly, "His bark has always been worse than his bite."

Marcus looked at her, then down at the stew. He wasn't so sure about that. He had felt Felcher's bite.

And he had a feeling he had only experienced the very tip of the man's teeth. He picked up his spoon and began to eat, the rich flavor of the stew now mingled with the cold taste of fear and the dizzying, terrifying prospect of a future he could not begin to comprehend. The game board was bigger and more complicated than he had ever dreamed, and he was just a single, ignorant pawn, being taught the first, painful rules of how to move.

Chapter 12

The sun, when it rose, did not filter into the small guest room as a gentle greying. It arrived as a sharp, clean blade of golden light, slicing through the gap in the curtains and painting a bright, uncompromising stripe across the far wall. The light was different here. It was a statement, not an apology. It smelled not of damp and decay, but of the faint, lingering scent of lavender from the freshly washed linen of his bedding. Marcus woke to this new light, this new smell, and for a disoriented moment, he didn't know where he was. The familiar, crushing weight of The Scar was absent, leaving a strange, unnerving emptiness in its place.

Then, memory returned in a cold, brutal flood. Felcher. The journey. The Commander. The wife. The stew. The decree. Your education begins.

He sat up, his body a cacophony of aches. The deep, throbbing pain in his knee was a dull, familiar drumbeat, but the myriad of other bruises and scrapes from a hundred fights seemed to be making themselves known with a new, sharp intensity in the comfort of a real bed. He was acutely aware of his own body in a way he never had been in The Scar. There, pain was just a part of the background noise. Here, in the quiet, clean room, it was a loud, insistent signal.

The clothes he had worn, the ghost clothes of the boy named Thomas, were folded neatly on a chair beside the bed. He dressed slowly, the soft fabric a constant, gentle reminder of his alien surroundings. He ran a hand through his hair. It was clean, soft, and free of tangles for the first time in his memory. The sensation was so strange that it felt like wearing a stranger's scalp. He was being remade, scrubbed clean of his past, piece by piece.

He found Felcher and Alyvia already in the kitchen. The room was filled with the warm, rich aroma of brewing chicory and toasted bread. It was a scene of such placid, domestic normalcy that it felt like a carefully constructed illusion. Felcher sat at the table, a pair of spectacles perched on his nose, reading from one of the thick, leather-bound books as his finger traced a line of the elegant, yet incomprehensible, script. Alyvia was at the stove, humming a soft, tuneless melody as she turned slices of bread on a griddle.

They both looked up as he entered.

"Good morning, Just Marcus," Alyvia said, her smile as warm and bright as the light streaming through the window. "Did you sleep well?"

Marcus froze in the doorway, unsure of the correct response. Sleep had been a battleground of disjointed, terrifying dreams, but he sensed that wasn't the answer she was looking for. "Yes, ma'am," he mumbled, his eyes on the floor.

"Good. Come, sit. Breakfast is almost ready."

He moved to the table and sat in the same chair as the night before, his movements stiff and deliberate. He placed his hands in his lap and waited.

Felcher closed his book with a soft thud. He took off his spectacles and polished them with a cloth, his gaze analytical and piercing. "Today," he said, his voice flat and devoid of any morning warmth, "you will learn the first and most important lesson of your new life. More important than reading, more important than fighting, more important than anything else I will ever teach you."

He paused, letting the weight of his words settle in the quiet room. "You will learn to see."

Marcus frowned, confused. "I can see."

"No," Felcher corrected him, his tone sharp, "You look. You react. You identify immediate threats based on a very narrow set of criteria learned in a gutter. That is not seeing. Seeing is an act of deliberate, disciplined observation. It is the art of understanding a landscape, a person, a situation, not just by what is visible, but by what is absent. It is the art of reading the subtle language of the world around you. It is the foundation upon which all intelligence, all strategy, is built. Without it, you are not a weapon, you are just a blind, thrashing animal."

Alyvia placed a plate in front of him. On it were two slices of toasted bread, dark and crusty, spread with what looked like apple butter, and a hard-boiled egg. The simple meal looked like a feast.

"Eat," Felcher commanded, "And listen."

Marcus ate, the simple, wholesome flavors a stark contrast to the complex, intimidating lesson he was being given.

"We will begin with this room," Felcher continued, his gaze sweeping the space. "Tell me what you see."

Marcus looked around, his mind racing. He saw what he had seen before. Books. Maps. Weapons. A comfortable, lived-in space. "I see... books. A lot of books. Maps. Some training swords. A kitchen." He listed the objects, his voice uncertain.

"That is an inventory," Felcher said with a sigh of profound disappointment. "A clerk could give me an inventory. I asked you what you see. What does the inventory tell you?" He pointed to the bookshelves. "The books. What do they tell you about the man who owns them?"

Marcus looked at the chaotic, overflowing shelves. "That he... reads a lot?"

"A stunning deduction," Felcher said, his voice dripping with sarcasm. Marcus flinched. "Look closer. Observe the details. Are the books new or old? Are they uniform or varied? Are they pristine or well used?"

Marcus looked again, forcing himself to see past the simple fact of their existence. "They're old," he said slowly, "The covers are worn. Some are falling apart. They're all different sizes and shapes. Not a matching set."

"And what does that imply?" Felcher prompted, his voice like a drill instructor's.

"That... they're for reading, not for show," Marcus ventured. "And that he's had them a long time. Or he buys them used."

"Better," Felcher conceded, a crumb of approval. "It implies that the knowledge within the books is more important than their value as objects. It suggests a mind that is pragmatic, not vain. A mind that values substance over appearance. Now, the maps." He gestured to the table covered in charts. "What do they tell you?"

"They show different places. The kingdom. Other lands."

"Look at the details," Felcher insisted, his voice sharp with impatience. "The pins. The notes in the margins, even if you cannot read them, you can see their presence. The worn fold lines. What does this tell you?"

Marcus stared at the maps, trying to see them as Felcher did. He saw the clusters of colored pins. He saw the dense scribbles of ink along the borders. He saw the creases where the maps had been folded and unfolded a thousand times. "They're not just for looking at," he said, the realization dawning slowly. "They're tools. They're being used to... plan something. The pins are marking places. The notes are information. They're... active."

"Precisely," Felcher said, a flicker of satisfaction in his eyes. "They tell you that the owner is not merely a student of history or geography. He is an active strategist. He is engaged in an ongoing campaign or planning a new one. He is a man who thinks in terms of terrain, logistics, and troop movements. By observing these simple, inanimate objects, you have learned that the inhabitant of this room is a pragmatic, experienced strategist who values knowledge over vanity and is actively engaged in some form of conflict. You have begun to see. Now, apply that same observation to Alyvia."

Marcus's head snapped toward Alyvia, who was sipping her chicory, watching them with a quiet, amused smile. He felt a hot flush of embarrassment. He was supposed to analyze her?

"Go on," Felcher commanded.

Marcus looked at Alyvia, his mind a blank. She was… a kind woman. She smelled of flowers. She was a good cook. How was he supposed to analyze that?

"Start with the obvious," Felcher guided him, his voice softening slightly, becoming more instructional. "Her hands."

Marcus looked at her hands. They were resting on her cup. They were not the soft, pale, unblemished hands of an upper-class lady. Her knuckles were slightly swollen, the skin on her fingers calloused. There was a faint, dark stain under one of her fingernails, a trace of soil. "They're… working hands," he said. "She uses them. In the garden, maybe. From the flower shop."

"And?"

"They're… strong," he added, thinking of the way she had scrubbed his back. "But the way she holds the cup… her fingers are gentle."

"Excellent," Felcher said. "You see the contradiction. Strength and gentleness. What else? Her clothes."

He looked at her dress. It was simple and homespun, but immaculately clean and well-mended. A small, neat patch was sewn onto the elbow, the stitches so fine they were almost invisible. "She takes care of her things," he said. "The patch is neat. She's patient. Precise."

"Her demeanor," Felcher pressed. "How did she treat me this morning?"

"She… scolded you. For burning your tongue."

"And what does that tell you about our relationship?"

Marcus hesitated. This felt like a trap. "That she's… not afraid of you," he said carefully.

"It tells you that our relationship is not based on a hierarchy of fear," Felcher corrected, "It is based on a partnership of mutual respect and long affection. It tells you that within this home, her authority in domestic matters is absolute. Therefore, if you wish to remain in my good graces, you will afford her the same respect and obedience you afford me. A vital piece of strategic information for your survival in this new environment, wouldn't you agree?"

"Yes, Commander," Marcus whispered, the lesson landing with the force of a physical blow. He had been looking at a kind woman. Felcher had been teaching him how to read a power structure.

"This is the art of seeing," Felcher concluded, standing up from the table. "You must practice it constantly. Every room you enter, every person you meet, every street you walk down. Ask yourself What do I see? And what does it tell me? Your life may one day depend on the details you observe, or the ones you miss. Your lesson in letters begins now. Alyvia."

Felcher gave a nod to his wife and then strode out of the room, leaving a profound, humming silence in his wake.

Marcus sat at the table, his half-eaten breakfast forgotten. His mind was reeling. He felt as if a door had been opened to a room he never knew existed, a world of hidden meanings and subtle clues that had been around him all along, but that he had been completely blind to.

Alyvia came and sat in Felcher's chair, her presence instantly transforming the atmosphere from a drill sergeant's classroom to something softer and less intimidating. She placed a small, smooth piece of slate on the table, along with a nub of white chalk.

"Don't let him frighten you," she said, her voice gentle. "He's been a teacher for a very long time. He just forgets that not all of his students are hardened soldiers." She smiled. "He once tried to teach me the principles of a defensive siege using my vegetable patch as a model. I told him if his soldiers trampled my carrots, they wouldn't be getting any of my stew."

Marcus risked a small smile. "Did they trample the carrots?"

"Not a single one," she said with a wink. "Even a Commander knows not to cross a cook. Now, then. Reading and writing are not as scary as they look. It's just a different kind of pattern. Like learning the rules of a new game." She picked up the chalk. "We'll start with the first letter. This," she said, drawing a clean, strong, vertical line with two shorter horizontal lines at the top and bottom, "is A."

For the next three hours, Marcus was plunged into a world of bewildering shapes and sounds. Alyvia was a patient and methodical teacher. She showed him the shape of each letter, told him its name, and made him repeat the sound it made. She had him trace the letters on the slate with his finger, then try to draw them himself with the chalk.

His hand, accustomed to the brutal grip of a fighter, was clumsy and awkward. The chalk felt alien in his fingers. His first attempts at the letters were shaky, malformed squiggles. He grew frustrated, the chalk dust coating his fingers feeling like a symbol of his own stupidity. This was harder than any fight. In the pit, the rules were simple: hit or be hit. Here, the rules were abstract, slippery. He couldn't punch a letter into submission.

"It's all right," Alyvia would say whenever he let out a growl of frustration. "It's like learning to walk. You fall down a lot at first. No one expects you to run a race on your first day."

She taught him the letters of his own name. M A R C U S. She showed him how they fit together to form the sound that was him. He stared at the five shapes on the slate. It was the first word he had ever recognized. It felt like a strange, powerful magic to see his own name captured in white dust on a grey stone.

By the time the three hours were up, his head was swimming. He had learned ten letters. They were a jumble of hooks and lines in his mind, a code he was only beginning to understand. His hand ached from gripping the chalk. He felt more exhausted than he had after two fights in one night.

Alyvia seemed pleased with his progress. "You have a good eye for the shapes," she said, wiping the slate clean. "You're a quick study, Just Marcus. Gerald was right about that."

The praise felt strange, but not unwelcome. Just as he was beginning to relax, the door opened and Felcher re-entered the room. He had changed out of his domestic clothes and was now wearing a simple, practical training tunic and trousers. The Commander was back.

"Time's up," he announced. "To the barn."

The transition was jarring. One moment, he was a student, painstakingly learning the building blocks of language. The next, he was a recruit being summoned to the training yard.

The barn, which had seemed a peaceful refuge for the great warhorse, was transformed. Felcher had cleared a space in the center. The rack of training weapons had been moved to the side. The air smelled of hay, horse, and the faint, metallic scent of old sweat.

"Your fight with The Butcher," Felcher began, without preamble. He began to circle Marcus, his eyes narrowed in analysis, a predator sizing up its prey. "It was effective, but it was inefficient. You won through endurance and brutality. You outlasted him. A valid strategy against a mindless brute, but it will get you killed against a trained opponent."

He stopped in front of Marcus. "You have three primary weaknesses. First, your stance is sloppy. It's reactive, not foundational. It leaves you open to trips and throws, as you so effectively demonstrated on your opponent. Second, you waste energy. Every move you make is too large, too telegraphed. You swing with your arms, not with your core. You rely on speed to compensate for poor technique. Third, and most critically, you have no defense. Your entire strategy is based on not being where the punch lands. A true defense is not about evasion. It is about control. It is about receiving, redirecting, and countering an attack in a single, fluid motion."

He picked up the heavy ironwood quarterstaff from the rack. It was as tall as he was and thick as his wrist. "We will begin by correcting your foundation. Assume your fighting stance."

Marcus did as he was told, sinking into the familiar, low crouch he used in the pit.

Whack.

The staff moved in a blur, striking him sharply on the back of his calf. The blow was not crippling, but it was hard enough to make his leg buckle. He stumbled.

"Pathetic," Felcher spat, "Your weight is on your heels. Your back is curved. You are prepared to spring away, not to hold your ground. Again."

For the next hour, Felcher dismantled him. He didn't attack him. He simply... corrected him. Every time Marcus settled into his stance, the staff would strike, a sharp, punishing blow to a part of his body that was out of alignment: his calf for being too far back, his thigh for not being engaged, his lower back for being hunched, and his shoulder for being too tense. Each blow was a painful, punctuated lesson.

"Your power comes from the ground," Felcher lectured, his voice a low, rhythmic counterpoint to the sharp whack of the staff. "The earth is your anchor. Your feet are the roots. Your legs, your hips, your core, that is the trunk of the tree. Your arms, your fists, they are merely the branches. The force must flow from the ground up. You are trying to fight with the branches alone."

By the end of the hour, Marcus was drenched in sweat, his body a canvas of fresh, stinging welts. He was more tired than he had been during his lesson with Alyvia, but it was a different kind of exhaustion. This was a deep, muscular fatigue. But something was happening. His body was learning, bypassing his conscious mind. He began to feel the difference between a stable stance and an unstable one. He could feel the flow of energy when he engaged his core. He was being broken down, yes, but he was also being rebuilt, piece by painful piece.

"Enough," Felcher finally said, lowering the staff, "For today." He looked at Marcus's battered, sweating form. There was no pity in his eyes, but there was a flicker of something else. A grudging approval. "You learn. Pain is a good teacher, and you are an attentive student. Go. Wash up. Your chores are next."

"Chores?" Marcus asked, confused.

"You will not be an idle guest in this house," Felcher said. "You will earn your keep. You will muck out the horse's stall. You will chop the wood for the stove. You will carry water for Alyvia. You will do whatever she asks of you. Labor builds discipline. And discipline," he said, tapping the ironwood staff on the ground, "is the forge in which a weapon is tempered."

That evening, after a dinner he was too tired to fully appreciate, Marcus lay on his cot, his body a universe of pain. Every muscle ached. His mind was a chaotic jumble of letters and fighting stances. His skin smelled of horse manure, woodsmoke, and rosemary soap.

He was a thing being unmade and remade. He was a boy learning to read and a killer being taught to kill more efficiently. He was a student, a recruit, a stable hand, a prisoner. The contradictions were dizzying, but beneath it all, a single, terrifying thought was beginning to take root.

For the first time in five years, he wasn't just surviving. He was learning. He was changing. The straight, brutal, and simple line he had been walking had ended. He was now on a new path, a complex and winding road being laid out for him by a master architect of pain and purpose. And for the first time, he found himself wondering, with a flicker of something that felt dangerously like hope, where it might lead.

Chapter 13

The day ended as it had begun, with the slow retreat of a light he was still unaccustomed to. The setting sun painted the slate rooftops outside his small window in hues of bruised purple and soft, dying orange. The sounds of the capital were winding down; the sharp, chaotic noises of commerce and transport were replaced by the more muted, domestic sounds of evening: the distant chime of a bell tower, the low murmur of conversations from neighboring houses, and the clatter of a pot being washed.

Marcus lay on his cot, his body a universe of new and exquisite pain. It was not the familiar, jagged pain of a split knuckle or a cracked rib. This was a deeper, more profound ache, the pain of muscles that had been dormant for a lifetime being violently awakened. His legs, his back, his core, every part of him that Felcher had "corrected" with the ironwood staff, throbbed with a low, insistent fire. His mind was a similar landscape of exhaustion. The ten letters Alyvia had taught him swam behind his closed eyelids, a jumble of abstract, alien shapes that refused to settle into any coherent order.

He had performed his chores in a state of weary automatonism. Mucking out Euphrates's stall, the warm, earthy smell of the horse was a strange comfort. Chopping wood, the rhythmic thud of the axe a familiar, percussive task, though his arms protested with every swing. Carrying buckets of water for Alyvia, his steps slow and measured, his focus entirely on not spilling a single drop. He had worked until his body screamed for rest, and now, in the quiet of his room, there was no escape.

He stared at the ceiling. The plaster was old, a web of fine, hairline cracks spreading from the center like a frozen spiderweb. He began to trace the lines with his eyes, a familiar ritual to quiet the storm in his head. The main crack branched into two smaller ones, which then split again. It was a pattern, a system. He focused on it, letting the aches of his body and the jumble of letters in his mind fade into a dull, peripheral hum.

The cracks began to sharpen, to define themselves. The pale, uneven plaster between them seemed to darken and lighten, a subtle but definite shift. The fine, web-like lines thickened, straightened, becoming a perfect, luminous grid that overlaid the ceiling. The familiar, humming silence of the dream space descended, and the small, safe room dissolved around him.

He was back on the board.

He stood as the Black Rook, a silent, iron tower in his castled corner, a guardian to his still hazy King. The air was cold and sterile, smelling of ozone and dust. Across the vast, checkered plain, the pieces of the Ivory Blight stood poised, their bone white forms radiating a cold, dead light. The Apothecary Pawn. The Silas Bishop. The hulking, brutish Knight. They were waiting, their malice a palpable pressure in the silent air.

But tonight, something was different. The pieces on his own side, the shadowy forms of his allied army, were not solid. They shimmered, and as he focused on them, he saw that they were not made of smoke or shadow at all. They were made of letters.

The pawn in front of him was a towering, three-dimensional effigy of the letter 'P.' The Knight beside it was a capital 'N,' its form sharp and angular. The Bishop, a 'B.' His Queen, a majestic, curving 'Q.' His King, a solid, regal 'K.' The entire army was an alphabet, a code he was only just beginning to learn.

And then he looked at the enemy. Their pieces, too, had changed. They were also letters, but they were twisted, malformed, their shapes sharp and unfamiliar, belonging to an alphabet he did not know. They were the very embodiment of the incomprehensible script he had seen in Felcher's books.

The game was not just one of strategy and violence. It was a game of language. A war between a language he was struggling to learn and one he could not even begin to understand.

His Player, the silent, commanding presence of Felcher, was absent. It was his turn to move, but he had not been given a command. He was alone on the board, faced with an impossible task. He had to make a move, but how could he command an army whose very essence was a mystery to him?

He focused on the letters on his side of the board. The ten shapes Alyvia had taught him. A, B, C, D, E... L, M, N... R, S... He saw them scattered amongst his ranks. He saw the 'M' of his own name, a solid, dependable shape. He saw the 'S' of Silas, a curving, serpentine form. He saw the 'A' of Alyvia, of Apothecary, of Abigail.

He felt a sudden, desperate urge to create order from the chaos. He tried to move the pieces, not with the strategic logic of a chess player, but with the fumbling, nascent logic of a new reader. He tried to slide the 'A' next to the 'M'. The pieces wouldn't budge. They were locked in place, awaiting a command he didn't know how to give.

He tried to force it, his will pushing against the silent, unyielding rules of the board. He had to make a word. If he could make a word, he could make sense of it all. M A R C U S. His name. A word of power. A word of identity. He strained, his entire being focused on the task of moving the letters, of forcing them into a coherent whole.

The board began to resist. The grid lines wavered, the air grew thick and heavy, like trying to breathe water. The enemy letters seemed to mock him, their twisted, alien shapes pulsing with a faint, malevolent light. He was an illiterate fool, trying to play a game of poets and scholars. He was out of his depth, a creature of the gutter trying to read the stars. The frustration and helplessness were so profound, so absolute, that a wave of pure despair washed over him. He was going to fail.

The sound of a slammed door ripped him from the board.

His eyes snapped open. He was back in his room, staring at the cracked ceiling, his heart hammering against his ribs, a cold sweat slicking his skin. The dream, or whatever it was, had been more vivid, more terrifying, than ever before.

The sound had come from the main living area. It was followed by the sound of raised voices. The muffled tones of a sharp, angry argument. He couldn't make out the words, but he could read the emotional language of the sounds. Alyvia's voice, usually so warm and gentle, was sharp, high pitched, and insistent.

Felcher's voice was a low, rumbling thunder, a sound of controlled, dangerous anger.

Marcus sat bolt upright, every muscle tensed. He swung his legs off the cot, his feet finding the cold floorboards. He was a creature of The Scar. He knew this sound. He had heard it a thousand times, echoing through the thin walls of the tenements. It was the sound that came before the real violence. The sound of a man's patience wearing thin, of a woman pushing too far. It was a sound that almost always ended with a sharp slap and a woman's cry.

He crept to his door, his movements silent, instinctual. He pressed his ear against the cool wood. The argument continued, the voices rising and falling in a tense, angry cadence. He couldn't understand the words, but he could feel the vibrations of their anger through the wood. He was a silent observer again, but this time, the details he was gathering were terrifying. The placid, domestic illusion he had witnessed was shattering.

Suddenly, he heard a sharp, cracking sound.

Slap.

It was unmistakable—the sharp, ugly sound of flesh striking flesh.

It was followed by an absolute, profound silence. A dead, ringing stillness that was a thousand times more frightening than the shouting.

Marcus froze, his blood running cold. Then, the cold was instantly consumed by a fire. A white hot, incandescent rage, hotter and purer than any anger he had felt in the pit. It was a rage born of a lifetime of seeing the strong prey on the weak, of seeing women like his mother worn down by the casual cruelty of men.

How dare he?

How dare this man, this Commander, who spoke of discipline and control, who lived in this beautiful home with this kind, warm woman, raise a hand to her? The hypocrisy of it, the sheer, brutal injustice of it, was a physical blow. The fear he held for Felcher, the deep, abiding terror of the man's power, was burned away in an instant, consumed by this new, righteous inferno. He didn't think. He didn't strategize. He reacted.

He wrenched his door open and rushed out into the main room, his fists clenched at his sides, his body coiled for a fight he knew he could not possibly win, but which he was compelled to engage in all the same. He was no longer a pawn, no longer a rook. He was a boy from The Scar, and he was about to defend a woman from a bully.

He burst into the kitchen, his eyes blazing, ready to see... what? Alyvia, cowering and crying? Felcher, standing over her with a look of smug, brutal satisfaction?

The scene that met his eyes stopped him dead in his tracks. His rage, his momentum, his entire sense of reality, screeched to a halt.

Alyvia was not cowering. Felcher was not standing over her.

She had him pressed against the far wall. One of her hands was braced against his chest, and the other was raised, her fingers slightly curled. There was a bright, red handprint, the clear, five-fingered mark of a powerful slap, blooming on Commander Felcher's cheek. And Felcher... Felcher was not angry. He was not retaliating. He was... smiling. A slow, predatory, wolfish grin that held no humor, only a raw, dangerous intensity.

And then, before Marcus could process this impossible tableau, Felcher moved. He snaked an arm around Alyvia's waist, pulling her flush against him with a force that should have been brutal but was instead possessive, claiming. His other hand came up to cradle the back of her head, his fingers tangling in her hair. He lowered his head and kissed her.

It was not a gentle, affectionate kiss. It was a fierce, passionate, consuming kiss —a kiss of fire and fury, a deep, tempestuous love that was as much a battle as it was an embrace. It was a raw, unfiltered expression of the storm that raged between them, a storm that had been brewing for decades. Alyvia, far from resisting, seemed to melt into him, her arms wrapping around his neck, returning the kiss with an equal, fiery passion.

This was not for his eyes. This was not for anyone's eyes. This was a private, primal language being spoken between two people who knew each other on a level he couldn't begin to comprehend. It was indecent. It was embarrassing. It was a glimpse into the raw, molten core of their relationship, and he felt like a voyeur who had accidentally stumbled upon a sacred, secret rite.

He stood frozen in the doorway for a heartbeat, his own rage feeling foolish and childish in the face of this... this elemental force. Then, his senses returned, and with them, a wave of humiliation so profound it was a physical sickness. He had to get out. He had to disappear.

He began to back away, his steps agonizingly slow, trying to make no sound. He turned, his back to the scene, and tried to slip away, to retreat to the sanctuary of his room. He held his breath, praying they hadn't seen him, that they were too lost in their own world to notice the boy who had blundered into their private war.

He reached his door. His hand was on the latch. He was safe.

"Make sure you're up early tomorrow."

Felcher's voice came from directly behind him.

Marcus's heart stopped. He hadn't heard him move. He hadn't heard a single footstep, not a whisper of movement. The man had crossed the entire room with the silence of a hunting cat, with the speed of a striking snake. He had been a ghost. A silent death.

Marcus didn't turn around. He couldn't. He stared at the wood grain of his door, his entire body rigid.

"The physical conditioning will be... more strenuous," Felcher continued, his voice a low, calm murmur, back to its familiar, commanding tone. There was no trace of the passion from a moment ago, but there was something else in his voice now. A thread of dark, dangerous amusement. "And after your letters, we will begin your real education. The study of history. The art of the lie. The politics of the court. You have a great deal to learn, boy."

He was sending a message. A clear, unmistakable message. I know you saw. I know you misunderstood. I know you were about to do something incredibly foolish. And I am reminding you who is in control. This is my house. This is my life. You are merely a piece in it. Do not forget your place.

A hand, heavy and firm, clapped him on the shoulder. "Get some rest," Felcher said. The words were an order, not a kindness. Then, the hand was gone, and Marcus heard the soft, retreating footsteps as Felcher returned to his wife.

Marcus stumbled into his room and leaned against the closed door, his knees weak, his body trembling. He slid down the door to sit on the floor, his head in his hands. The world was not just complex. It was insane. It was a place of violent love and controlled rage, of domesticity and deadly force, of lessons taught with both a primer and a quarterstaff. He was a boy from the slums, a creature of simple, brutal truths, and he had been dropped into a universe of impossible, terrifying contradictions. He had no idea how to navigate it. He only knew that he had to survive it. And that his education had just entered a new, and far more dangerous, phase.

Chapter 14

Marcus woke with a jolt, not to the sharp blade of morning light, but to a diffuse, gentle luminescence that filled the small room. The quality of the light was different, softer, less demanding, as if it had been filtered through fine muslin. It was the light of a day already well underway, a day that had started without him.

A wave of pure, cold panic washed over him, a physical sensation that started in his gut and radiated outward, making his skin prickle. He was late.

He scrambled out of the cot, his heart hammering against his ribs in a frantic, panicked rhythm that was sickeningly familiar. It was the same adrenaline-fueled terror he felt in the pit when he'd made a mistake, when he'd seen an opponent's fist coming and knew he couldn't move away in time. He had overslept. Felcher had ordered him to be up early. Failure is not an option. The Commander's words echoed in his mind, not as a memory, but as a sentence of doom about to be carried out. He imagined Felcher standing over him, the ironwood staff held loosely in one hand, his obsidian eyes cold with a disappointment that was far more terrifying than any rage, and the promise of a brutal, painful correction.

He threw on the clothes of the ghost boy, Thomas, his fingers fumbling with the simple laces of his tunic, his mind a chaotic whirlwind of potential punishments. He was a recruit who had failed his first test of discipline. He was a sentry who had fallen asleep at his post. Why hadn't anyone woken him? Was this another one of Felcher's cruel, intricate tests? A test of his own internal discipline, which he had already failed so spectacularly? He braced himself for the confrontation, for the sharp, cutting words that would flay him more effectively than any whip, for the sharp, stinging impact of the staff against his already aching muscles.

He crept out of his room, his bare feet silent on the smooth, clean floorboards, every nerve ending screaming, hyper aware of every creak of the building, every distant city sound. He moved like a spy in his own home, expecting to be ambushed at any moment. He peeked into the main living area, a space that still felt alien and hostile in its domesticity. It was empty. The books and maps sat on their tables, silent and waiting, repositories of a knowledge he did not possess. The training weapons leaned in their rack, untouched and menacing. The entire apartment was filled with a profound, unnerving quiet.

He made his way cautiously to the kitchen, the space that had become the nexus of his new, bewildering life. The warm, inviting scents of the previous day's stew and baking bread were gone, replaced by the simple, clean, and slightly bitter aroma of brewing chicory. The room was tidy, everything in its proper place, a testament to Alyvia's quiet efficiency. And sitting at the small wooden table, bathed in a pool of soft morning light that illuminated the dust motes dancing in the air, was Alyvia.

She was not cooking. She was not bustling about with her usual energetic purpose. She was simply sitting, a steaming earthenware mug cradled in her hands, a thick, open book resting on the table before her. She was reading, her expression placid and thoughtful, a mask of calm. But as Marcus watched from the shadows of the archway, he saw the tightness around her eyes, the subtle tension in the set of her shoulders. It was the posture of a woman holding a great deal of worry at bay. She looked up as he entered, and her face broke into a small, gentle smile that did not quite reach her eyes.

"Good morning, Just Marcus," she said, her voice quiet, lacking its usual vibrant warmth. "I was beginning to wonder when you'd surface. Did you rest well?"

Marcus stood frozen in the archway, his carefully rehearsed anxiety momentarily short-circuited by the unexpected tranquility of the scene. Felcher was nowhere in sight. The confrontation he had braced for was absent. The quiet, he realized, was more terrifying than any shouting would have been.

"I… I'm sorry," he stammered, the words tumbling out, a confession of his failure, "I overslept. I didn't mean to."

Alyvia took a slow sip from her mug, her gaze returning to the incomprehensible script in her book. "Don't be sorry," she said, her voice taking on a flat, carefully neutral tone that was a poor imitation of nonchalance, "I let you sleep in. You looked like you needed it." She paused, her finger tracing a line on the page as if the words there were of paramount importance. Then she added, still without looking up, "Gerald has been called away on… business. He'll be out of the city for a few days."

She didn't look happy about it. And then, it clicked. A series of connections fired in Marcus's brain with the shocking clarity of a lightning strike. The argument from the previous night. The slammed door. The fierce, angry, possessive kiss. And now, Felcher was suddenly gone. This "business" wasn't business. It was the fallout—the cause of their fight.

"I was told to tell you," she continued, her eyes still on the page, as if she were reading a script, "that after your letters, you are to help me with chores and running errands until he returns."

She had intentionally let him sleep in.

The realization was staggering. It reconfigured his entire understanding of the power dynamics in this house. This wasn't just an act of kindness for his benefit. This was an act of petty, domestic rebellion. A wife's subtle revenge. She was mad at Felcher, and her way of expressing it was to disrupt the rigid, disciplined schedule he had laid out for his new recruit. It was an act of defiance so subtle, so personal, and so utterly alien to Marcus's world of brutal, straightforward power dynamics that he didn't know how to process it. She was using him, his sleep, his schedule, as a pawn in her own private war with the Commander.

And in that moment, a new and far more terrifying emotion than the fear of punishment settled over him a crushing, suffocating sense of responsibility.

Felcher was gone. And he, Marcus, a boy of the gutter, a creature of violence, had been left here, in Felcher's home, with Felcher's wife. The Commander, a man of immense power and, as Marcus was learning, immense and complex passions, had entrusted him, implicitly, without a single word, with the safety of the one thing in the world he seemed to truly love. The unspoken weight of that trust was heavier than any physical burden, more terrifying than any threat. If anything were to happen in his absence, if the house were robbed, if Alyvia were threatened, if a single hair on her head were harmed, the blame would not fall on some abstract circumstance. It would fall squarely, and with crushing, unimaginable finality, on him.

He could feel the cold fury of the absent Commander, a phantom presence that seemed to emanate from the very stones of the house. He could picture Felcher's obsidian eyes, and he knew, with a certainty that chilled him to the bone, that any failure to protect this home, this woman, would result in a correction far more permanent than a blow from a training staff. He was no longer just a recruit being honed into a weapon. He was a sentry. The Black Rook, left behind to guard the Queen while the King was away on the battlefield.

Alyvia seemed oblivious to the storm of anxiety she had just unleashed in him. She finally closed her book with a soft sigh and looked at him directly. "So," she said, her tone now deceptively casual, "after breakfast, I was thinking we could go to the market first to pick up a few things, and then we can do your letters this afternoon. It will be good for you to see a bit more of the city, get your bearings."

She was changing the routine.

The schedule Felcher had laid out —letters in the morning, conditioning in the afternoon, and chores in the evening —was a lifeline for Marcus. It was a clear, predictable set of rules, a structure he could cling to in this new, bewildering world. It was hard, it was painful, but it was known. And now, she was changing it. Casually. Willfully. A quiet act of defiance against her absent husband.

The anxiety in his stomach tightened into a hard, painful knot. His first instinct was to protest, to insist on the established order. No, letters first. The Commander said letters first. The words rose in his throat, a desperate plea for the safety of predictability. But he clamped his jaw shut before they could escape. He looked at the quiet determination in Alyvia's face, the subtle, stubborn set of her jaw. To go against her would be to fail at the first test of his new, unspoken duty. He had to keep her happy, keep her safe. And if that meant enduring the terrifying chaos of a disrupted schedule, then he would endure it.

He sat down at the table, his movements stiff. "Yes, ma'am," he said, his voice quiet. He pinched his thigh hard under the table, a sharp, grounding pain, a private punishment for the chaos that was roiling inside him. He would not dare go against her. He would be the perfect, obedient sentry. His survival, and possibly hers, depended on it.

Breakfast was a quiet, tense affair. Alyvia made them both toast and chicory, and they ate in a silence that was thick with unspoken things. Marcus focused on the mechanics of eating, the rough, crumbly texture of the toasted bread, the bitter, earthy taste of the chicory, anything to avoid thinking about the crushing weight of his new responsibility and the unpredictable woman sitting across from him.

After they had eaten and cleaned their plates, Alyvia stood up. "Alright, then. Let's get our shopping list together."

The journey to the market was a fresh sensory ordeal. Alyvia had given him a large, woven basket to carry, its rough texture a constant reminder of his duty. He followed a half step behind her, his eyes constantly scanning, his senses on high alert. He was no longer just an observer, a student of Felcher's lessons. He was a bodyguard. Every person who passed them, every shout from a vendor, every rumbling cart was a potential threat to be assessed and categorized.

He catalogued them all. The two burly dockworkers with tattooed arms arguing on a corner, loud and unprofessional, posed no threat. The trio of young, swaggering apprentices, laughing too loudly, arrogant yet soft, posed no threat. The quiet, hawk-faced man in a dark cloak who seemed to be watching them from across the street, this one he noted, logged away, his eyes tracking the man until he disappeared into the crowd. Potential Bishop, diagonal influence, observe from a distance. He was trying to see as Felcher saw, to separate the noise from the signal. The sheer number of potential signals was exhausting.

The market itself was a chaotic explosion of life, a place where all of Felcher's lessons in observation seemed to break down under the sheer, overwhelming volume of data. It was a vast, open square, crammed with stalls selling everything imaginable. The air was a thick, overwhelming soup of a thousand competing smells the sharp, briny scent of fresh fish laid out on beds of ice the sweet, earthy aroma of mounds of cabbages, carrots, and potatoes the heady, spicy fragrance of exotic herbs and powders from a stall run by a dark skinned man from the southern isles the warm, greasy smell of sizzling sausages from a food vendor's cart, a scent so delicious it made his stomach ache.

The sounds were a deafening roar, the shouts of a hundred vendors hawking their wares, "Fresh mackerel, caught this morn," "Fine silks, fit for a queen," "Pies! Hot meat pies," the loud, aggressive haggling of customers the frantic squawking of chickens crammed into wooden cages the joyous laughter of children chasing a stray dog the high, lively music of a lone fiddler playing a reel in a corner, his foot stomping out the rhythm on a wooden board.

For a moment, Marcus felt the familiar, overwhelming urge to retreat, to shut down. The sensory input was overwhelming, a tidal wave that threatened to drown him. He felt his mind begin to slip, to seek the safety of its own internal, ordered world. He pinched his thigh again, hard, but it was too late. The world began to waver, the chaotic colors and sounds bleeding together, and the familiar, luminous grid of the chessboard started to impose itself over the scene.

But this was not the clean, epic battlefield of his dreams. This was a corrupted, chaotic mockery of the game.

He was still the Black Rook, but he was lost in a sea of pieces. The cobblestones of the market square became the checkered board, but the pieces were all wrong. The milling crowd resolved into hundreds of Pawns, far too many for a normal game, moving not in straight lines but in erratic, unpredictable patterns, blocking paths, creating bottlenecks. They were a mindless, churning tide of humanity.

He saw the swaggering apprentices resolve into Knight pieces, but they weren't the lean, vicious wolves of his dream army. They were clumsy, braying donkeys, their L-shaped moves jagged and foolish, posing no real threat but getting in the way. He saw the hawk-faced man he'd noted earlier as a Bishop, a creature of shadow and observation, but his diagonal line of sight was constantly being blocked by the swirling mass of Pawns.

He saw Rooks, not as towers of power, but as the lumbering, overloaded dray carts, powerful in a straight line but slow, clumsy, and easily trapped. Their drivers were the petty Kings of their own small, mobile domains, shouting orders that were lost in the greater din.

And the Queens. There were Queens everywhere. Their power was absolute but utterly irrational. He saw the beautiful, richly dressed noblewoman, her nose in the air, a Queen of social standing, her "moves" dictated by vanity and whim as she inspected a bolt of silk. He saw the flower vendor at her stall, a Queen of her own fragrant domain, surrounded by a court of bees and admiring customers. He saw a sharp-eyed matron, the undisputed Queen of her household, berating her husband, a cowed, shuffling Pawn. Each was a center of immense, localized power, but their motivations were a mystery, their strategies incomprehensible.

And Alyvia. Alyvia was the most powerful Queen on the board. She moved through the chaos with a serene, unhurried grace, the Pawns parting before her as if by magic. She haggled with a fishmonger Bishop, her words a sharp, diagonal attack that won her a better price. She smiled at a child Pawn, and it beamed back, its erratic movement stilled for a moment by her kindness. She was a force of nature, her influence radiating outward, reshaping the game around her without any apparent effort.

He, the Black Rook, was supposed to be guarding her. But how could he guard a piece so powerful, so unpredictable, a piece whose moves he couldn't begin to anticipate? He felt useless, a clumsy, iron-bound tower in a game of fluid, chaotic grace. There was no clear objective here. There was no enemy King to topple. There were a hundred petty kings, a dozen powerful queens, and a thousand mindless pawns. The rules were broken. The system had failed. This wasn't a game of strategy; it was a riot.

"Marcus?"

Alyvia's voice cut through the chaos of his mind, a clean, clear note that shattered the illusion. The board dissolved. The pieces turned back into people. The roar of the market rushed back in, almost knocking him off his feet. He blinked, finding himself standing dumbly in front of a stall piled high with vibrant green cabbages and earthy brown potatoes. Alyvia was looking at him, a faint line of concern between her eyebrows.

"Are you alright? You looked a thousand miles away," she said.

"I'm fine," he said quickly, his voice rough. He shifted the weight of the basket in his arms, the physical sensation a welcome anchor. "Just... a lot of people."

She gave him a knowing look. "It can be a bit much if you're not used to it," she said. "The Scar is loud, but it's a different kind of loud. This is the noise of life, of abundance. It takes some getting used to."

She turned to the vendor, a stout woman with arms as thick as hams. "A head of cabbage, please, Martha. And a dozen of your best potatoes."

He watched her interact with the vendor, the easy back and forth, the shared laugh. He realized Felcher's lesson was continuing, even in his absence. He was supposed to be "seeing" all this. But his attempt to apply the strategic, predatory gaze of the Commander to this vibrant, chaotic scene had failed. The system was too complex.

He took a deep breath, forcing the phantom chessboard from his mind. He couldn't see the whole board. It was too big, too confusing. He had to narrow his focus. He couldn't be a grand strategist. He had to be a bodyguard.

His new objective was simple, tactical, and immediate. A bubble of space. A three-foot radius around Alyvia. That was his board now. Nothing was allowed to breach that perimeter without his express permission. His gaze sharpened, no longer trying to categorize every person in the square, but focusing instead on the immediate vicinity. The man jostling too close. The boy running with a stolen apple, who might knock into her. The shifting weight of the crowd.

This he could do. This was the discipline of the pit, applied to a new ring. A smaller, more manageable board. He shifted his stance, placing himself slightly behind Alyvia and to her left, the basket held in front of him like a shield. His eyes were constantly moving, tracking the flow of bodies, anticipating movements, creating a small, invisible wall of pure, focused intent around her.

He was still the Black Rook. But he was no longer lost on a vast, incomprehensible board. He had found his file. He had found his rank, and he would hold the line. The weight in the basket grew heavier as Alyvia added vegetables, a small fish wrapped in paper, and a bag of flour, but the weight of his responsibility felt, for the first time, manageable. It was a simple, brutal, and straightforward task. And that, he could understand.

Chapter 15

He maintained his silent, watchful orbit around Alyvia as she moved through the market. The three-foot bubble of space around her became his entire world, a small, mobile fortress he defended with a quiet, simmering intensity. He learned to anticipate the chaotic surges of the crowd, subtly shifting his position to shield her from a lurching drunk or a group of boisterous children. He held the increasingly heavy basket like a shield, its weight a grounding, physical manifestation of his duty.

The riotous sensory input of the market, which had initially threatened to overwhelm him, was now filtered through this new, narrow lens of purpose. He no longer tried to process the entire chaotic scene. He focused only on what was relevant to his perimeter. The smells, the sounds, the sights, they were all just data points to be analyzed for potential threats to the queen of this small, temporary kingdom. He was a Rook, controlling his file, and the simplicity of the task was a relief.

Alyvia seemed completely oblivious to his silent, intense vigilance. She moved with an unhurried grace, greeting vendors she knew by name, her laughter a warm, bright sound in the cacophony. She bartered with a good-natured firmness, her knowledge of prices and quality clearly earning the respect of the tough, seasoned merchants. She was a master of this environment, a different kind of commander than her husband, her authority rooted not in fear, but in a currency of kindness and familiarity that Marcus found both baffling and fascinating.

They were at a stall piled high with fragrant, brightly colored fruits, including pears, apples, and late-season plums, when the perimeter was breached.

He approached from Alyvia's blind side, moving with a practiced, gliding step that was designed to seem humble and unobtrusive. He was a man dressed in the faded, slightly too large black robes of a lesser clergyman. His face was thin and pale, his eyes held a look of pious, sorrowful sincerity, and his hands were clasped before him in a gesture of meek supplication. A small, wooden alms box was slung around his neck on a frayed leather cord.

To Marcus's hyper-vigilant senses, the man was a cacophony of wrong signals. The robes, while appearing humble, were of a decent wool, not the rough burlap of a truly impoverished order. His boots, peeking out from beneath the hem, were worn but well made, not the scuffed, broken things of a man who walked everywhere. His face, though arranged in an expression of piety, had a flicker of something sharp and assessing in the eyes as he scanned the crowd, his gaze lingering for a fraction of a second too long on the women with fuller purses. And his smell, beneath the faint, musty scent of old wool, there was a trace of cheap, sweet wine on his breath.

This was not a man of God. This was a predator wearing a costume. In the internal, strategic landscape of Marcus's mind, a new piece appeared on the board. A Bishop, cloaked in black, its movements diagonal and insidious, its purpose to exploit belief and compassion.

"Good lady," the Bishop began, his voice a soft, unctuous purr that was perfectly calibrated to inspire pity and guilt. He timed his approach perfectly, catching Alyvia just as she had paid for a bag of apples, and her coin purse was still in her hand. "Forgive my intrusion, but I am collecting for the Chapel of the Merciful Hand. A small donation, perhaps? A generous subscription to help the poor and the dispossessed of our great city?"

Marcus saw right through it. The overly formal language, the well-rehearsed plea, the strategically timed approach — it was a game as old as The Scar itself, just played with a better costume and a more pious vocabulary. He had seen a hundred variations of this grift, from beggars faking crippling injuries to "orphans" with suspiciously well-fed faces. He tensed, his grip on the heavy basket tightening. He waited for Alyvia to give the man a polite but firm dismissal, to shoo him away as she would a buzzing fly. It was an obvious trick, a transparent piece of trickery.

And then Alyvia spoke, and Marcus's world, which he had just managed to bring into a semblance of ordered control, shattered once again.

"The poor?" she said, her face instantly transforming, the shrewd, bargaining market goer replaced by a woman of boundless, heartbreaking compassion. "The homeless people of the city? Oh, my word! Of course!"

Marcus froze, his muscles locking in disbelief. He watched, horrified, as she not only bought the man's story but embraced it with a fervent, wide-eyed sincerity. She was totally, completely taken in. The Bishop piece on the mental chessboard seemed to swell, its aura of corruption growing stronger as it fed on her pure, undiluted goodness. She was fumbling with the strings of her coin purse, ready to give her heart and soul, as well as a significant portion of her household budget, away to this charlatan.

He had to intervene. The thought was a bolt of pure, cold panic. But how? He couldn't physically step in; that would be an overreach, an insult to Alyvia. He couldn't call the man a liar; that would create a scene, drawing the exact kind of attention Felcher had warned him against. And worse, it would humiliate Alyvia, forcing her to see that her own good nature had been turned into a weapon against her. That felt like a betrayal of his duty to protect her, not just physically, but also from this kind of ugly truth.

He needed a different strategy. Not a Rook's move of brute force. He needed a Bishop's move of his own. A subtle, diagonal attack.

He stepped forward slightly, just enough to be included in their conversation, his expression a carefully constructed mask of boyish, innocent curiosity. He looked at the false clergyman, his eyes wide.

"Which church is it, sir?" he asked, his voice deliberately pitched to sound young and guileless. "The Commander, Mr. Felcher, sometimes likes to make donations directly to the parishes."

He was using Felcher's name as a weapon, a subtle application of pressure. He was also beginning to see, to read the man in front of him. The flicker of avarice in the man's eyes as he looked at Alyvia's purse. The slight tightening of his lips at the mention of a name associated with authority. The way his clasped hands shifted, a small, nervous gesture. The Bishop was a powerful piece, but it had its weaknesses.

The man's pious smile didn't falter, but a new, wary light entered his eyes. He had been a predator sizing up a lone sheep, and now a young, unpredictable wolf had just stepped out from behind a tree. "It is the Chapel of the Merciful Hand, my son," he said, his voice smooth as oil.

"A small but devout congregation."

"And where is your chapel located?" Marcus pressed, his innocent tone unwavering. He felt a strange, cold thrill, a sense of power that was completely different from the physical domination of the pit. This was a different kind of fight.

The man hesitated for a fraction of a second. A lie was being constructed. "It is on... on Willow Creek Lane. By the old weir."

Alyvia, who had been listening to their exchange, frowned. Her natural compassion was now being filtered through a lens of specific, local knowledge. "Willow Creek Lane?" she said, her brow furrowed in thought. "That's down by the dyers' district, isn't it? I don't recall a church there. Just warehouses and tenements."

The Bishop on the mental board had just made a fatal error. It had moved to a square where it was vulnerable. It had stumbled into the queen's line of fire.

Marcus saw his opening. Another diagonal move, feigning innocence to deliver the killing blow.

"I know Willow Creek Lane!" he said, his voice full of false, boyish enthusiasm. "We can help you find it! I can carry the alms box for you, sir; it looks heavy. We can walk you right to the door."

He was offering help, but it was a threat. He was calling the man's bluff, offering to expose the lie by walking him to a place that didn't exist.

The man's composure finally cracked. A bead of sweat trickled down from his temple. His pious smile tightened into a grimace. He looked from Marcus's wide, innocent eyes to Alyvia's now suspicious frown. The grift had collapsed. The sheep had suddenly grown teeth, and the shepherd dog was looking at him with dawning suspicion.

"Tha.. that's quite all right, my boy," the man stammered, taking a hasty step backward. His eyes darted around, looking for an escape route through the crowd. "Very kind of you, very kind indeed. But I... I have other parishioners to visit. On the other side of the market. Thank you for your kindness."

He turned and slipped away into the throng, his humble, gliding walk replaced by the quick, furtive scuttle of a rat leaving a sinking ship. He disappeared into the sea of Pawns before Alyvia could give him a single coin.

The Bishop was off the board. Checkmate.

Alyvia watched him go, a look of profound disappointment on her face. "Oh, well," she sighed, her compassion seemingly undimmed by the near deception, "There will always be more mouths to feed, I suppose." She turned to Marcus, a bright, slightly forced smile on her face. "All this haggling has made me thirsty. How about we stop and get something to drink?"

Before Marcus could protest, to suggest a respectable tea shop or a simple water vendor, she led him toward the mouth of a narrow, noisy alley. The sign above the door was a crudely painted, snarling boar's head. The sounds from within were a low thrum of male voices, punctuated by bursts of rough laughter. Warning bells, loud and clear, started going off in Marcus's head. This was not a place for her.

She pushed through the door and casually strolled into the rough-looking tavern. The air inside was thick with the smell of spilled ale, unwashed bodies, and cheap pipe smoke. It was a smell that was uncomfortably close to the taverns of The Scar. The clientele was a collection of shady-looking characters, off-duty laborers, river men with hard faces, and a few men who just had the cold, quiet look of professional troublemakers.

The older man at the counter, a burly figure with a scarred face and a belly that strained his apron, looked up as they entered. His eyes widened in surprise to see a woman like Alyvia in his establishment. A slow, greasy smile spread across his face. "Well, now. What's a pretty flower like you doing in a dusty old bar like mine?" he asked, his voice a low rumble, casually flirting with her.

Marcus stiffened, his hand tightening on the basket. He scanned the room, his mind instantly populating the space with chess pieces. The bartender was a Rook, powerful and immovable in his own territory. The shadowy men at the tables were a mix of dangerous Knights and Pawns, their intentions unknown.

He relaxed slightly when he saw two off-duty city guards in a corner booth, their armor unbuckled, mugs of ale in their hands. They were a stabilizing presence, two of his own Rooks, though their allegiance was to the city, not to him.

Alyvia seemed completely oblivious to the undercurrents in the room, to the way the men had stopped their conversations to watch her. She beamed at the bartender. "It's a hot day, and my throat is dry," she said, her voice as clear and bright as a bell, "I would like a cup of your cleanest water, please. And one for the boy as well."

The bartender's smile widened. He clearly enjoyed the attention. As he turned to get their water, one of the city guards from the corner booth stood up and approached their table. He was younger than his partner, with a handsome, arrogant face and a swagger in his step.

"Ma'am," he said, his voice oozing a practiced charm as he leaned against their table, "a place like this is no spot for a lady of your quality. You need someone to escort you around the city? I can show you some... much nicer places."

More bells were going off in Marcus's head. This Knight was making an aggressive, forward move, directly threatening his Queen. And she, in her radiant innocence, just thought the man was being polite.

Alyvia laughed, a sound of genuine, unflustered amusement. "Oh, that's very kind of you, young man! But I'm quite alright. It would be nice if my husband, Gerald, was here; he knows the city so well..."

The guard's eyes lit up at the mention of a husband in the past tense. He pressed on, thinking she was a lonely widow, a vulnerable piece on the board. "A good man, was he? I know how to help a lady through being lonely..."

Suddenly, the other guard from the booth was on his feet. He was older, more seasoned, his face a roadmap of long nights and hard days. He grabbed his partner's arm, his grip like iron. "Oi, Corvan! Are you stupid?" he whispered, his voice a low, urgent hiss that Marcus, with his heightened senses, could hear clearly. "Do you know whose wife this is?" He leaned closer, his whisper dropping even lower, laced with a genuine terror. "That's Felcher's wife. Gerald Felcher..."

The younger guard, Corvan, looked horrified. The color drained from his face, his arrogant charm evaporating like mist in the sun. He looked from his partner to Alyvia, who was still smiling, completely oblivious to the near disaster, then to Marcus, who was watching them both with cold, unblinking eyes.

Corvan straightened up, snatching his hand away from their table as if it were on fire. "My... my apologies, ma'am," he stammered, his voice cracking, "I... I mistook you for someone else. Please, enjoy your water." He practically dragged his partner back to their corner booth, where they both stared intently into their mugs, trying to make themselves as small and unnoticeable as possible.

Marcus watched them retreat, and a sudden, profound realization dawned on him. This was not an isolated incident. This must happen all the time. Felcher, the terrifying Commander, was married to a woman who was not only beautiful but possessed a radiant, almost childlike innocence and a complete inability to recognize the predatory nature of the world around her.

No wonder the man was always on edge. No wonder his lessons were so brutal; they were so focused on exposing the threats beneath the surface. He lived with this every day. People saw his wife as a target, a piece of naive meat to be preyed upon. He probably spent half his life fending off foolish, arrogant men who saw only a pretty flower and not the iron hard, impossibly dangerous thorn bush that surrounded her.

They finished their drinks in silence and left the tavern. As they stepped back out into the bright, chaotic noise of the market, Marcus looked at Alyvia with a new understanding. She was not just a Queen to be protected. She was a liability. A walking, talking, smiling vulnerability that her husband had to constantly account for. And now, for a few days, that impossible, terrifying job was his.

Chapter 16

The days that followed Felcher's departure unfolded in a strange, new rhythm, a tempo set not by the Commander's iron will, but by Alyvia's gentle, yet unyielding, domestic reign. The rigid, predictable schedule that had been Marcus's lifeline was gone, replaced by a more fluid, organic routine that he found both unnerving and, to his secret shame, strangely comforting. The immediate, physical fear of Felcher's presence had been replaced by the more abstract, yet somehow heavier, weight of his responsibility as Alyvia's protector.

Each morning began not with a jolt of panic, but with the warm, inviting smells of Alyvia's kitchen. She seemed to have taken it upon herself to fatten him up, preparing hearty breakfasts of porridge with honey, thick slices of toasted bread with jam, and endless cups of chicory. He ate everything she put in front of him, a silent, ravenous furnace. The simple act of eating a full meal, without having to wonder where the next scrap of food would come from, was a luxury so profound that it felt like a dream.

He performed his chores with a meticulous, focused intensity. Mucking out Euphrates's stall was no longer just a task; it was a ritual of service to the great, silent beast that was his Commander's most trusted companion. He spoke to the horse in low murmurs as he worked, not because he expected an answer, but because the horse's calm, intelligent presence was a steadying force in his chaotic new world. Chopping wood became a form of meditation; the clean, sharp scent of the split logs was a welcome antidote to the memory of The Scar's perpetual rot. The rhythmic thud of the axe was a way to channel the restless, violent energy that still hummed beneath his skin.

But the true center of his new existence was the lessons. With Felcher gone and the brutal physical conditioning sessions on hold, Alyvia doubled their time with the slate and chalk. The kitchen table became their classroom, the battlefield where Marcus waged a silent, frustrating war against the tyranny of his own ignorance.

Alyvia was a relentless and endlessly patient teacher. She seemed to understand, with an intuitive grace, the way his mind worked. She didn't just show him the shapes of the letters; she taught him their architecture. The 'B' was a straight line with two curved rooms attached. The 'D' was a line with one large, round room. The 'R' was a 'P' with a supporting leg kicked out. She turned the abstract squiggles into logical, physical structures, and his mind, so accustomed to understanding the geometry of a fight, began to find purchase.

And then, she introduced him to phonetics.

"Every letter," she explained, her chalk tapping against the slate, "is not just a shape. It's a sound. A piece of a sound. And when you put them together in the right order, they talk. They sing. Watch."

She wrote the three letters he knew best: M A R.

"Mmm," she said, her lips pressed together, the sound a low hum. "Aaaah," her mouth open, the sound bright and clear. "Rrrrr," the sound of a growl at the back of her throat. "Mmm aaaah rrrr. Mar. You see? You put the sounds together, and they make a new sound."

It was a key. A secret, magical key that unlocked the entire system. He had been trying to memorize the letters as individual, meaningless symbols. But now he understood. They weren't just pictures. They were notes in a symphony. They were pieces in an army, each with its own unique move and power, and their strength was magnified when they worked together.

His progress, once agonizingly slow, became explosive. He was ravenous for it. He demanded more letters, more sounds, more combinations. During the day, he would sit at the kitchen table with Alyvia, his brow furrowed in concentration, the chalk a constant, dusty presence on his fingers. At night, in the quiet of his room, the real work began.

As he lay on his cot, staring at the ceiling, the familiar grid of the chessboard would descend upon him. But it was no longer a place of frustration and helplessness. It was his private training ground, his mental forge. The pieces of his army were no longer just static letters; they were alive with the sounds Alyvia had taught him. He had unlocked the entire alphabet in this 8x8 realm. The 26 pieces of his language army.

He found he could move them now, not with the strategic logic of a chess master, but with the emerging, phonetic logic of a new reader. He would slide the consonant Knights and the vowel Bishops across the board, trying to arrange them into formations that made sense. He would bring a 'C' pawn forward, then an 'A' pawn, then a 'T' pawn. C A T. Kuh ah tuh. Cat. The word would form in his mind, and the three pawn pieces would shimmer and merge, transforming for a moment into a sleek, shadowy feline that would stalk across the board before dissolving back into its component letters.

He spent hours in this silent, internal world, playing his strange, solitary game. He learned the power of the Queen vowels, the way they could move in any direction and connect disparate consonant Rooks and Knights into powerful, cohesive words. He discovered

the subtle, tricky power of the silent 'E' pawn, a piece
that made no sound of its own but could march to
the end of a word and completely change the sound
of the vowel before it. Rat. Rate. A simple pawn had
changed the entire value of the word, had altered
its very soul.

The enemy army of twisted, alien letters still stood
across from him, silent and menacing. He still could
not read them, still could not understand their language. But he no longer felt helpless. He was forging
his own weapons. He was building his own army. He
was learning the rules of his own power.

One evening, after three days of this intense, im-
mersive education, he was lying on his cot, lost in
his phonetic chessboard. He was trying to assemble
a particularly difficult word Alyvia had shown him
that afternoon: S T R E N G T H. It was a powerful,
ugly word, a dense cluster of consonant Rooks and
Knights, with only a single vowel Queen to hold them
all together. He was struggling to get them in the
right order, the sounds a guttural jumble in his mind.

He was so deeply engrossed in his mental battle that
he didn't hear the front door open. He didn't hear
the heavy tread of familiar boots on the floorboards.
He didn't hear the low murmur of Alyvia's greeting.
The first thing that broke through his concentration
was the scent.

It was the smell of the road, of horse sweat, of dust, of cold night air, and beneath it all, the faint, unmistakable, metallic scent of iron.

Felcher was back.

Marcus's eyes snapped open. The chessboard dissolved. He was back in his room, his heart suddenly pounding with a new, sharp anxiety. The quiet, predictable, and safe routine of the past few days was over. The Commander had returned to the board.

He swung his legs out of bed and crept to his door, his senses on high alert. He could hear them in the main room, their voices low. This time, there was no anger. Alyvia's voice was full of a soft, anxious concern. Felcher's was tired, a deep, rumbling weariness that seemed to settle into the very foundations of the house.

And then he heard Alyvia's voice, taking on a new tone. It was a wheedling, cajoling tone, a tone he was beginning to recognize. It was the sound she made when she wanted something from her husband.

"Dear..." she began, the word a soft, strategic opening move.

Marcus pressed his ear to the door, shameless in his need for information.

"The boy, Gerald," Alyvia said. "He's... remarkable. You were right about him. His mind is like a dry sponge. He absorbs everything. He has nearly all his letters, and he's starting to sound out simple words. He works so hard at it, I've never seen anything like it."

Marcus felt a hot flush of pride, quickly followed by a cold spike of fear. What was she leading up to?

"But this," she continued, "this kitchen table tutoring... it's not enough. He needs a proper teacher. He needs structure. He needs books and proper materials. I think... I think you should enroll him in the Academy."

There was a long, profound silence from the other room. Marcus held his breath. The Academy. He knew of it only as a place for the sons of nobles and wealthy merchants, a place of high walls and higher learning, a world as alien to him as the moon.

"The Royal Academy?" Felcher's voice was flat, incredulous. "Alyvia, be serious. They don't accept... boys like him. He has no family name, no patronage, no history. He's a ghost. That's the entire point of him."

"Then give him a history!" she retorted, her voice gaining a passionate fire. "Give him your name! You're a Commander. You have influence. You pulled strings to get that Vaelen boy a promotion he didn't deserve.

You can pull strings to get a boy who does deserve it a chance!"

"It's not that simple," Felcher rumbled, "Enrolling him in the Academy makes him visible. It puts him on the ledgers. It creates a paper trail. It undermines the very reason I chose him. He needs to remain a shadow."

"He needs to remain a boy!" Alyvia's voice cracked with emotion. "He needs a chance at a life, Gerald, not just a function! You can't forge him into a weapon in the dark and expect him to have a soul left at the end of it! He'll be reading in no time at all, I promise you. He'll make you proud. Just... give him this. Give him a chance to be more than just your rook."

Another silence, longer this time. Marcus could picture the scene in his mind. Alyvia, her face full of passionate, earnest pleading. Felcher, his face an impassive mask, weighed the variables and calculated the risks. His entire future, the entire trajectory of his life, was being debated in the next room. He was a piece being fought over by the two most powerful players he had ever known.

The floorboards creaked. He heard Felcher sigh, a deep, weary sound that seemed to carry the weight of the entire world. "I will... consider it," he said, his voice grudging. It was not a promise. It was not a yes. But it was not a no. It was a concession, a chink in the Commander's iron armor, forced open by the relentless, passionate love of his wife.

Marcus backed away from the door, his mind reeling. The Academy. Reading. A future that was not just about fighting and killing. A future where he could understand the books that lined the walls, where he could read the maps, where he could decipher the language of the enemy on his mental chessboard.

A terrifying, exhilarating, and utterly impossible thought began to take root in his mind. For the first time, he saw a path that wasn't just about serving as Felcher's weapon. He saw a path that might, just might, lead to him becoming a player in his own right. The thought was so audacious, so dangerous, that it made him feel dizzy. He retreated to his cot and lay down, staring into the darkness. The silent, humming energy of the chessboard was already beginning to form above him, the letters of his new world waiting to be arranged.

Chapter 17

Absolutely not.

The thought was not a whisper; it was a violent, visceral rejection that coiled in his gut like a nest of snakes. The Academy. A place filled with the sons of nobles, boys who had been learning their letters while he was learning how to dodge a fist in a grimy alley. Boys who had tutors and warm beds and surnames that meant something. Boys who could read the books that lined these very walls.

He was trash. Scar trash. A pit fighter. A killer. A ghost who was only just now, at the age of seventeen, beginning to understand the difference between a 'B' and a 'D.' The idea of him walking through the hallowed halls of the Royal Academy was so grotesquely absurd, so profoundly wrong, that it made him feel sick.

He lay on his cot, the darkness of the small room a suffocating blanket, his mind a chaotic battlefield. The conversation he had overheard was a fire that had burned away the strange, tentative hope that had begun to sprout in the quiet of the last few days. He didn't want a "chance." He didn't want to be "more than a rook." He wanted out. This was getting too real, too complicated. The lines were blurring. He had been a weapon, a tool, a thing with a simple, brutal purpose. Now, Alyvia wanted him to be a student—a person. And the prospect was a thousand times more terrifying than any opponent he had ever faced in the pit.

He couldn't do this. They all had years on him. Decades. They had a lifetime of knowledge, of understanding the subtle rules of their world. He was an illiterate brute who had only just learned not to bite his nails in front of the Commander. He would be exposed, humiliated, and cast out. The thought of the other students, their casual cruelty, their easy confidence, their laughter directed at him, it was an enemy he could not fight, a battle he was guaranteed to lose.

He had to leave. Tonight.

The decision landed in his mind with the cold, hard finality of a thrown knife. It was the only logical move. The game had become too complex, the stakes too high. He had to reset the board, to flee back to a world with simpler, more brutal rules. He would go back to The Scar. He would find another pit in another city. He would become The Shadow again. It was a miserable existence, but it was an existence he understood. It was his.

He sat up, his heart pounding a frantic, desperate rhythm. He had to be strategic about this. He couldn't just walk out the front door. He began to pace the small room, his bare feet silent on the floorboards, his mind a whirlwind of calculation. He started hitting the side of his thigh with his clenched fist, a hard, rhythmic thumping. Thump. Thump. Thump. The familiar, self-inflicted pain was a grounding force, a way to focus his racing thoughts, a desperate attempt to beat back the rising tide of panic.

The plan formed a sequence of logical steps. The kitchen window was the furthest point from Felcher and Alyvia's bedroom. It overlooked the narrow alley behind the flower shop. He could feign getting a drink of water if he was heard. He would put his shoes on outside to avoid the sound of them on the floorboards. He would climb out the window, drop onto the low, sloped roof of the flower shop's back porch, slide down, and be gone. A clean, silent escape into the familiar darkness.

He took a deep, shuddering breath, the decision solidifying his fear into a cold, hard resolve. He moved to the chair where the ghost boy's clothes lay folded. He pulled on the trousers and the linen shirt. Then he picked up the worn leather boots. They felt heavy in his hands, the weight of a life he was about to steal and then discard. He held them tight against his chest and crept out of his room.

The apartment was dark and silent, save for the low, rhythmic sound of Felcher's soft snoring from the master bedroom. The sound was a steady, reassuring beat, a sign that his captor was asleep, his guard down. The floorboards were cool beneath his feet as he navigated the main living area, his movements as silent and practiced as any of the wraiths who had met them in the alley. He was a creature of the night again. He was in his element.

He reached the kitchen. The moonlight, filtered through the small window, cast a pale, silvery light on the room, illuminating the clean counters, the silent stove, the neat rows of pots and pans. It was a scene of a life he was rejecting.

He moved to the sink, his cover story ready. He held the boots in one hand, tucked against his side. With the other, he picked up a tin cup and worked the handle of the water pump. He let the water run for a few moments, the soft, gurgling sound a perfect cover for any small noise he might make. His eyes were fixed on the window, on the path to freedom just a few feet away.

His heart was a frantic drum, but his mind was cold and clear. This was it. The final move. He would set the cup down, unlatch the window, and be gone.

He set the cup down. He turned toward the window.

And the world stopped.

Ice, colder and more absolute than the water from the pump, flooded his veins. His breath hitched in his throat. His meticulously constructed plan, his entire strategy for escape, shattered into a million pieces.

Felcher was sitting on the windowsill.

He was perched there as casually as if it were a throne, one leg drawn up, his arm resting on his knee. He was fully dressed in a simple, dark tunic and trousers, a silent, motionless silhouette against the moonlit square of the window. He wasn't looking at Marcus. His gaze was directed out into the night, as if he were simply enjoying the cool air. But his presence was a wall, a fortress, an absolute and impassable barrier between Marcus and the outside world.

There was no way.

Marcus's mind, a machine of logic and calculation, tried to process the impossibility of it. There was no way he could have gotten there. Marcus had been silent. The floorboards hadn't creaked. The only possible way was if Felcher had exited the apartment through the front door, gone down the stairs, circled around the entire building through the dark alleyways, and then climbed up the sheer, two story brick wall to the kitchen window, all without making a single sound, all in the few moments it had taken Marcus to walk from his room and pump a cup of water.

It was impossible. It defied the laws of physics.

And Marcus realized, with a chilling, soul-deep resolve that went beyond mere fear, that this man wasn't entirely human. The silent wraiths in the alley, the impossible strength, the way he seemed to know things before they happened... it wasn't just skill and training. It was something more. Something... other.

Felcher finally turned his head, his movements slow and deliberate. His face was unreadable in the deep shadows, but Marcus could feel the weight of his gaze, a physical pressure.

"Hey, boy," Felcher said, his voice a low, casual rumble that was more terrifying than any shout. "Where are you going?"

The question was a trap. A lie would be pointless. The truth was an admission of treason. Marcus stood frozen, the heavy boots still clutched in his hand, his mind a complete and utter blank. He had no moves left. He had been outplayed, outmaneuvered by a player who didn't seem to be bound by the same rules as the rest of the world.

He simply stood there, silent, caught in the act, the evidence of his intended betrayal clutched in his hand. The silence stretched, thick and heavy.

Felcher unfolded himself from the windowsill and landed on the floor with a soft, cat-like sound. He took a step toward Marcus, and another. He stopped just a few feet away, his shadow eclipsing the moonlight.

"You were going to run," Felcher stated. It wasn't a question. It was a diagnosis. "Back to The Scar. Back to the pit. Back to the only life you think you deserve." He gestured with his chin to the boots in Marcus's hand. "You think these will help you outrun your own ghosts, boy? You think a change of scenery will silence the one in your head?"

Marcus flinched as if struck. The man saw right through him, not just his actions, but his motivations, his deepest, most secret fears.

"The Academy frightens you," Felcher continued, his voice a low, analytical murmur. "The prospect of failure in a world of letters is more terrifying to you than the prospect of death in a world of fists. You would rather be the king of a gutter than a novice in a palace. A predictable, if disappointing, response."

He reached out and took the boots from Marcus's unresisting hand. He looked at them for a moment, then set them on the floor. "You cannot run from this, Marcus. Not because these walls are strong, or because I am fast. But because I have already made the investment. You are my rook. And my pieces do not leave the board until I remove them."

He looked at Marcus, and for a moment, in the dim light, Marcus saw a flicker of something in his eyes that was not anger, not disappointment, but a deep, profound weariness. "Alyvia... she sees the boy in you. The one who deserves a chance. And she is not wrong. But I... I see the weapon. The tool. The survivor. And I know that the boy cannot survive what is coming. Only the weapon can."

He sighed, a sound like stone grinding on stone. "I will not punish you for this. Fear is a rational response to an unknown threat. But understand this. The next time you try to run, I will not be sitting in the window. I will simply let you go. And you will find that the world outside this apartment is a far more dangerous and unforgiving place than you can possibly imagine. You will be alone, without purpose, and the ghosts you are running from will catch up to you. And in the end, you will beg to be let back on the board."

He turned and walked toward the living area. "Your education has been disrupted," he said over his shoulder. "That will be corrected. Be ready at dawn. The physical conditioning will be... redoubled. You have shown me that your discipline is still a very raw and untempered thing. We will have to apply more heat to the forge."

He disappeared into the darkness of the main room, leaving Marcus standing alone in the moonlit kitchen. He was trembling, not with fear, but with the aftershocks of his shattered reality. He looked at the window, at the path to an escape that was no longer an option. He looked at the boots on the floor, the symbols of his failed rebellion.

Felcher was right. He was trapped. Not by walls, not by locks, but by a purpose that had been forced upon him, a purpose that was now the only thing standing between him and the howling void of his own past. He was a piece in a game he couldn't comprehend, played by a master who wasn't even human. And the only path forward was the one his player laid out for him.

He walked back to his room, his feet heavy as lead. He lay down on his cot, but he did not close his eyes. He stared up at the ceiling, waiting for the grid to appear. He knew, with a sinking, final certainty, that he would never truly leave the board again.

Chapter 18

Dawn did not arrive; it assaulted the small attic room. The light was a cold, grey, unforgiving thing, the color of wet stone and drawn steel. It held none of the soft, golden promise of the previous mornings. This was Felcher's light. It promised discipline and pain.

Marcus was already awake, lying rigid on the cot, listening to the house come to life. He had not slept, not truly. He had drifted in a shallow, restless state, his mind a tense battlefield where the memory of Felcher's impossible appearance in the window warred with the equally impossible prospect of the Academy. He had surrendered. The failed escape attempt had been the final, foolish thrashing of a snared animal. Now, there was only the cold, hard reality of the trap. He was a piece on the board, and the board was this house, this life, this purpose that was being hammered into him. His only move was to endure the will of his player.

He heard Felcher rise, the soft, economical sounds of a man who wasted no motion. There was no conversation from the kitchen, no scent of baking bread, only the faint, bitter aroma of chicory. The brief, bewildering interlude of Alyvia's domestic reign was over. The Commander was back in command.

Marcus dressed in silence, pulling on the rougher training clothes Felcher had first provided. They felt more appropriate now, a uniform for the day's coming trials. When he entered the main room, Felcher was waiting for him, not at the kitchen table, but standing by the door, a quarterstaff of dark ironwood held loosely in one hand. He was already dressed for the barn.

"No breakfast," Felcher stated, his voice flat, pre-empting a question Marcus would not have dared to ask. "You do not feast before a battle, and you do not feast before you train. A full belly makes a man sluggish and complacent. We work first. We earn our sustenance. A principle you will do well to remember."

He turned and led the way out of the apartment, his footsteps a steady, relentless rhythm on the stairs. Marcus followed, his own steps silent, his stomach a tight, empty knot of apprehension. The morning air was cool and damp, carrying the scent of wet earth and the distant promise of rain. It smelled like a day for bruises.

The barn was cold, the air thick with the scent of hay and horse. Euphrates watched them enter, his large, intelligent eyes following Felcher with a look of calm recognition. He huffed softly, a warm cloud of breath in the cool air, a greeting between old comrades. Felcher gave the horse a brief, affectionate pat on the neck before turning his full, undivided attention to Marcus. The brief flicker of warmth in his eyes was extinguished, replaced by the instructor's cold, analytical gaze.

"Your discipline is a wild, untamed thing," Felcher began, his voice echoing slightly in the high raftered space, "It appears in flashes of intense, brutish focus, but it has no foundation. It is the discipline of a cornered rat, born of desperation, not of will. Today, we will begin to build that foundation. From the ground up."

He pointed to the center of the cleared floor with the tip of his staff, "Assume the horse stance. Low."

Marcus obeyed, sinking into a crouch. He knew this from the pit, a low stance to spring from, to evade.

Whack.

The staff was a blur, striking the outside of his right thigh with a sharp, stinging impact that was expertly placed to disrupt his balance without causing real damage. "Lower," Felcher commanded. "Your center of gravity is too high. You are preparing to run, not to fight. Your feet are too close together. Widen your base. You are not a dancer."

Marcus corrected, spreading his feet, sinking deeper until his thighs began to burn, a low, insistent fire. He thought he had it right.

Whack.

This time, the blow landed on his lower back. "Straighten your spine. You are hunched like a beggar. Your power flows from the earth, through your legs, up your spine, and out through your arms. You have just dammed the river at its source. Hold your core tight. Imagine you are trying to crack a walnut with your stomach muscles."

Marcus adjusted again, his body screaming in protest. The stance was unnatural, a torture device of his own anatomy. The burn in his thighs intensified, becoming a searing, liquid fire. The muscles began to tremble, tiny, uncontrollable spasms that threatened to collapse the entire structure.

"Hold it," Felcher said, his voice a calm, relentless pressure. He began to circle Marcus, a silent predator observing its prey's weakness. "This is the root of all combat. Stability. The ability to absorb a blow without being moved. The ability to generate power from a solid, unshakeable foundation. All of your frantic, wasted motion in the pit, all of your dancing and dodging, was a compensation for the simple fact that you have no root. You are a leaf in the wind."

One minute passed. Then two. The fire in Marcus's thighs was a roaring inferno. His legs were shaking violently now, the trembling so intense it was making his teeth chatter. Sweat beaded on his forehead and trickled down his temples, stinging his eyes. He focused on his breathing, trying to find a rhythm, but the pain was a chaotic, screaming static that drowned everything out. He was going to fall. He couldn't hold it.

He needed an escape. Not a physical escape, but a mental one. His eyes, watering with strain, fixed on the floorboards of the barn. They were old, dark wood, warped with age, the gaps between them filled with dust and straw. He focused on a single board. A long, straight line. He began to trace it with his eyes, from one wall to the other. Beside it was another. And another. His mind, desperate for a refuge from the agony, latched onto the pattern.

The lines began to sharpen. The dust and grime between them faded, the wood itself lightening and darkening into a familiar, alternating pattern. The world of the barn, the smell of hay, the searing pain in his muscles, began to recede. The grid was descending, a welcome shroud of cold, clean logic.

The floor of the barn was now a perfect, eight-by-eight chessboard. He was not on it. He was above it, a disembodied observer. He felt the pain in his legs not as a personal agony, but as a data point, a status effect being applied to a piece on the board. Status Immobilized. Duration Unknown. Effect Structural integrity decreasing.

The trembling intensified. His physical body was about to fail. He needed to hold on. He needed a way to measure the time, to break this endless ocean of pain into manageable, sequential units. He began to count. He would count to sixty-four, one for each square on the board.

One. He pictured a single white pawn on square A1. Two. He moved it to A2. Three. A3. Each number was a step, a piece moving across the board, a small, logical victory against the screaming chaos of his own failing body. The pain was still there, a roaring, peripheral noise, but the focus of his mind was on the board, on the slow, deliberate march of the pawn.

Whack.

The staff struck his shoulder, a sharp, jarring impact that shattered the illusion. The grid dissolved. The barn rushed back in. The pain in his thighs, which had been a distant, academic data point, returned with a vengeance, a tidal wave of pure, physical misery. His legs, no longer supported by the cold logic of his mental fortress, gave out completely. He collapsed, his body folding like a wet cloth, and he ended up in a heap on the floor, gasping for breath, his limbs trembling with a violent, shuddering exhaustion.

"Five minutes," Felcher said, his voice holding a note of clinical disappointment. "Your physical endurance is adequate. Your mental fortitude is pathetic. You allowed the pain to master you. You did not master it. Get up."

Marcus pushed himself up, his legs feeling like jelly, his muscles twitching uncontrollably. He stood before Felcher, breathing heavily, his body slick with sweat.

"Again," Felcher commanded.

The next hour was a blur of methodical, repetitive torture. The horse stance. The collapse. The brief, gasping recovery. The command to do it again. Each time, Marcus held the stance a little longer. Each time, he retreated into the cold, clean world of the grid, his mind desperately seeking refuge. He learned to count the seconds by the steady drip of sweat from his chin. He learned to measure the time by the slow, imagined transit of a bishop across its diagonal. The grid was no longer just a symptom of his trauma; it was becoming a tool, a willed act of dissociation, a mental sanctuary he could build in the heart of his own private hell.

Felcher watched him, his expression unreadable. He saw the boy collapse, get up, and do it again, his face a mask of grim, stubborn determination. He saw the strange, inward focus in Marcus's eyes as he held the stance, a look of intense concentration that seemed disconnected from the physical agony he was obviously enduring. He saw endurance, yes, but it was a strange, brittle kind of endurance. It was not the flexible strength of tempered steel, but the rigid, unyielding hardness of glass. It would hold, and hold, and hold, and then, he suspected, it would not bend. It would shatter.

After the fifth collapse, Felcher changed tactics. "Enough of the foundation. Let us see the house you have built upon it." He gestured for Marcus to stand. "We will work on your defense. I will attack. You will block."

This, Marcus understood. This was the rhythm of the pit. He fell into a ready stance, his hands raised.

Felcher moved, but not with the explosive speed Marcus expected. He moved with a slow, deliberate grace, the quarterstaff held in a low guard. He executed a simple, telegraphed thrust toward Marcus's chest. It was a textbook move, a training dummy's attack.

Marcus reacted with the instincts of the pit. He didn't block. He swatted the staff away with a sharp, open-handed blow, simultaneously sidestepping, trying to get around the weapon and inside Felcher's guard.

Whack.

The butt of the staff, moving with a speed that seemed impossible from its slow initial thrust, flicked out and caught him squarely on the kneecap of his good leg. Not his injured one. Felcher was not a sadist. He was a teacher. The pain was a sharp, blinding flash. His leg went out from under him, and he was on the floor again, clutching his knee, a guttural cry of frustration and pain escaping his lips.

"You are a fool," Felcher said, his voice cold. "I said block. You did not block. You tried to counterattack. You evaded. You saw an opening that was not there. It was bait. And you, a hungry, foolish fish, leaped for it." He nudged Marcus with the tip of the staff. "Get up."

This became the new rhythm of their brutal dance. Felcher would attack, a slow, simple, obvious movement. Marcus, his mind and body screaming with the ingrained habits of five years of street fighting, would react with instinct. He would dodge, he would weave, he would try to parry with a slap instead of a solid block. And each time, Felcher would exploit the opening his evasion created. A flick of the staff to an exposed rib. A trip with the butt end as he sidestepped. A sharp jab to the solar plexus as he tried to duck under the main attack.

Again and again, Marcus found himself on the dusty floor of the barn, his body a canvas of fresh, stinging bruises, his frustration mounting into a cold, hard knot of rage. He was fast. He was strong. He knew how to fight. But none of it worked. Felcher wasn't fighting him. He was dismantling him, taking his strengths and showing him how they were, in fact, his greatest weaknesses.

His thigh began to twitch. The frustration was a physical pressure, a building storm that needed a release. Without thinking, his right hand came up and began to slap against his thigh, a hard, percussive, rhythmic sound. Thump. Thump. Thump. It was the tic, the pressure valve, the unconscious ritual he had developed in his room, now on full display.

Felcher stopped. He lowered his staff and simply watched, his head tilted slightly, his eyes narrowed. He observed the rhythmic, self-inflicted blows. He observed the grim, furious set of Marcus's jaw. He observed the way Marcus's eyes were not focused on him, but on some internal, middle distance.

And Felcher began to see.

He saw more than just a frustrated boy. He saw a pattern of behavior. He remembered Alyvia's words from the night before, her casual descriptions of Marcus's lessons. "He's so quiet, Gerald. He'll work for hours on a single letter, and if he can't get it, he doesn't ask for help; he just gets... angry at himself. He hits the table with his fist. Not hard. Just... a rhythm."

He connected it to his own observations. The boy's almost religious adherence to the harsh, structured routine. His visible discomfort with Alyvia's more fluid, emotional approach. The way his communication was limited to direct, functional responses. His thinking, as demonstrated in their fight, was brutally, almost pathologically, black and white. Block meant block. Attack meant attack. There was no room for the grey areas, the feints, the deceptions.

A flaw in the casting, Felcher thought, the phrase landing with the cold finality of a diagnosis. The boy's mind was not like other minds. It was a rigid, structured, and brittle thing. It craved order, routine, and clear, unambiguous rules. It excelled at repetitive, focused tasks, but it broke down in the face of social nuance and emotional complexity. This wasn't just a lack of training. It was a fundamental difference in the very architecture of his mind.

A different kind of man, a kinder man, might have seen this as something to be understood, to be nurtured. A man like Alyvia would have sought to build a bridge to this strange, isolated mind. But Gerald Felcher was not a kind man. He was a craftsman. And he was not building a bridge; he was forging a weapon.

And a weapon with a flaw was a liability. This rigidity, this black-and-white thinking, this inability to adapt to the grey chaos of the real world, was a weakness. A fatal one. It couldn't be trained out of him. It was too deep, too fundamental. Therefore, it had to be covered. It had to be encased in a shell of discipline so thick, so absolute, that the flaw would never be exposed in the heat of battle. The boy's strange, rigid mind couldn't be fixed, so it would have to be weaponized. His craving for rules would be satisfied with a doctrine of iron. His black and white thinking would be honed into an unwavering, unquestioning loyalty to a single, simple objective.

Felcher's expression did not change, but a new, cold resolve settled in his eyes. The training would not be lessened. It would be intensified. The pressure would be increased. The heat in the forge would be raised until the flawed metal either tempered into something unbreakable or it shattered completely.

"Stop hitting yourself, boy," Felcher's voice cut through the air, sharp and cold. "Your frustration is a useless indulgence. Channel it. Focus it. Now. Attack me."

The command shifted the dynamic entirely. Marcus's frustration, which had been a diffuse, helpless anger, was suddenly given a target. A low growl rumbled in his chest. He surged forward, not with a plan, but with a pure, desperate desire to land a single, solid blow.

The spar was a brutal, one-sided affair. Marcus attacked with the wild, desperate energy of a cornered wolf. He was a whirlwind of motion, his fists and feet a blur. But it was all noise. Felcher stood like a rock in a storm-tossed sea. He didn't retreat. He barely seemed to move. He used the staff not as a bludgeon, but as an extension of his own body, a tool of pure, economic defense.

A flick of his wrist would turn aside a powerful kick. A slight rotation of the staff would intercept a punch, the impact jarring Marcus's arm to the shoulder. A short, sharp jab with the butt end would strike a nerve cluster, momentarily paralyzing a limb. He dismantled Marcus's offense with an infuriating, almost casual ease. Every attack Marcus launched was turned against him, every ounce of his own momentum used to send him stumbling, off balance, and crashing to the floor.

After the tenth time he was sent sprawling into the dust, Marcus lay there, his body a symphony of pain, his lungs burning, his spirit utterly crushed. He had nothing left. He had thrown everything he had at this man, and it had been like throwing pebbles at a mountain. He had failed.

He pushed himself to his hands and knees, his head hanging, defeated. He was about to give up.

And then, something shifted. A memory from the day before. Alyvia, teaching him. "It's like learning to walk. You fall down a lot at first." And then, Felcher's own words, from this very morning. "Your power comes from the ground. The earth is your anchor."

He was on the ground. He was at his lowest point. He was anchored.

He didn't get up. He stayed low, on one knee, and looked at Felcher, not with rage, but with a new, cold focus. He saw the Commander's stance. The way his weight was perfectly balanced. The way the staff was held in a deceptively relaxed guard. He saw the patterns.

Felcher took a step toward him, the staff held ready to deliver another "correction."

As the staff came down in a sweeping arc meant to tap his shoulder and force him to stand, Marcus moved. He didn't try to get up. He didn't try to evade. He exploded forward from his low position, a low, driving lunge. He didn't attack Felcher's body. He attacked the staff itself.

He slapped the descending staff not with his hand, but with the full, hard length of his forearm, a solid, bone on wood block. At the same time, his other hand shot out and grabbed the staff lower down, near Felcher's hand. He used the momentum of his lunge to drive the butt of the staff into the hard-packed earth of the barn floor.

For a single, glorious, unbelievable moment, he had neutralized the weapon. He had anchored it to the ground. He had controlled it.

It was a small victory, a fleeting one, but it was a victory born not of instinct, but of observation and a glimmer of technique. He had seen the pattern. He had found the opening.

Felcher's eyes widened for a fraction of a second, a flicker of genuine surprise that was more satisfying to Marcus than any purse of coin he had ever won.

Then, the surprise was gone, replaced by a cold, thin smile. It was a terrifying smile, a smile that said, Good. You have finally learned to speak the first letter of my language. Now, let me show you the rest of the alphabet.

Felcher released his grip on the staff. In the same fluid, impossible motion, his hand snapped forward and seized Marcus by the front of his tunic. He used Marcus's own forward momentum, twisted, and threw.

The world became a spinning, incomprehensible blur of brown and grey. Marcus was airborne for a moment, his body completely out of his control, before he crashed onto his back with a force that knocked the wind from his lungs and made his teeth rattle in his skull.

He lay there, staring up at the high, dusty rafters of the barn, the world swimming back into focus. He was defeated, broken, and in more pain than he had ever been in his life. But as he gasped for breath, a strange, new sensation bloomed in his chest. It wasn't despair. It wasn't rage.

It was the cold, clean, and terrifying thrill of understanding. He had lost, but he had learned. The weapon was being tempered. The pain was the fire, and the Commander was the hammer. And the forge was just getting hot.

Chapter 19

The world had shrunk to the size of a single, aching bruise. It wasn't the sharp, specific agony of a fresh blow, but a deep, pervasive throb that had settled into his bones, a hum of misery that was the new background music of his existence. He woke not to light or sound, but to this pain, a familiar and unwelcome companion. The rain had come in the night, a soft, persistent drumming against the slate roof, a sound that should have been soothing but instead felt like a cage, each drop another bar in the prison of the quiet, clean room.

He didn't need to be told the rules had changed. The air in the house was different. The brief, bewildering warmth of Alyvia's reign had been extinguished, snuffed out by the cold, formidable presence of her husband. The scent of brewing chicory that morning had been sharp and bitter, unsoftened by the aroma of toasted bread or porridge. Felcher had eaten his meager breakfast standing up, a piece of hardtack washed down with water, his eyes fixed on some middle distance, his presence a vortex of controlled impatience that sucked all the warmth from the room. He was a Commander preparing his theater of operations, and Marcus was the primary terrain to be conquered.

The barn was a forge, and Marcus was the flawed, brittle iron. The days bled into one another in a relentless, structured cycle of pain and revelation. Felcher's promise of "redoubled" conditioning had been a grotesque understatement. The Commander was not merely training him; he was attempting to dismantle him, to break him down to his constituent parts and reassemble him into something stronger, something more useful, something that would not, under any circumstances, run.

The horse stance was the anvil upon which he was hammered. He would hold it until his thighs were screaming monoliths of fire, until sweat stung his eyes and his vision blurred at the edges, until the world dissolved into a roaring, grey static. He learned to hate the very floor beneath his feet, the unyielding wood that offered no mercy. He would collapse, his body a trembling, shuddering ruin, only to hear the flat, implacable command "Again." And he would push himself up, his muscles screaming, and do it again. The pain was a constant, a known variable in an equation he was beginning to understand. It was no longer just a punishment; it was a tool. It was the heat that exposed the impurities in the metal.

His mind, in a desperate act of self-preservation, retreated to the only sanctuary it had ever known. The chessboard. It was no longer a hazy, involuntary escape. It was now a willed act of dissociation, a fortress he constructed in the heart of the inferno. As the fire in his thighs built to an unbearable crescendo, he would close his eyes and see the grid. He would focus on the cold, clean logic of the sixty-four squares, on the silent, geometric purity of the pieces. He learned to count his breaths by the slow, diagonal slide of a Bishop. He measured the agonizing seconds by the deliberate, one square at a time march of a Pawn. The pain became a peripheral storm, raging outside the walls of his mental citadel. He was not a boy whose legs were on fire; he was an observer, watching a piece on the board endure a status effect. His physical endurance grew, but it was his mental control —his ability to detach from the agony —that truly began to harden.

Felcher saw it. Marcus could feel the Commander's sharp, analytical gaze on him, noting the shift. He saw the boy's eyes glaze over, the subtle change in his breathing, the way his body, though trembling violently, seemed to find a new, rigid stability. Felcher didn't comment on it. He simply increased the pressure.

The staff work was the hammer. It was a relentless, percussive education in his own inadequacy. Every flaw in his stance, every wasted motion, every flicker of his old pit fighter instincts was met with a sharp, stinging, expertly placed blow. He learned the geography of his own body through a map of fresh bruises. The staff corrected his balance, his posture, and his footwork. It taught him that power came not from the wild swing of an arm, but from the rooted, coiled strength of the core. It taught him that a true block was not a panicked slap, but a solid, unyielding wall that absorbed and redirected energy.

One afternoon, after a particularly brutal session, as Marcus was sent sprawling into the hay for the dozenth time, something inside him finally shifted. He lay there, gasping, the taste of dust and his own blood in his mouth. The rage and frustration that had been his constant companions were gone, burned away by sheer, bone-deep exhaustion. All that was left was a cold, empty clarity.

He pushed himself up, not with anger, but with a slow, weary deliberation. He stood before Felcher, his body a symphony of aches, and for the first time, he did not assume a fighting stance. He simply stood, waiting.

"Tired of the taste of dirt, boy?" Felcher asked, his voice a low rumble.

"Yes, Commander," Marcus said, the words simple, devoid of defiance.

"Good," Felcher said, "Frustration is a closed loop. Submission to the lesson is the only way out." He motioned with the staff. "Assume the first defensive posture. As I showed you."

Marcus moved. He did not fall into the instinctive crouch of The Shadow. He deliberately, painfully, placed his feet, widened his stance, straightened his spine, and tightened his core, mimicking the form Felcher had been trying to beat into him for days. It felt awkward, slow, and horribly vulnerable.

Felcher attacked, a simple, probing thrust. Marcus did not evade. He brought his forearm up, catching the staff with a solid thud; his other hand moved to support the block, and his body absorbed the impact without giving ground. He had held the line.

A flicker of something not praise, not even approval, but a cold, clinical acknowledgment of a successful test passed through Felcher's eyes. "Again," he commanded.

For the rest of the hour, they worked. A slow, methodical, repetitive drill. Attack. Block. Reset. The dance was no longer a chaotic flurry of violence, but a structured, geometric exercise. Marcus's body was learning the new language, the new architecture of combat. He was being unmade and remade, and the process was agonizing.

The forge of the barn was balanced by the quiet classroom of the kitchen. Alyvia, seemingly oblivious to the brutal physical regimen Marcus was undergoing, continued her lessons with a gentle, unwavering persistence. His mind, sharpened and honed by the intense focus required to survive Felcher's training, devoured the letters.

The chessboard in his head became his primer. He would spend his nights arranging the phonetic pieces, the consonant Knights and vowel Queens, into words. He started with simple things. R O O K. H A N D. P A I N. Then, he moved on to more complex structures, including the silent pawns and consonant clusters. S T A F F. S H A D O W. S T R E N G T H. The words were no longer just sounds; they were concepts, ideas with weight and texture. He was learning to read not just the letters, but the world they represented.

One evening, after a day that had left him feeling as though every muscle in his body had been individually tenderized, he sat at the kitchen table with Alyvia. She had given him a new task. She had written a single, simple sentence on the slate and asked him to read it aloud.

T H E B O Y R A N.

He stared at the letters, the familiar shapes now beginning to connect in his mind. He sounded them out, his voice a low, hesitant murmur. "Th uh. The. B oy. Boy. R an. Ran."

He looked up at her, his eyes wide with a dawning, terrifying understanding. "The boy ran."

He had read it. He had taken the abstract, meaningless squiggles and decoded them into a thought, an image, a story. A jolt, more profound than any blow from Felcher's staff, went through him. It was a feeling of pure, unadulterated power. The locked boxes of the books on the shelves, the secret language of the maps, the entire world of knowledge that had been barred to him, he suddenly held the key. It was a small, clumsy key, but it was real.

A slow, unbidden smile spread across his face. It was a genuine smile, the first one that had touched his lips in so long he had forgotten what the muscles felt like. It felt strange, foreign, a cracking of the stone mask he had worn for five years.

Alyvia beamed, her face alight with a teacher's pure joy. "You see?" she said, her voice full of pride. "I told you! It's just a pattern. A game. And you, Just Marcus, are a very, very good player."

It was into this moment of quiet, triumphant breakthrough that Felcher walked. He had been cleaning the training weapons, and he carried a faint scent of oil and whetstone. He stopped in the doorway, taking in the scene. The boy, whose face was usually a mask of sullen defiance, was lit from within by a fragile, unfamiliar joy. His wife was looking at the boy with an expression of profound, maternal pride.

Felcher's own face remained a mask of stone, but his eyes narrowed. He saw the connection between them, the bridge of warmth and learning Alyvia had built. And he saw it not as a success, but as a potential contamination. The weapon was growing fond of its handler. It was developing attachments. Attachments were vulnerabilities. It was time to reassert control. It was time to address the fear that had been festering in the boy since the night he had tried to run.

"The boy ran," Felcher said, his voice cutting through the warm atmosphere of the kitchen like a shard of ice. He walked to the table and looked down at the slate. "An appropriate first sentence. But a lesson you have failed to learn."

Marcus's smile vanished. The warmth in the room curdled. He straightened in his chair, his back going rigid, the familiar posture of a recruit awaiting judgment. Alyvia's expression faltered, a look of disappointment and annoyance directed at her husband.

"Gerald," she began, her tone a warning.

Felcher ignored her. His gaze was locked on Marcus, his eyes cold and hard. "Your progress with your letters is... adequate," he said, the word a calculated insult. "But your progress in courage is nonexistent. You are still the same terrified boy who was ready to flee from a shadow. You fear the Academy. You fear being seen. You fear being found wanting."

He leaned forward, placing his hands flat on the table, his presence an intimidating weight. "I have made my decision. Your fear is a liability. A rot. And the only way to cure rot is to burn it out. I have sent a letter to the Proctor of the Royal Academy. I have informed him that my ward, after a period of private tutelage under my wife, is now prepared to sit the entrance examinations. They are in two weeks."

The air left Marcus's lungs in a silent rush. Two weeks. It was real. It was happening. The abstract terror he had been trying to suppress was now a concrete, looming reality.

"No," the word escaped his lips, a raw, desperate whisper. "I can't. I'm not ready. I can barely read three-letter words. They'll... they'll laugh at me." The humiliation of it, the thought of standing before the sons of lords and merchants, a grown boy stumbling over the alphabet, was a prospect more terrifying than any physical pain.

"I do not care if they laugh at you," Felcher said, his voice a low, brutal snarl. "I do not care if they mock you, or spit on you, or trip you in the hallways. You think their laughter is a weapon? I have seen men disemboweled with sharpened spoons. I have seen villages put to the torch for a misplaced word. The scorn of pampered little boys is not a threat. It is a distraction. And you will learn to ignore it."

His eyes were burning now, a cold, furious fire. This was the anger Marcus had sensed the night he was caught. Not a hot, impulsive rage, but a cold, deliberate, weaponized fury. He was angry that Marcus had shown a weakness, and he was going to punish that weakness by forcing him to confront it head-on. It was not just a lesson; it was an act of spite.

"You tried to run from this," Felcher growled, his voice dropping to a dangerous, conspiratorial whisper that was meant for Marcus alone. "You tried to choose the coward's path. So now, you have no choice at all. You will go to that Academy. You will sit for their examinations. And you will pass. Because failure," he said, the words landing like hammer blows, "is not an option. Your fear is an enemy. I am simply giving you the opportunity to face it on the battlefield. You should be thanking me."

Marcus stared at him, his mind reeling, his heart a trapped bird beating against the cage of his ribs. He looked to Alyvia for help, for an intervention, but she was silent, her lips pressed into a thin, unhappy line. She had started this, but she could not stop it. The Commander had made his move, and it was absolute.

"To be enrolled, you will need a name," Felcher continued, straightening up, his tone shifting back to one of cool, pragmatic administration. The storm had passed, leaving a chilling calm in its wake. "A full name. One that can be entered into the official ledgers." He looked at Marcus, a flicker of something unreadable in his eyes. "You will need a surname. A house to belong to. You will be Marcus Felcher."

It was the ultimate move. The final act of possession. To give him his own name was to brand him, to claim him as property, to erase any last vestige of the boy from The Scar and replace him with an artifact of his own creation. Marcus Felcher. The Rook of the Commander.

And in that moment, in the face of that absolute, crushing declaration of ownership, something inside Marcus broke. Or perhaps, something was finally forged. He had been bent, broken, and remade for days. He had submitted to the pain, to the lessons, to the will of this terrifying man. But this... this was a line he could not let him cross. To take his name was to take his soul.

He looked up from the table, and for the first time since he had been brought to this house, he met the

Commander's gaze without flinching, without fear, without a trace of defiance. His own eyes were as cold and hard as Felcher's.

"No," Marcus said.

The word was quiet, but it landed in the room with the force of a thunderclap. It was not the desperate, pleading "no" from a moment ago. It was a flat, un-yielding, absolute statement.

Alyvia gasped softly.

Felcher's eyes narrowed, the only sign of his surprise. He had expected fear, or anger, or a sullen, resentful submission. He had not expected this—this calm, solid wall of refusal.

"Explain yourself," Felcher commanded, his voice dangerously soft.

Marcus took a breath. He chose his words carefully, using the new, fragile power of the language he was learning. He spoke not with the emotion of a boy, but with the cold, hard logic of a player making a counter move.

"The name Felcher," he said, his voice steady, "is the name of a Commander. It carries weight. It carries a history. It is a name of power and respect." He paused, holding the Commander's gaze. "I have not earned it. And I will not hide behind it."

He was using Felcher's own lessons and philosophy as a shield. He was demonstrating that he had learned more than just letters.

"The other students, the sons of lords, they will look up the name Felcher. They will know who you are. And they will see me as nothing more than your shadow, your pet project. They will treat me with a false respect born of fear for you, or with a deeper scorn for being an imposter riding on your name. Either way, I will not be seen for what I am. I will be invisible behind your legacy. And you taught me," he said, the words a sharp, precise jab, "that invisibility can be a weapon, but not when it is wielded by your enemies."

Felcher was silent, his face an unreadable mask of stone. He was being outplayed at his own game; his own logic turned against him.

"I need to forge my own path," Marcus continued, the words feeling true and real in his mouth for the first time. "I need to build my own history. But," he added, a deliberate, strategic concession, "I will not forget the man who set me on it. I will not dishonor the hand that forged the blade."

He took another breath. This was his move. His gambit.

"Your middle name," Marcus said, "Philip. It is a good, strong name. It is connected to you, a quiet honor that only those who truly know you will understand. But it is not the name of the Commander. It is a name I can make my own." He looked Felcher directly in the eye, his voice dropping to a firm, declarative statement. "I will be Marcus Phillips."

The silence that followed was absolute. The tension in the room was a physical thing, a high, humming wire. Alyvia watched them both, her hand covering her mouth, her eyes wide. Marcus had not just refused an order. He had made a counterproposal. He had asserted his own identity, his own will, within the framework of the Commander's world. He had claimed a piece of the board for himself.

Felcher stared at him for a long, unblinking moment. He was seeing something new. The boy was gone. The frightened rat from the gutter was gone. The sullen, resentful pit fighter was gone. In their place stood something else. Something cold, hard, and intelligent. Something that had taken his lessons and was beginning to shape them into a weapon of its own. He was no longer just a Rook. He was a Rook that was beginning to think.

A slow, cold, and utterly terrifying smile spread across Gerald Felcher's face. It was not a smile of warmth or pride. It was the smile of a master craftsman seeing his creation suddenly, unexpectedly, display a spark of the genius he had tried to hammer into it. It was the smile of a player realizing his favorite piece had just learned a devastating new move.

"A rook that seeks to control its own square," Felcher murmured, more to himself than to anyone else. "Interesting."

He straightened up, the moment of tension broken. He gave a single, curt nod. "Very well. Marcus Phillips it is." He turned to his wife, "See that he can spell it by week's end."

He strode from the room, leaving Marcus sitting at the table, his heart pounding, his body trembling with the aftershocks of the confrontation. He had faced the Commander and had not broken. He had forged an identity from the ruins of his past. He had a name. His name.

Alyvia came and placed a hand on his shoulder. Her touch was warm and steady. "I am very proud of you, Marcus Phillips," she said softly.

He looked down at the slate on the table, where the simple sentence still lay. The boy ran. He picked up the chalk, his hand surprisingly steady, and beneath it, he began to write, the letters awkward and shaky, but his own.

MARCUSPHILLIPS.

He stared at the words. It was his name. It was his future. The Academy was a terrifying, unknown battlefield. But for the first time, he felt like he was entering it not as a nameless ghost, but as a player with a piece on the board. And he would not run again.

Chapter 20

The war in the barn ended. The war in the kitchen began.

Felcher, in a move of cold, strategic pragmatism that Marcus was beginning to recognize as the man's native language, declared a truce with his body. The brutal physical conditioning ceased. The ironwood staff was returned to its silent vigil in the rack. The horse stance, the endless cycle of muscle failure and agony, was suspended. The Commander had decreed that the flawed iron of his recruit's body had been heated enough for now it was the mind that required the forge.

The next two weeks were an exercise in a different kind of pain. A quieter, more insidious agony that left no bruises but carved deep, invisible lines into the landscape of his soul. His world shrank to the kitchen table, to the smooth, cool grey of the slate, and the dusty, ephemeral whisper of the chalk. He was no longer a fighter being honed; he was an ignorant brute being civilized, and the process was a thousand times more humiliating.

The days fell into a new, relentless rhythm. He would wake in the predawn quiet, his body a map of fading aches, and find Alyvia already waiting for him. She was his general in this new campaign, her patience a formidable weapon, her gentle encouragement a strategic flanking maneuver that left his frustration with no place to hide. They would work for hours, the only sounds the scrape of chalk on stone and Alyvia's soft voice, dissecting the architecture of the alphabet.

"No, no, Just Marcus," she would say, her finger gently guiding his clumsy hand. "The curve of the 'S' is a serpent, not a broken stick. Feel the flow of it."

He poured every ounce of the fierce, desperate focus he had once reserved for the pit into this new battle. The alphabet was his opponent. Each letter was a feint, a parry, a complex posture he had to master. The twenty-six shapes were a hostile army, and he attacked them with a grim, obsessive determination. He would spend an hour on a single letter, his hand cramping, the chalk grinding down to a useless nub, until the malformed squiggle on his slate finally resembled the clean, perfect shape in Alyvia's primer.

At night, sleep offered no refuge. It was merely a different training ground. The moment he closed his eyes, the familiar grid would descend, but it was no longer a sanctuary from physical pain. It was the classroom, magnified. He was a lone, ignorant Rook on a vast, empty board, and the enemy pieces were the letters themselves. He would spend hours in that cold, silent space, shunting the consonant Knights and vowel Bishops into formations, trying to build the simple, three-letter words Alyvia had taught him. D O G. H A T. S U N. Each successfully formed word was a small, triumphant capture, a piece of the enemy army brought under his control.

But while his days were consumed with this new, quiet war, his nights were haunted by the sounds of another. Every evening, after he had retreated to his room, the argument would begin. It was a low, rumbling storm that started in the main living area, its vibrations traveling through the solid floorboards, a physical manifestation of the discord in the house.

He would lie on his cot, every muscle tensed, and listen. He was seeing now, as Felcher had commanded, but what he saw terrified him. The sounds were a language he understood far better than the letters on his slate. It was the universal language of conflict.

Alyvia's voice, usually a warm, melodic thing, would sharpen, taking on a high, insistent edge. It was the sound of a plea turning into a demand. He imagined her as a Bishop on the chessboard, her attacks diagonal and sharp, striking at Felcher's logic from unexpected angles.

Felcher's voice never rose. That was the most terrifying part. It remained a low, controlled rumble, a sound of immense, contained pressure, like a volcano grumbling before an eruption. He was a Rook, holding a defensive line, his position immovable, his logic a fortress of stone. Marcus had never heard the Commander raise his voice to his wife, not once. There was no hot, impulsive anger. There was only the cold, unyielding weight of his absolute will.

The subject was always the same. Him. He could not make out the specific words, but he could piece together the shape of their conflict from the emotional contours of their voices. The Academy. Too soon. He's not ready. He needs more time. He needs a chance. It's cruel. It's necessary. Failure is not an option.

The nightly arguments cast a pall over the house. During the day, Alyvia would pretend as if nothing was wrong, her smile bright, her lessons cheerful. But Marcus could see the strain. It was in the faint, purple shadows under her eyes. It was in the way her hand would tremble almost imperceptibly as she poured their chicory. It was in the moments when she would stare out the window, her gaze a thousand miles away, her face a mask of worry. Her cheerfulness was a feint, a brave pawn sent forward to screen the vulnerable pieces behind it.

Felcher was in a perpetually foul mood. The truce with Marcus's body was clearly a concession he had been forced to make, and he resented it. He would spend his days in the main room, ostensibly reading his books or studying his maps, but his stillness was predatory. Marcus would feel the weight of the Commander's gaze on him as he worked with Alyvia, a silent, disapproving pressure that made the back of his neck prickle. Felcher wouldn't speak, wouldn't interfere, but his presence was a constant, brooding storm cloud on the horizon.

Marcus learned to navigate the emotional landscape of the apartment as carefully as he would a booby trapped alley in The Scar. He saw the cause and effect. The nightly argument would be more intense, and the next morning, Felcher's silence would be heavier, Alyvia's smile more brittle. He understood that he was the epicenter of this domestic earthquake, the stone dropped into the placid pool of their lives, and the ripples were threatening to swamp them all. He kept his head down, worked harder, and spoke only when spoken to. He was a ghost in their house, a silent, walking embodiment of their conflict.

The two weeks passed in this state of tense, suspended animation. His reading improved at a phenomenal rate. He moved from three-letter words to four, from simple nouns to complex verbs. He could now read the simple sentence on the slate without hesitation. The boy ran. He could also read the new ones Alyvia wrote. The dog is big. The sun is hot. Each sentence was a new world unlocked, a new piece of the puzzle falling into place. But with each new word he learned, the dread of the Academy grew, a cold, dark counterweight to his fragile new confidence.

Finally, the day of the exam arrived.

The morning was still and grey, the air heavy with the promise of more rain. The usual silence in the apartment was different today. It was not the silence of routine, but the charged, humming silence of a held breath. Marcus couldn't eat. The piece of toast Alyvia placed in front of him felt like a stone in his throat. His stomach was a tight, writhing knot of pure, unadulterated terror.

He was dressed in the best set of Thomas's old clothes, a dark wool tunic, and well-mended trousers that Alyvia had pressed the night before. The clothes felt like a costume for a play he had not rehearsed, for a role he was not fit to perform. He felt like a scarecrow dressed in a prince's finery.

When it was time to leave, both Felcher and Alyvia walked him to the door. Alyvia fussed with his collar, her hands warm but trembling slightly. "You'll do wonderfully, Just Marcus," she whispered, her voice thick with an emotion he couldn't decipher. "Just remember what we practiced. Take your time. Sound it out. You know this." She gave his arm a reassuring squeeze, but he could feel the frantic, bird-like flutter of her own anxiety through her fingertips.

Felcher stood a few feet away, his arms crossed over his chest, his face an unreadable mask of stone. He said nothing. His silence was a physical weight, an accusation, a command. Do not fail me. The unspoken words were louder than any shout. He simply gave Marcus a short, sharp nod, a dismissal that was also a final, terrifying order.

Marcus turned and walked down the stairs, his own footsteps echoing in the quiet stairwell. He felt their eyes on his back until he stepped out into the street. The walk to the Royal Academy was a journey through a nightmare. The grand, stone buildings of the capital seemed to lean in, their windows like a thousand disapproving eyes. The other people on the street, the well-dressed merchants and chattering students, all seemed to be looking at him, their gazes a mixture of curiosity and contempt. He was an interloper, a creature of the gutter who had dared to walk on their clean, paved stones.

The Academy itself was a fortress of knowledge, a place of soaring spires and vast, arched windows that seemed to look down on him with an ancient, scholarly disdain. He presented the letter Felcher had given him to a stern-faced proctor at the gate, his hand trembling so badly he could barely hold the paper steady. The proctor read it, his eyebrow arching in a gesture of faint surprise, and then waved him through with a dismissive flick of his wrist.

He was directed to a large, vaulted hall. The room was immense, with a ceiling so high that it was lost in shadows. The air smelled of old paper, beeswax, and the faint, sharp scent of ink. It was the smell of a world he did not belong in. And then, he saw them.

Dozens of boys, all around his age or younger, were already seated at rows of long, dark, polished wooden desks. They were the sons of the elite, their clothes of fine wool and cut velvet, their faces alight with the easy, unthinking confidence of those who had never known a moment of true hunger or fear. Their chatter filled the vast hall, a low, buzzing hum of privilege.

As he walked down the central aisle to find his assigned seat, a hush fell over the room. The chatter died. Every eye turned to him. They saw his ill-fitting, though clean, clothes. They saw the jagged scar through his eyebrow, a brand of a life they couldn't imagine. They saw that he was seventeen, which was a good two or three years older than most of the other applicants. He was an anomaly, a strange, rough-hewn piece that did not fit on their polished, elegant board.

He found his desk, his name, Marcus Phillips, written on a small, neat card. He sat down, his movements stiff, his face a carefully blank mask. He could feel their stares, hundreds of them, like the pricking of a thousand tiny needles.

And then, the world began to dissolve.

The silence was the first sign. The low buzz of their renewed whispers, the scrape of a chair, the distant cough —all faded away, replaced by the profound, humming stillness of the board. The polished floor of the hall, the dark wood of the desks, the pale faces of the boys, it all began to waver, to lose its substance.

The floor beneath him resolved into a vast, polished grid of alternating light and dark squares. The long rows of desks became the ranks and files of the board, each desk a perfect, empty square. He was sitting on D4, a forward, exposed position in the center of the battlefield.

He looked at the other boys. Their features were blurring, smoothing away, their individual identities dissolving into a uniform, ovoid shape. They were becoming the Pawns, featureless and unformed, their potential unknown, their sheer numbers a daunting, oppressive presence. There were dozens of them, a sea of white, featureless eggs on the squares around him.

He looked to the front of the hall, where the head proctor sat at a large, imposing desk on a raised dais. The man's severe, academic robes shimmered and transformed, becoming the elegant, powerful silhouette of a Queen. He was the most powerful piece in this room, his authority absolute, his gaze a withering, diagonal attack that could remove any piece from the board with a single, sharp word.

Marcus sat frozen in his chair, a lone, dark piece in a sea of white. He was a Rook, out of place, a creature of straight lines and brute force in a game of subtle, social maneuvering. He felt exposed, vulnerable, and utterly, completely alone.

The physical world tried to reassert itself. He could feel the cool, smooth wood of the desk beneath his hands. He could smell the sharp, clean scent of the ink in the small well set into the desk. But his mind was trapped on the board, a prisoner of its own defensive architecture.

And then, it started.

Thump. Thump. Thump.

His right hand, of its own accord, began to tap against the side of his thigh, a hard, rhythmic, percussive beat. It was the tic. The pressure valve. The unconscious, frantic drumming that betrayed the screaming chaos in his soul. It was a sound that did not belong in the profound silence of the chessboard, a frantic, animal noise in a world of cold, silent logic.

The Pawns turned their smooth, featureless heads toward him. The whispers started, not as sound, but as psychic assaults, as moves on the board.

A Pawn on E5 slid forward one square. "*Why is he doing that?*" The thought was a sharp, probing question, a feint to test his defenses.

Another Pawn on C5 mirrored the move. "*He's weird.*" The thought was a blunt, frontal attack, an attempt to undermine his position.

He tried to stop his hand. He clenched his fist, digging his ragged fingernails into his palm, trying to will the muscles to be still. But the tapping continued, a frantic, unstoppable rhythm of its own. Thump. Thump. Thump. Thump.

A third Pawn, this one directly in front of him on D5, advanced. It was older than the others, its egg-like form carrying an aura of smug, aristocratic superiority. "*Isn't he a little old to be taking this exam?*" The whisper was a direct challenge, a poisoned piece offered in a trade he couldn't refuse. "*He must be slow. A simpleton from the provinces.*"

The words were a physical blow. Simpleton. Scar trash. Gutter rat. The old names, the old ghosts, rose up from the depths of his memory. The Pawn's attack was not just a move; it was a mirror, reflecting his deepest, most secret fears back at him. He was an imposter. A fraud. A piece of filth that had been washed and dressed up, but was still filth underneath.

Thump. Thump. Thump. Thump. Thump.

The tapping grew faster, harder, a desperate, frantic drumbeat against the rising tide of their scorn. The Queen at the front of the room rapped a gavel on her desk. The sound was a cannon shot on the silent battlefield.

"You may begin."

A proctor, a lesser Bishop piece, moved down the aisle and placed a sheaf of papers on his desk. The exam.

Marcus stared at the page. The letters, which had been his allies in the quiet of the kitchen, his soldiers on the training ground of his mind, were now a hostile army. They swam before his eyes, a chaotic, mocking jumble of black shapes on a white field. He couldn't make them out. He couldn't form the words. The key Alyvia had given him had turned to dust in his hand.

The whispers continued, a relentless psychic siege. "Look at him. He can't even read the first question." "I heard the Commander Felcher sponsored him. Must be some charity case." "He'll be gone by midday."

The Pawns were advancing, their featureless faces a wall of silent, unified contempt. They were boxing him in, their moves coordinated, their pressure relentless. The board was shrinking, the walls of their scorn closing in around him. He couldn't breathe. The air was thick and heavy, tasting of chalk dust and failure.

He looked at the first question on the page. The letters danced and blurred. He saw an 'A.' He saw an 'R.' He saw an 'S.' He saw the ghost of his own name. He was going to fail. He was going to fail Alyvia. He was going to fail the Commander.

And in the cold, logical calculus of his new world, failure was not an option.

He closed his eyes. The frantic drumming of his hand against his leg ceased. The whispers faded. The pressure of the advancing Pawns receded. He deliberately, willfully, banished the chaotic, hostile board of the exam hall.

He retreated. Deeper.

He built a new board in his mind. Not the vast, intimidating battlefield of the hall, but the small, familiar, eight by eight grid of his own room. The clean, safe space where he was the master. He placed a single piece on it. The Black Rook. His piece. Solid. Grounded. Anchored.

He opened his eyes. He was still in the hall. The Pawns were still there, their silent judgment a palpable force. The Queen still watched from her dais. But they were on the outside of his new fortress. He was on his own square now. He was in control.

He looked at the paper again. The letters were still a jumble, but they were no longer a threat. They were just an opponent. A puzzle to be solved. A code to be broken.

He took a deep, steadying breath. He picked up the pen. The battle had begun.

Chapter 21

The pen felt strangely light in his hand.

It was a slender, delicate thing of carved wood, its metal nib sharp as a needle. He was used to the feel of a sword hilt, a splintered axe handle, the rough, satisfying weight of a stone. His hand, a crude instrument of violence, a landscape of calloused flesh and scarred knuckles, was not made for this. His fingers, trained to clench into a fist of brutal finality, struggled to find a grip that was both firm and precise. He held it like a weapon he didn't know how to wield, a dagger held by the blade.

He was on the board. The great, vaulted hall had dissolved, its stone pillars and arched windows melting into the misty, indeterminate horizon of his mental battlefield. The polished floor was a vast, unforgiving grid of sixty-four squares, stretching into an infinity of cold, logical possibilities. The other boys, the sons of the elite, had become a sea of white Pawns, their featureless, ovoid faces turned toward him, a silent, unified chorus of judgment. Their whispers were no longer just sounds; they were moves, psychic probes launched across the checkered expanse, testing the integrity of his defenses. The proctor, a stern Queen on her dais, watched with an impassive, regal authority, the final arbiter of his success or failure.

He, Marcus Phillips, was a lone, dark Rook on square D4, stranded in the center of the enemy's territory, exposed and utterly alone.

And he was not alone.

To his left, on the adjacent dark square, a new piece coalesced from the shadows of his own mind. It was a Rook, like him, but its form was not solid iron. It was a swirling, turbulent vortex of black smoke and smoldering embers, a piece of living, breathing darkness. It was a ghost of a piece, its edges indistinct, its shape constantly shifting, but its presence was a font of pure, familiar poison. It was The Shadow. His past. The five years of blood and sawdust and hollow, echoing grief. It was the part of him that reveled in the simplicity of violence, the part that had thrived in the brutal logic of the pit.

To his right, on the adjacent white square, another piece stood sentinel. This one was sharp, clear, and formidable. A Queen, carved from what looked like dark, polished ironwood, the same material as the Commander's staff. Her form was severe and regal, her posture one of unshakeable, absolute authority. She wore the face of Gerald Felcher. She was his new reality, the embodiment of the iron will that was being hammered into him, the silent, judging presence of his new master.

The battle for his soul was arrayed on the squares beside him. The Shadow Rook and the Felcher Queen. His past and his future. The gutter and the game.

He looked down at the exam paper. The first section is Reading and Comprehension. The letters, which had been his allies in the quiet of the kitchen, his soldiers on the training ground of his mind, were now a hostile army arranged in incomprehensible formations. They swarmed across the page, a chaotic, mocking jumble of black shapes on a white field.

"Look at him," the whisper came from a Pawn on his left flank, "He's frozen. He can't even begin."

"Simpleton," hissed another from the right.

The Shadow Rook beside him seemed to pulse, a low, guttural chuckle echoing in his mind —a sound like the grinding of stone and old, bitter rage. "See?" it whispered, its voice the rasp of a thousand forgotten fights. "I told you this was a fool's game. This is not our world, boy. Their weapons are ink and lies. Our weapons are fists and bone. You don't belong here. Let's leave. Let's go find something we can break."

The temptation was a physical thing, a sweet, siren song of simplicity. The thought of the clean, honest crunch of a jawbone under his fist, the straightforward logic of a fight, was a powerful lure against the bewildering, intellectual terror of the page in front of him. His hand, the one not holding the pen, began its frantic, unconscious rhythm against his thigh. Thump. Thump. Thump. The beat was a desperate S.O.S., a signal of his rising panic.

The Felcher Queen on his right did not speak. It did not need to. It simply stood there, its ironwood form radiating a silent, crushing disappointment. Its judgment was more damning than any insult. You are failing; its silence screamed. You are weak. You are proving me right.

He had to do something. He had to make a move. He forced his eyes to focus on the first question. The letters swam, a black, chaotic tide.

W H A T I S T H E P R I M A R Y T H E M E O F T H E F O L L O W I N G P A S S A G E ?

The words were a mountain range, an impassable barrier of alien symbols. He saw the individual letters, the familiar shapes Alyvia had taught him, but they refused to cohere. They were just squiggles, just noise. The panic was a physical presence now, a cold hand closing around his throat.

"Give up," the Shadow Rook hissed, its smoky form swirling with a dark, triumphant energy. "This is their magic, not ours. You are a dog trying to read a scroll. Let's go back to the kennel. At least there, we are the strongest dog."

He was about to put the pen down. He was about to surrender. The humiliation was a taste of ash in his mouth. He was going to fail.

Then, a new voice entered his mind. It was not the taunting rasp of The Shadow, nor the silent judgment of the Commander. It was the calm, instructional voice of the drillmaster in the barn.

"Break it down. Analyze the components."

The memory was so vivid that it was like a physical blow. Felcher, standing over him as he struggled with a complex defensive posture. "You are trying to fight the entire army at once. You are overwhelmed. Focus on a single soldier. One opponent. One move. Deconstruct the threat."

He took a deep, shuddering breath. He was trying to read the sentence. He was trying to fight the entire army. He had to break it down.

He looked at the first word. W H A T. Four letters. Four opponents. He focused on the first one. W. He knew that shape. He knew its sound. H. He knew that one, too. Alyvia had called it the "breathing sound." He sounded them out in his head, his lips moving silently. W h a t. What.

The word clicked into place. It was no longer a hostile squiggle. It was a concept. It was a question. It was a captured piece.

He moved to the next word. I S. Two letters. Easy. A simple pawn to be taken. Is.

The next word. T H E. Another one he had drilled a hundred times with Alyvia. The.

He was no longer reading a sentence. He was fighting a series of small, individual skirmishes. Each word was an opponent. He would isolate it, analyze its components, sound out its weaknesses, and defeat it. Then he would move to the next. It was a slow, agonizing, painstaking process—a war of attrition.

The whispers of the Pawns continued. The taunts of The Shadow Rook still echoed in the periphery of his mind. But they were just noise now. Background static. His entire world had shrunk to the single word in front of him, the single opponent he had to defeat before moving to the next.

He finished the first question and moved to the passage it referred to. It was a dense block of text, a veritable army of hostile letters. It was an excerpt from a history of the Second Border War, the very war Felcher had served in.

"The legion's flank was exposed. Commander Valerius, knowing that a retreat would mean the complete collapse of the western front, made a decision born of cold, brutal calculus..."

He fought his way through it, word by painful word. He stumbled over "legion." He had to break it down into its phonetic components, l e g i on, a multi-step combination move he had practiced on his mental board. He wrestled with "calculus," a word as foreign and menacing as any beast from a forgotten legend. But he did not give up. Each word was a square on the board, and he would not cede a single one.

Felcher's lessons, the ones from the barn, began to surface, their brutal logic applying not just to a physical fight, but to this mental one.

"Your power comes from the ground. The earth is your anchor." He felt the solid wood of the chair beneath him, the floor under his feet. He was anchored. He was stable. The whispers of the Pawns could not move him.

"Do not waste energy. Every move must have a purpose." He stopped letting his eyes roam over the whole page. He focused only on the word in front of him, conserving his mental energy, applying it with a sharp, singular focus.

"A true defense is not about evasion. It is about control." He was no longer trying to avoid the difficult words. He was meeting them head-on, dissecting them, controlling them, forcing them to yield their meaning.

He was using the Commander's own ruthless discipline to fight this battle. The Felcher Queen on his right remained silent, but he could feel its imposing presence shift, the aura of crushing disappointment lessening almost imperceptibly, replaced by a cold, analytical observation. The weapon was being tested. The weapon was performing.

The Shadow Rook on his left grew more agitated, its smoky form churning. "This is slow," it snarled. "This is weak. This is not who we are. Smash the desk. Break the pen. Show them what real power is." But its voice was weaker now, a desperate, fading echo. It was a creature of impulse and rage, and it had no place in this battle of cold, deliberate, intellectual attrition. Its moves were useless here.

Time became a blur. The vast hall, the sea of Pawns, the watching Queen, it all faded into an indistinct background. His universe was the black ink on the white page, the slow, methodical conquest of one word after another. He answered the questions, his hand cramping from the unfamiliar act of writing, his letters a clumsy, almost childish scrawl compared to the elegant print of the exam paper. He wrote about the primary theme of the passage: duty versus survival. He identified the strategic error made by the opposing general in overextending his supply lines. He explained the meaning of the word "pyrrhic" in the context of a victory that costs too much.

He was so engrossed in his silent, brutal war that the proctor's voice was a jarring intrusion, a cannon shot that shattered his fortress.

"Pens down. The first section is complete."

Marcus looked up, blinking. The page in front of him was full of his clumsy, spidery writing. He had answered every question. He had no idea if his answers were right. He only knew that he had not surrendered. He was drenched in sweat, his neck and shoulders aching with tension, his mind a wasteland of exhaustion. But he had held the line.

There was a fifteen-minute break before the next section. The hall erupted in a buzz of confident chatter. The Pawns around him stood up, stretching, comparing their answers, their voices full of the easy, untroubled certainty of the privileged.

"That passage on the Second Border War was dreadfully simple, wasn't it?"

"I thought Valerius's gambit was brilliant, if a bit obvious."

"My father knew Valerius. Said he was a solid tactician, but no true strategist."

Marcus sat frozen at his desk. He felt a wave of nausea. They spoke of the history, of the Commander's war, with a casual, academic detachment. To them, it was a story in a book. To him, it was a living, breathing thing, a force that had shaped the man who was now shaping him. They hadn't fought for every word on that page. They had simply read them.

The Shadow Rook was back, its form dark and triumphant. "See?" it whispered, its voice dripping with a venomous, self-loathing satisfaction. "You struggled and bled for what they consumed like a sweet cake. You don't belong. You are an animal in a scholar's robes. You passed, perhaps, but you are not one of them. You will never be one of them."

The despair was a physical weight, crushing the air from his lungs. The Rook was right. He had survived the battle, but he had lost the war. The chasm between him and them was too vast to be bridged by a few weeks of study. He had just endured the most difficult mental ordeal of his life, and to them, it had been a triviality.

He put his head in his hands, the rough wood of the desk cool against his forehead. He was an imposter. A fraud. And soon, everyone would know it.

"The second section will now begin," the Proctor Queen announced, her voice cutting through his despair, "Mathematics and Logic."

Another sheaf of papers was placed on his desk. Marcus looked at it with a sense of numb, defeated dread. If letters were a hostile army, then numbers, with their strange, arcane symbols and their mysterious, hidden rules, would be a legion of demons. He had failed. He just hadn't received the official notice yet.

He picked up his pen, his hand heavy as lead. He forced himself to look at the first question.

And the world shifted.

It wasn't the slow, creeping dissolution of before. It was a sudden, violent, instantaneous snap. As his eyes fell upon the page, the chaotic, hostile world of the exam hall vanished, and the cold, clean, perfect world of the grid slammed into place with the force of a physical blow.

The page was not a jumble of incomprehensible symbols. It was a language. A language he knew. A language he had been speaking his entire life.

Question 1: A merchant buys 30 barrels of wine at 8 silver crowns per barrel. He must pay a 15% tax on the total cost. If he sells each barrel for 12 silver crowns, what is his total profit after tax?

His mind didn't see words. It saw a sequence of moves.

30 x 8 = 240. The initial position. The cost of the goods. A simple multiplication, a Rook moving down an open file.

240 x 0.15 = 36. The tax. The opponent's move. A Bishop's diagonal attack, taking a piece of his value.

240 + 36 = 276. The total investment. His position after the opponent's move.

30 x 12 = 360. The potential return. His counterattack. A Queen sweeping across the board.

360 x 276 = 84. The final position conversion then simplified. The profit. Checkmate.

The answer was 84 silver crowns.

He blinked. The connection was so sudden, so profound, it was like a lightning strike to his brain. This was not some abstract, academic exercise. This was the math of survival. This was the cold, hard calculus of The Scar.

He thought of Silas, the oily parasite, and his "small finder's fee." Twenty percent. He had spent years doing that calculation in his head after every fight, his mind a bitter, silent abacus, ensuring the leech never took a copper more than he was owed. He knew percentages.

He thought of the endless, complex bartering in the market. The weight of a purse, the shifting value of coppers to bronze to silver. He had lived and breathed a world of complex, multi-step financial transactions just to ensure he and his mother didn't starve. He knew profit and loss.

And then, he thought of the chessboard in his head. For years, he had been playing a silent, solitary game, a game of pure logic and multi-step application. He would visualize a sequence of moves: Pawn to E4, the opponent responds with E5, Knight to F3, and the opponent responds with C6. He was constantly calculating positions, threats, and future possibilities, three, four, five moves ahead. He had been training his mind for this exact kind of logical combat without even knowing it.

The letters had been a foreign language he had to learn from scratch. The numbers... the numbers were his native tongue.

A new kind of power surged through him. Not the hot, brutish power of the pit, but a cold, clean, exhilarating power of the mind. He looked at the exam paper, and it was no longer a hostile army. It was a series of tactical puzzles. It was a game—a game he knew how to win.

On the mental chessboard, a profound shift occurred.

The Shadow Rook on his left recoiled as if struck by a physical blow. Its smoky form seemed to shrink, its taunting whispers silenced. This was a kind of power it could understand and respect the cold, efficient, and brutal dismantling of a problem. There was no room for its chaotic rage here. This was the work of a killer, but a different kind of killer. A killer of variables.

The Felcher Queen on his right remained silent, but its ironwood form seemed to stand taller. He felt, rather than saw, a single, almost imperceptible nod of approval. This was discipline. This was focus. This was the weapon performing its function with ruthless, beautiful efficiency.

Marcus picked up his pen. His hand was no longer clumsy. His grip was firm, precise. He was no longer a terrified boy. He was a player.

The pen flew across the page. He moved through the problems with a speed and confidence that was breathtaking. He calculated the trajectory of a catapult stone using geometry. He determined the logistical requirements for a legion marching through hostile territory. He solved complex algebraic equations that were, to him, simply a more elegant way of saying, "If X is my attacking force, and Y is the enemy's defense, what value of Z do I need to achieve victory?"

The whispers of the Pawns around him started again, but their tone had changed.

"Look at him... he's flying through it."

"Is he just guessing? No one can work that fast."

"He hasn't stopped since he started."

Their scorn had been replaced by a confused, grudging awe. Their probing attacks had been repulsed. He was on the offensive now, his pen a sword, each correct answer a captured piece.

He finished the entire section with a full thirty minutes to spare. He did not put his pen down. He went back to the beginning, not out of uncertainty, but with the cold, dispassionate professionalism of a master craftsman inspecting his work. He checked every calculation and verified every step, ensuring there were no flaws, no weaknesses, and no openings for the enemy to exploit. It was a perfect, elegant, brutal campaign.

When the Proctor Queen finally called time, Marcus calmly placed his pen on the desk. His heart was steady. His breathing was even. The frantic tapping of his hand against his leg had long since stopped. He was calm. He was centered. He was in control.

The boys filed out of the hall, their confident chatter now tinged with a new, uncertain note. They cast strange, sidelong glances at the silent, scarred boy who had finished the exam before any of them. Marcus ignored them. He walked out of the Academy, his steps steady, his gaze fixed straight ahead. The battle was over. Now, he just had to wait for the final score.

He didn't have to wait long. The results were posted on a large board in the main courtyard the following afternoon. He walked through the crowd of anxious, chattering boys, a silent island in their sea of privilege. He found the list. He scanned the names, his eyes searching for the one he had claimed as his own.

There it was. Marcus Phillips.

He forced his eyes to the first column, his heart beginning to pound again.

Reading & Comprehension Score 61/100. Pass Mark 60

A wave of dizzying, bone deep relief washed over him, so powerful it almost buckled his knees. He had done it by a single, solitary point. He had not failed. He had survived. It was not a victory, but it was not a defeat. He had held the line.

Then, his eyes moved to the next column.

Mathematics & Logic Score 98/100. Class Rank 3rd

He stared at the number. Third. In the entire class. He read it again, and then a third time, the letters and numbers clear and sharp and undeniable. It wasn't a mistake.

A new feeling, one he had never experienced before, began to bloom in his chest. It wasn't the hollow triumph of the pit. It wasn't the quiet satisfaction of reading his first sentence. It was a feeling of deep, profound, and undeniable power. He had not just survived their game. He had beaten them at it. He had walked onto their board, a despised and underestimated piece, and he had shown them he was not a Pawn. He was a player.

He looked around at the other boys, at their stunned, disbelieving faces as they saw his name and his rank. He saw their expressions shift from open contempt to a new, wary respect. He had established his position. He had put a major piece on the board and declared his presence.

He turned and walked away from the results board, away from the whispers and the stares. He was still an outsider. He was still a creature of The Scar. But something fundamental had changed.

He was beginning to understand. The forge wasn't just in the barn. It was here, in his mind. The lessons Felcher was hammering into him weren't just about fighting stances and physical pain. The discipline, the analysis, the breaking down of a problem into its component parts... it was a universal weapon. It could be used to defeat an opponent in the pit, to deconstruct a sentence on a page, or to solve an equation that baffled the sons of lords.

He was still Felcher's Rook. But for the first time, he felt the thrill of controlling his own square, of seeing the entire board, of choosing his own move. The path ahead was still a terrifying, unknown battlefield. But he was no longer just a weapon waiting to be aimed.

He was a weapon that was learning how to think. And that made him infinitely more dangerous.

Chapter 22

The city was a different country on the walk back. The stones beneath his feet were the same, the grand facades of the capital buildings had not changed, but the lens through which he viewed them had been violently, irrevocably altered. He walked out of the Academy's gates not as a trespassing ghost, but as a recognized entity, a name on a list, a rank in a class. He had not been cast out. He had earned a square on their board.

The air itself seemed to have a different texture. Before, it had been a hostile medium, thick with the silent judgment of a world he did not belong to. Now, it was just... air. The scent of baking bread from a distant shop, the sharp tang of coal smoke on the breeze, the damp, earthy smell of the coming rain, they were no longer accusations of his own filth, but simply data points, sensory information to be cataloged and filed. He was seeing, as the Commander had commanded, and for the first time, he was not just seeing threats. He was seeing a city.

His mind was a battlefield in the aftermath of a shocking, contradictory victory. He had fought two separate wars in that examination hall, and the outcomes were a paradox that his mind, which craved simple, brutal logic, struggled to reconcile.

The first war, the one against the letters, had been a desperate, grinding affair. A battle of attrition fought word by painful word. He had survived, but just barely. A score of sixty-one. One point. A single, solitary point was the only thing that separated him from abject, humiliating failure. It was the victory of a man who throws himself on a grenade and lives, but with every bone broken, his body a ruin. It was a victory that, in its own way, felt like a defeat. It confirmed his deepest fear in the world of words, of culture, of the knowledge these people were born into; he was a cripple. He would always be a step behind, a clumsy brute stumbling through their elegant libraries.

The Shadow Rook inside him, the ghost of the pit, was grimly satisfied by this. "See?" it whispered, its voice a rasp of dark validation. One point. "You are a fraud. You scraped by on a sliver of luck. You do not belong. This is not your strength."

But then there was the second war. The war against the numbers. And in that war, he had not just survived. He had conquered. A score of ninety-eight. Third in the class. In the realm of pure, cold, unadorned logic, in the universal language of calculation and consequence, he was not a cripple. He was a prince. He had moved through those problems with a speed and an intuitive grace that had left the sons of lords choking on his dust. He had not just fought their army, he had annihilated it.

The Felcher Queen in his mind, the ironwood embodiment of his new master, was a silent, formidable presence. It did not offer praise. Praise was a useless emotional indulgence. It simply acknowledged the data. Literacy functional. Logic exemplary. The weapon is calibrated. It was the cold, satisfying click of a well-oiled machine seating itself into place.

These two truths warred within him as he walked. He was a simpleton and a genius. A failure and a prodigy. The contradiction was a dizzying, internal vertigo. Who was he? Was he the clumsy, barely literate brute who had clawed his way to a passing grade? Or was he the cold, calculating strategist who could see the elegant, brutal mathematics beneath the surface of the world?

He looked at the people passing him on the street, no longer as a sea of potential threats, but as pieces on a board he was beginning to understand. The portly merchant, hurrying past, his face a mask of anxious calculation, was a creature of numbers, a man whose entire existence was a series of profit and loss equations. The two young nobles laughing by a fountain, their conversation a flurry of witty, layered insults and social maneuvering. They were creatures of words, their power derived from a language of subtlety and influence. He was only just beginning to decipher it. He was caught between their two worlds, a citizen of neither, a ghost who could speak a little of both their languages but was fluent in neither.

He reached the quiet street of the flower shop. The scent of damp earth and blossoms hung in the air, a familiar, comforting perfume now. He walked up the stairs to the apartment, his hand surprisingly steady as he reached for the door latch. The anxiety of the morning, the gut-wrenching terror of the exam, was gone. It had been replaced by a quiet, humming un-certainty, a sense of standing on the precipice of a new and far more complex battlefield. He had won the first skirmish. Now, it was time for the debriefing with the Commander.

He opened the door and stepped inside.

The apartment was still and quiet. The air was thick with tension, a palpable, humming energy that was a thousand times more intimidating than the empty silence he had left that morning. Alyvia was standing by the window, staring out at the grey, rain-streaked sky, her arms wrapped around herself as if to ward off a chill that had nothing to do with the weather. Felcher was sitting at the kitchen table, not reading, not studying his maps, but simply sitting, his hands clasped before him, his face an unreadable mask of stone. He looked like a statue carved from granite, yet impatience was etched on his face.

They both turned as he entered. Their movements were sharp and simultaneous, like two predators re-acting to a sound in the brush. Two sets of eyes, one warm and filled with a desperate, pleading hope, the other cold and sharp and demanding, fixed on him.

This was the final test. More terrifying than any question on the exam.

Alyvia took a step toward him, her hands clasped together so tightly her knuckles were white. "Marcus?" she breathed, her voice a fragile whisper. She didn't need to ask the question. It was written in every line of her body.

Marcus looked at her, at the raw, undisguised hope and fear in her eyes. He thought of the two weeks she had spent with him, her endless patience, her unwavering belief that the gutter rat could be taught to read. He had passed by one point. A single, pa-thetic point. He could not give her the triumphant victory she so clearly craved. But he could not give her failure.

He gave a slow, deliberate nod. "I passed," he said, his voice quiet, revealing nothing of the tumultuous battle he had just fought.

The relief that washed over Alyvia was a physical thing. It was as if a set of invisible strings holding her rigid had been cut. Her shoulders slumped, a small, choked sob of pure, unadulterated joy escaped her lips, and she closed the distance between them in two quick steps. She wrapped her arms around him in a fierce, trembling hug.

He froze. His entire body went rigid. It was the first time she had hugged him, the first time anyone had since his mother passed away. The sensation was a shock to his system, an invasion of his carefully guarded personal space. Her body was warm and soft against his, her scent of lavender and rainwater a dizzying, intimate cloud. He stood there, stiff and awkward as a training dummy, his arms pinned to his sides, not knowing how to respond. He was a creature of blows and bruises, not of embraces.

"Oh, I knew it," she whispered into his shoulder, her voice thick with tears, "I knew you could do it. You clever, clever boy. I am so proud of you."

He felt a strange, painful lump form in his throat. Pride. Someone was proud of him. The concept was so alien, so powerful, it felt like a brand against his soul. A small, wounded part of him, a part he thought had died in that cold room with his mother, wanted to melt into the embrace, to soak up the warmth, to finally, after all these years, feel safe. But another part, the larger part, the part forged in the pit and hammered into shape in the barn, recoiled. This was a weakness. This was an attachment. This was a vulnerability that the enemy could, and would, exploit.

He endured the hug, his body a battlefield of conflicting impulses, until she finally pulled back, wiping at her eyes with the back of her hand, her face alight with a joy so pure it was almost painful to look at.

And then he turned to face the Commander.

Felcher had not moved. He had watched the entire exchange with the detached, analytical gaze of a biologist observing the mating ritual of a strange and unfamiliar species. Now, his obsidian eyes were fixed on Marcus, cold and demanding.

"The results," he said. It was not a question. It was an order for a report.

Marcus met his gaze. He recited the numbers from memory, his voice flat, a soldier delivering a battlefield assessment. "Reading and Comprehension: sixty-one out of one hundred. Pass mark was sixty. Mathematics and Logic: ninety-eight out of one hundred. Class rank third."

Felcher was silent for a long moment, processing the data. He steepled his fingers, his gaze unwavering.

Marcus stood before him, awaiting the verdict. He had not failed. But had he succeeded?

"Functional," Felcher said finally, the word a cold, clinical diagnosis. "Your literacy is functional. Barely. It will require significant, ongoing improvement. One point is not a victory; it is a stay of execution. It means you were not the most ignorant man in the room, and nothing more."

Alyvia, who had been beaming, let out a small noise of protest. "Gerald! He worked so hard! It's a wonderful achievement!"

Felcher held up a hand, silencing her without looking at her. His focus was entirely on Marcus.

"Your performance in logic and mathematics, however," he continued, his tone shifting almost imperceptibly, a subtle change in pressure, "is exemplary. It confirms my initial assessment. The raw material is sound. The processing power is high. You have a mind that sees in systems, in patterns, in cause and effect. This is a far more valuable asset than a talent for pretty words."

He stood up from the table, his movements fluid and purposeful. "You passed the test. Not the Academy's test. My test. You demonstrated an ability to learn, an ability to function under pressure, and, most critically, an ability to apply disciplined logic to a chaotic problem. Your training is far from over. In fact, it has only just begun. The preliminaries are concluded. Now, it is time for you to understand the nature of the war you have been drafted into."

He gestured with his chin toward the main living area, the war room. "Come."

Marcus followed him, his heart beginning to pound a new, slow, heavy rhythm. The relief of the exam was gone, replaced by a cold, sharp sense of anticipation. This was it. The reason he had been taken from the gutter. The purpose behind the pain.

He entered the room with the maps and the books. Felcher went to the large table, and with a sweep of his arm, he cleared a space in the center, pushing aside the ancient charts of forgotten lands. He unrolled a new map. It was fresh, the ink dark and sharp, the vellum crisp. It was a minutely detailed schematic of the capital city. Not the sprawling, chaotic map of a cartographer, but the clean, geometric layout of a military strategist. Every street, every alley, every major building was marked with a cold precision.

"This," Felcher said, his finger tapping the center of the map, a complex cluster of buildings marked with a royal crest, "is the board." He looked at Marcus. "You understand the game of chess?"

"Yes, Commander," Marcus said. He was an expert.

"Good," Felcher said, "It will save us time. The game being played for the future of this kingdom is not so different. It is a game of position, of influence, of calculated sacrifice. And right now, our side is in a very precarious position."

He began to move his finger across the map, his voice a low, dispassionate lecture, a general briefing of his new operative. "Our King," he said, his finger resting on the Royal Palace, "King Theron, is old. His health is failing. He is a good man, but he is a creature of tradition, his moves predictable, his strategy defensive. He seeks only to maintain the status quo, to hold the line. But the line is crumbling."

His finger moved to another location on the map, a series of opulent manors in the noble quarter. "The enemy. The Ivory Blight, as you have come to know them in your... particular way of thinking. A faction of powerful, reactionary nobles. Men who see the world in black and white their own power and the threat to it. They see the King's weakness. They despise his heir. They believe the kingdom is rotting from the head down, and they are preparing to perform their own brutal surgery."

He looked up at Marcus, his eyes like chips of flint. "And at the center of the board, the piece that will determine the outcome of the entire game, is our most valuable and most vulnerable asset."

He paused, letting the weight of the moment build.

"Prince Alexander."

The name landed in the quiet room with the force of a physical blow. A Prince. The heir to the throne. Marcus stared at Felcher, his mind struggling to process the scale of this. He had thought this was about some petty court intrigue, some factional squabble. He had not imagined... this.

"The Prince," Felcher continued, his voice a low, intense rumble, "is his mother's son. He is an idealist. He believes in justice, in compassion, in a kingdom where the common man is not just a pawn to be sacrificed. He has seen the rot in The Scar, and he wants to cut it out, not with a sword, but with reform. This makes him a mortal threat to the Ivory Blight. They see his idealism not as a virtue, but as a poison that will destroy the traditions that grant them their power. They will not allow him to take the throne. They are planning to remove him from the board. Permanently."

He let that sink in, the ugly, final word hanging in the air.

Marcus finally found his voice. It was a raw, croaking whisper. "Why... why are you telling me this?"

Felcher leaned forward, his gaze so intense it felt like a physical pressure. "Because you, Marcus Phillips, are the solution to this problem. You are the unexpected move. The piece that does not belong on their board. You are a ghost from a world they pretend does not exist. Your loyalty is not to a noble house, not to a family name, not to a tradition of power. Your loyalty," he said, his voice dropping to a near whisper, "has yet to be earned. But your purpose is clear."

He straightened up, and his voice resumed its cold, commanding tone. "Your purpose, your entire reason for being, the reason I have invested my time and my wife's patience in your forging, is that you will enter the Academy. You will excel. You will find a way to get close to the Prince. You will become his shadow, his shield, his unseen guardian. You will be the wall of night that stands between him and the knives in the dark. You will protect the future of this kingdom."

He stopped, his pronouncement complete, the order given.

Marcus stared at him, his mind a howling void. Protect a Prince. Him. A pit fighter. A killer. A boy who had failed to protect the one person in the universe he had ever truly loved.

The memory was a physical agony, a knife twisting in an old, unhealed wound. His mother, her breath a fragile rattle, her hand cold in his. The ten silver crowns he had failed to earn. The single agonizing point by which he had just passed his exam. He was a creature of failure, of just barely surviving. And this man, this Commander, was entrusting him with the life of a Prince, with the future of the entire kingdom.

The absurdity of it, the sheer, crushing, cosmic irony, was so immense that it was almost funny. A harsh, broken sound, half laugh, half sob, escaped his lips.

"You... you want me?" he choked out, the words tasting of ash and self-loathing. "A boy who couldn't even save his own mother? You want me to protect a Prince? I failed. I failed the one time it mattered. What makes you think I won't fail again?"

The confession, the deepest, most secret shame of his soul, was laid bare on the kitchen table. He expected Felcher to dismiss it, to mock his weakness.

But the Commander did not. He simply looked at him, his gaze steady, and for the first time, Marcus saw something in those obsidian eyes that was not calculation, not command, not disappointment. It was a flicker of something that looked almost like... understanding.

"I know," Felcher said, his voice surprisingly soft. "I know you failed. That is precisely why you will not fail again. Your grief is not a weakness, boy. It is the finest, hardest, most unbreakable armor you will ever possess. The memory of your failure is the fire that will fuel you. You will not allow another person to die on your watch because you were not strong enough, not fast enough, not smart enough. You will protect this Prince with the ferocity of a man who has already stared into the abyss and knows exactly what lies at the bottom."

He reached across the table and placed a thin, leather-bound dossier in front of Marcus. "Your education begins now. This is no longer about letters and numbers. This is about the game."

Marcus looked down at the dossier. His hands, which had been trembling, were now steady. The despair in his chest had not vanished, but it had been transmuted, forged by the cold, brutal logic of the Commander's words into something else. A purpose. A terrible, crushing, and unavoidable purpose. He was a weapon being aimed. He was a Rook being placed on its square. He was being given a chance, not to erase his past, but to redeem it.

He opened the dossier. The first page contained a charcoal sketch of a young man, not much older than himself. He had a noble, serious face, intelligent eyes, and a mouth that seemed on the verge of a compassionate smile. Beneath it, in clear, block letters that Marcus could now agonizingly read, was the name:

PRINCE ALEXANDER

He stared at the face of the boy he was meant to die for. The battle was no longer in his head. The board was no longer a mental construct. It was real. It was here. And the first move had just been made. He had been given his King. And he would not let him fall.

About the Author

Rachel Stone grew up in a lively Pennsylvania home with six siblings, learning early to find quiet patterns within chaos. Living with autism and ADHD, she developed a deep appreciation for structure, logic, and the systems people create to bring order to the world. This perspective shapes her storytelling, allowing her to craft intricate worlds and characters who navigate the overwhelming sensory and emotional noise of life.

Her fiction explores the tension between internal order and external unpredictability, following outsiders and thinkers who see the world differently. For Rachel, these stories are as much about mastering the mind's own labyrinth as they are about surviving the world beyond it.

A mother of two and advocate for accessibility in literature, she ensures all her novels are published using dyslexia-friendly fonts, creating a more inclusive experience for every reader. She lives on the East Coast with her family, usually outlining a new world—or searching for her keys.

www.ingramcontent.com/pod-product-compliance
Lightning Source LLC
Chambersburg PA
CBHW040854010826
48978CB00013BA/1024